The Reluctant Bandit: Lawlessness & the Law, Book 1

Ami Hicken King

The Reluctant Bandit: Lawlessness & the Law, Book 1

Ami Hicken King

To three of the best men I
know and love:
Jon, Max, and Stuart

❦ 1 ❦

Arizona Territory, 1878

Charlie's fingertips pinched the brim of his hat, pulling it further forward on his face. His other hand adjusted the bandana obscuring the rest of it. Long, dusty strides chewed up the distance to the front door. He had chosen the short straw.

It was finally his turn to rob the mercantile. He knew the drawing was rigged, but played their game anyway. The gang had been chomping at the bit to have him prove his mettle. He pushed the door open, bell ringing. Striding in, he barked at the clerk, "Give me the money."

Three long strides brought him to the counter as the clerk lowered his hand to the register to open the drawer. Others in the mercantile froze as they watched him. The clerk didn't hesitate, sliding the money across the counter, despite not having a gun pointed at him.

Wouldn't have happened, anyway—Charlie's holster was empty. Being broad and tall had its benefits. Sweeping the money into a burlap sack, he eyed a woman, frozen, to the left of him. A jangling door chime behind him startled the woman and pulled her out of her trance.

When the door fully opened behind him, she covered her mouth, her eyes widening. "Papa—" she whispered.

Damn! Charlie clutched the bag and lunged for the woman. One arm pulled her snugly to his chest while the other still clutched the bag. Whirling around, he came face to face with the town's sheriff.

"Step aside, Sheriff." When the sheriff didn't move, he simultaneously squeezed and lifted the little bit of a woman off the floor, giving her a shake. She released a tiny gasp. "Wouldn't want your darlin' daughter to get caught in the crossfire." His eyes never left the sheriff's.

They locked eyes until the sheriff finally stepped aside, shaking his head. His face fell as Charlie walked the woman past him. Charlie's gut churned as he watched the father and daughter's exchange out of the corner of his eye and heard the sheriff murmur, "Hang tight, Annabelle. I'll find you, no matter what."

The gruffness in his voice made Annabelle turn her head completely to look back at her father's pained expression. Charlie broke their moment. "Now Sheriff, give us ten minutes before you come on out. We've got the mercantile covered. I don't want Annabelle, here, to get hurt. 'Kay?"

Charlie dragged his two new acquisitions out into the daylight. Who knew his first robbery would garner him a sack of money and a pretty woman to boot?

Annabelle remained snug to Charlie's front as they walked out of the mercantile toward his horse. Despite their height disparity, they fit and moved well together. He loosened his grip a little so as not to hurt her. Putting his mouth close to her ear, he said, "Keep walking politely and no one gets hurt. We're goin' to my horse and then riding out of town. Do you understand?"

Annabelle nodded, bumping her head against Charlie's firm chest. Not trusting the sheriff, he moved her slightly to his side while gripping her arm and extending his stride. Charlie lifted her onto his horse and pulled himself up behind her. Wrapping thick, corded arms around her waist, he flicked the reins and sent his horse racing.

They rode hard for about twenty minutes before turning toward the mountains at a slower pace. The terrain was rough and the path grown over. Neither spoke a word. The sun was now at its zenith, and the day grew hot. Their clothing stuck to them like a second skin and molded the pair together from the intense heat. Charlie leaned away from her, loosening his hold to provide relief from both the heat and her proximity. She was a pretty woman, petite and delicate—a perfect fit in his arms. She also had lots of dark, curly hair that smelled nice, which was beginning to embarrass him below the belt. It was difficult to gain much space between them, as Annabelle was beginning to slouch in the saddle, although she didn't complain.

After another hour of nonstop riding, the forest opened up and there were signs of a mining camp ahead. Clomping hooves drew men from all directions. A slow progression of men moved into the main area of camp—they wanted to see if Charlie had been successful. Many had placed bets on him. Some had clear surprise on their faces, but it was hard to say whether it was because he had returned in one piece or because he had a woman with him. They were especially curious about who she was. Some craned their necks to see better; others pushed and shoved to stand in front.

Charlie rode the horse into a large clearing where the men were beginning to gather. He could feel Annabelle's tremor the closer they came to the gang, but it wasn't from the drop in temperature as they rode lower into the valley. The men were moving in on them with curiosity, and they were a motley bunch, ranging from moderately tidy to outright filthy. From the opposite direction, Wrighty, a blond man with a medium build, came marching toward them. His eyes were narrowed and his arms swinging as they propelled him forward. The men cleared a path to let him through.

Wrighty marched directly up to the horse just as Charlie dismounted, catching him off guard and knocking him out of the way. He grappled for Annabelle's waist, but she thrust her boot out and clipped his jaw, snapping his head backward. He threw out his arms for balance, grabbed her ankle, yanking Annabelle so that she slid out of the saddle and bumped her head on the pommel. She would've hit the ground hard if Charlie hadn't caught her.

"What the hell, Wrighty! You could've hurt her." Instead of being thankful for Charlie's reflexes, Annabelle turned on him, kicking and hitting him as he tried to set her to rights. Tiring of her antics, he grasped her shoulders, stood her upright, then gave her a shake for good measure. Wrighty watched with his hands on his hips, clearly interested.

"Looks like you caught a wildcat. Why'd you bring her? You were told to rob the mercantile, not go hunting for a woman." Even as he was saying this, Wrighty reached out and tried to catch a lock of Annabelle's hair. She jerked away from him a couple of times before he finally grabbed a fistful and pulled her hard toward him. Trying not to get close, she planted her feet. Regardless, this just placed her in a physically awkward, as well as humiliating, position, with her head faced toward Wrighty and her bottom toward Charlie. Mesmerized, Wrighty twirled her hair between his fingers before she managed to pull it away, glaring at him. Charlie stepped between them, irritated with Wrighty's harassment.

"She smells as pretty as she looks." Wrighty grabbed for her again, but she snarled and swung at his face before he caught her wrist. Using the momentum of her thwarted swing, he easily yanked her from Charlie's side, pulling her toward him just as Charlie got a good hold on her middle and hauled her back. All the while, Annabelle was hollering at them while ineffectively twisting and turning to get free, like an animal caught in a trap. By now, the men had circled around them as they watched Annabelle get tugged and pulled between the two. Charlie raised his arm to bat Wrighty away but was interrupted.

"Cease!" a booming voice sounded from behind them, halting all motion. Even Annabelle froze.

An imposing figure lumbered down the path. Despite a slight limp and shoulders that curled inward, he was tall and broad. His relaxed posture belied the dangerous, coiled energy beneath his calm façade. The stark contrast of his salt-and-pepper hair, grey mustache, and icy blue eyes was a warning that all was not as it seemed.

When he saw Annabelle shudder, he gave a cold smile. Looking between the two men, then at Annabelle, he asked Charlie, "What do we have here?" He lifted his chin toward Annabelle.

Charlie shot a glare at a smirking Wrighty before turning to the man. "This is Sheriff O'Donnell's daughter, Annabelle." An eerie silence hung in the air. No one moved.

The man continued to stare at Annabelle until she started shifting her feet, unconsciously moving herself halfway behind Charlie for protection. He finally let out a hoot of laughter before slapping Charlie on the shoulder. "Damn, son! I send you to rob the mercantile and you come back with a better prize. How'd you do it?"

Charlie could feel Annabelle's eyes boring into the back of his head. He had the decency to blush. He pushed back his hat and scratched his head. "Well, I robbed the mercantile, and she happened to be there…then the sheriff showed up, you see. By the look on her face when she saw her daddy walk in, I'm guessing she wasn't supposed to be there." He threw a look back at Annabelle. It was her turn to blush.

The man nodded, waiting expectantly. After a brief pause, Charlie relayed how the robbery went down and waited for the yelling to start. It never did. The men surrounding them started murmuring and talking amongst themselves.

"We should kill her and send her body back to the sheriff!" This was met with some approval. Annabelle paled, clutching Charlie's arm now instead of fighting to get away from him.

Another man nodded. "That damn sheriff has double-crossed us for the last time. We'll show him." Annabelle looked at him with shock, her mouth falling open and eyes growing wide. A few men nodded and grunted in agreement.

"Let's keep her for—" Orrin looked around as if needing approval, nodding his head before dramatically adding "*ransom*." His fist pumped into the air. Annabelle gasped, swiveling toward him in dismay. More of the men seemed to like that idea. Others just wanted to use her.

Annabelle shrank further away from the crowd, grabbing Charlie's arm with both hands. He shifted to reassure her, creating a barrier between the gang and Annabelle.

Charlie raised his voice, cutting through the mayhem. "That's not why she's here."

But there was no reasoning with them. He'd have to try that later. The men were now talking to, or mostly over, each other. Wrighty kept his eyes on Charlie and Annabelle the entire time. Charlie's body was tense—jaw set, shoulders stiff, and fists clenched—ready to defend Annabelle, which wasn't lost on Wrighty or the tall man. Annabelle clung to Charlie as if her life depended on it, and it was starting to sound as if it did.

Finally, Wrighty said to the tall man, "Boss, I think I should have her. We can always ransom her later. Sheriff owes us, and Charlie owes me." He emphasized the last part by jabbing his thumb into his chest while clenching his jaw, and shooting a narrowed side-eye at Charlie.

Wrighty's grudge against Charlie went deeper than the cut Charlie had given him, and it bothered him worse than the ugly scar it left behind. He told Goat that the scar felt like it ached when Charlie made him angry. Goat just laughed at him, which made matters worse for Charlie, at least in Wrighty's eyes. Even now, his eyes burned, daring Charlie to say something, rubbing his upper right arm all the while.

Van Der Kamp, the tall man, held up his hand, calling for silence. He looked between the two men, then momentarily at Annabelle. His voice was low and modulated, but carried far, asking no one in particular, "How big was the haul?" A voice from the back of the group answered, calling out a large sum. It was Orrin. He had gone through Charlie's saddlebag while the three of them were tussling. Van Der Kamp nodded once and looked thoughtful for a moment.

Turning to Charlie, he said, "What would you have us do?" He waited a moment before adding, "You seem to have brought in a considerable amount of money, and our nemesis's daughter—a lucky boon, I'd say. Not bad for a first-timer. So, what say you?"

Everyone turned to look at Charlie. They still weren't sure what to expect from him. He was a hard worker, toed the line like the rest of them—better than most of them, in fact. He still didn't seem to be embracing the gang, but neither was he undermining it or trying to escape. He was a valuable member because of his work ethic. Visibly swallowing, he said, "If it's all right with you, Van Der Kamp, I'd like to think about it for a spell." He slowly bobbed his head down and back up, emphasizing his point.

"Fine idea, son. Tie her up, and by the time Goat has supper ready, we'll hear what you have to say." With that, Van Der Kamp turned and walked away. His limp was a little more prominent from behind.

Charlie released a long breath and turned toward Annabelle. She stepped away from him and crossed her arms over her chest, to keep some distance between them, despite having used him as a shield minutes prior.

"Come on." He held his hand out to her. "Let's find a good place to put you."

Wrighty latched onto Charlie's outstretched arm at the wrist and clamped down hard. "I still think she needs to be making a visit to *my* tent, greenhorn." Charlie tried to shake him off, unsuccessfully, before taking his other hand and prying off Wrighty's fingers.

"I disagree. You heard Van Der Kamp. *You* don't want to make him angry, *do you?*" No one said anything while they stared at each other. The air was hot, as it was nearing noon-time, without the benefit of a breeze. Sweat trickled down Charlie's brow.

Finally, Wrighty pulled back his arm and leaned toward Charlie. "This isn't over, *son.*" He walked a few steps away before turning around to cast one more angry look at them, then stalked off. Charlie and Annabelle stood watching him for a moment before Charlie looked at her. He opened his eyes wide and jerked his head in the direction of camp. Reluctantly, she shrugged her shoulders and began walking with him.

Two weeks earlier…

"I've told you, time and again, you need to wait for MaryAnne or you don't go out at all. There's also Deputy Collins. He's offered to take you places when it's quiet at the jail—all you need to do is ask."

Sheriff Daniel O'Donnell ran his hand through his hair in exasperation. Annabelle was on another roll about going out and doing errands. He knew what she really wanted—adventure. He suspected she might be needing at least some break in the monotony. There wasn't much for a gentlewoman to do around this mining town other than keep house or whore— the latter clearly not a consideration for Annabelle. Women didn't walk alone on these streets, especially unmarried ones. Like hell he was going to let anything happen to his little girl.

Annabelle sat primly on the edge of the sofa with her hands folded on her lap. She played the penitent as she stared down at her hands and avoided eye contact, but that wasn't fooling him, either.

"Annabelle, I realize I still treat you like you're a little girl— shoot, I still think of you as my little girl. But that doesn't change the fact that it's dangerous for a lone woman in this town." He pointed toward the window. "Hell, the whores in this town rarely go out alone. They all know better—and they've been around a time or two." Everyone knew that it was too easy to cull a lone woman from the herd. He threw up his hands in frustration while raising his voice. Annabelle looked up at him. He responded by immediately holding up his hands in a placating manner. "I know you're tired of hearing this but it's true. I don't want anything to happen to you, honey. Neither do I want what happened to your mom to happen to you." His eyes took on a slight sheen.

Annabelle's face softened when Papa mentioned Mama. It was more because of the feelings she imagined Papa having for his wife than any she had for her mother. She didn't really remember the woman because she disappeared so long ago. Well, run away most likely. At least, that's what some of the gossips said. She must've been about two or three years old when her mother didn't return to the jail for her after dropping her off to run a quick errand. In Annabelle's mind, it didn't matter. For as long as she could remember, it was all about her papa, the sheriff. He was good to her, and she never missed her mother. She wasn't sure why that was, but she had a sneaky feeling it wasn't just because she couldn't remember things—especially since she had no good memories or good feelings about her mother, either. Perhaps Papa always cared more for her than her mother did. He certainly was hands-on. He had some help with Mrs. Johansson, but he didn't let her take over or do everything. He did more than his fair share. Everyone loved Sheriff O'Donnell, and the sheriff sure did love his daughter, Annabelle, and the town he was in charge of. He was dedicated and fair.

She felt for her dad because he'd never remarried and had raised her on his own. He never said a word about it, nor did he intentionally make her feel bad or guilty. She thought Papa deserved more than what her mother seemed to be able to give him—if the running away part was true. The problem for her, right now, was getting him to loosen up so she could have some independence. It also meant that he couldn't keep assigning keepers to her, especially that nasty deputy of his. She shuddered just thinking about him.

"Papa, I know you mean well. I do—and I love you for it. But I've always felt safe in this town. No one will bother me—I'm the sheriff's daughter. They wouldn't think of it. Besides, I only go to the mercantile, and sometimes the bakery. I—"

The sheriff sighed deeply, his shoulders dropping before kneeling in front of Annabelle. He placed his large, calloused hand on her delicate, folded ones. "Honey, the Van Der Kamp gang has been sighted not far from here. They're butchers, and I don't want you near anybody like that. It's definitely dangerous for a lone woman—she'll always be a prime target for these types. While it can be a rough town, the people drifting through tend to be even more dangerous. Can you understand where I'm coming from, at least with that?"

Begrudgingly, Annabelle nodded her head. Frustration had her biting her lower lip to stave off tears. She was still feeling sold out by the baker's wife, who tattled on her earlier, but she couldn't deny her father had a point. Still, that left her no closer to the freedom or independence she'd been craving so much lately. The desire for this independence hit her like spring fever—relentless and brutal.

Sheriff O'Donnell smiled a sad smile. Standing, he gently kissed her forehead before reaching his hand down to help her up. He tucked her hand into the crook of his arm before saying, "I told Jake we'd bring dinner by for him tonight. I thought we'd grab a bite to eat at Ma's inn and then drop some by for him. What do you say?"

Annabelle paused for longer than necessary. She didn't want to upset her father again, but Deputy Jake Collins was someone she really could do with less of.

"That sounds wonderful—but, Papa, I don't really want to be around the deputy."

The sheriff tilted his head and looked at Annabelle for a long time before asking, "Why?"

"Papa, I've told you this before—he makes me feel uncomfortable. He stands too close to me and is always trying to take my hand or have me hold on to his arm. He—"

"Annabelle, he's just trying to be a gentleman. You know I require all my men to use their manners."

"I know—but—this goes, well, beyond *manners*. He—" Annabelle stopped talking when she saw the pained expression creep onto his face. She'd already caused him enough trouble today, so she decided to quit while she was ahead. Switching paths, she rubbed her belly like she used to as a child, because it always made him laugh. "I'm pretty hungry—you?" She smiled brightly, trying to wash away the pain she seemed to keep bringing with her lately.

"I'm having some mighty big hunger pains, myself—it was a busy day. Did I tell you I had to chase down this little filly?" He gave her a wry look, which told her he knew what she was up to, and they both laughed. They walked out of the house, arm in arm, and down to Ma's inn for her excellent chicken and dumplings.

After dinner, Ma wrapped up a plate for Jake, and they headed back toward their home, which was next to the jail. Sheriff O'Donnell stopped in front of their house and patted Annabelle on the arm. "Honey, you go on and get ready for bed. It's been a long day. I'll take this to Jake and check in on him."

"Are you sure? I was just being petulant before. I—"

"Go on, it's all right. Nothing you have to worry about." Daniel watched his daughter go into the house before he headed next door. He felt eyes on him as he waited. He knew where they were coming from.

The sheriff walked through the jailhouse door and handed the plate to his deputy. "What're you looking out the window at us for, there, Jake?" He tilted his hat back on his head and pierced him with a sharp look. He didn't much appreciate being spied on.

"Just making sure Annabelle got in okay. It's been a long day for her."

"You don't think I can handle my own daughter?"

Jake's eyes went wide as he realized the error in his words. "No. NO! I was just worried about Annabelle and all. You do right fine by her, Daniel. You're a good man and a good father."

"It's mighty kind of you to look out for her and to offer help and all, but she's not yours. She's not your responsibility, you know." Daniel leaned forward, emphasizing the last comment. Something about Annabelle's words stuck with him, especially after seeing Jake watch them through the window. It felt proprietary, which added to his discomfort. Daniel grabbed the pot of coffee Jake had warming on the stove. He poured himself a cup before sitting down at his desk, kicking up his feet. He didn't break his eye-lock with Jake the entire time. Tilting his head, he asked, "Care to explain yourself?"

Jake flushed to his hairline as he cleared his throat. "Well, considering Annabelle seems to be grown up and all…" Daniel didn't move a muscle. He was still piercing Jake with his glare, a combination of law enforcement and angry, protective father. Jake's throat, once more, echoed loudly in the jailhouse, with all the hacking and clearing it was doing. "I thought, maybe. Well, maybe, I could get permission to court her. You know, with your…permission, and all."

Daniel continued staring at Jake in disbelief. He had thought the deputy was being helpful, but all this time, he was really bellying up to the bar, so to speak. Annabelle was right—Jake was probably being somewhat inappropriate with her, and that didn't sit well with him. He liked Jake. He was a good man and a good deputy. But this felt fairly underhanded, as well as out of the blue.

Jake couldn't stand the silence, so he added, "What do you think? May I wait on Annabelle?"

Daniel stood up so quickly that it caused Jake to jump out of his chair, as well, turning his head in either direction, looking for the threat, before realizing that *he* was the threat. Daniel stood with his jaw and fists clenched as he glared at his deputy. If it were anyone else, he'd have hauled off and hit him. Jake had been with him for the past eleven years—eleven years! He'd watched Annabelle grow up, for Christ's sake. Daniel had mentored him, to get him ready to take over the sheriff's duties, one day.

And it wasn't as if he'd picked up some greenhorn off the street; Jake had come to him through his friend Frank Johnson, a sheriff in a nearby little boomtown that didn't have need for another deputy. Frank thought Jake had potential that shouldn't be wasted. So, when Larson, Daniel's deputy, wanted to retire, Frank sent Jake to replace him—and now Jake was prowling around his daughter. Daniel shook his head, feeling the fool. Annabelle tried, God bless her. She was always trying.

Daniel didn't answer Jake's question. He picked up the coffee mug and took it with him. He turned and walked out the jailhouse door without so much as a goodbye.

Jake watched Daniel storm out of the jail. *That was a close one.* He shook his head, trying to clear it. Daniel had thrown him for a loop when he jumped out of his chair ready to do battle. It took him a minute to realize that Daniel was ready to pummel him and not some outside threat. Blowing out a breath of relief, he found himself shaking his head again.

You'd think Annabelle was the only game in town, the way Daniel protects that girl. Sure, she's pretty, a good cook and house-keeper, and smart—oh, yeah, and smells really good and all—but Daniel needs to lighten up. Girl has to get married someday. I'm suitable for her and I'm ready. He puffed his chest out at that thought. *So, she's still on the young side at nineteen. She wants adventure.* He shrugged, his face twisting into a smirk. *That, I can give her. She just doesn't understand that kind of adventure, yet.*

He lost himself in thought about all the things he'd been planning to do to Annabelle, as well as with her. If Daniel ever got wind of his thoughts, he'd be a dead man. He'd nearly been there before with that rancher's daughter down in Texas. *Dodged that bullet.*

Jake sat back down and thought up ways to get back into Daniel's good graces—as well as Annabelle's. He'd have to work a little harder this time. *Be a little more contrite. Maybe even a little more humble?* He chuckled to himself as if he'd told a funny joke. *Yup, that's a good one. I'll try humble on for size.*

❧ 3 ❧

orning dawned bright. The light seeped in between the curtains, caressing Annabelle's face. She hadn't slept much the night before. Guilt weighed heavily on her for the trouble she'd caused her father. Then he excused her from having to deal with Jake even though he wanted both of them to go by the jail. Even more surprising was the fact that he came home almost immediately, which was very out of the ordinary for him. He usually liked to catch up on things and have a cup of coffee while talking. Lazily rolling over, she stretched with a yawn. *Better get up and get breakfast going. If something's wrong, Papa will be awake. Maybe he never even went to bed.*

She padded down the hallway, sensing him before seeing him. Papa was sitting at the table looking at his hands, which were wrapped around a coffee cup. He didn't move when she entered the kitchen. Not even when she put the pan on the stove or moved around to get eggs and other items she needed to start breakfast.

She threw a big pat of grease on the pan and turned toward Papa with her hands on her hips. "Penny for your thoughts." It was something he'd always said to her as a little girl, especially when she was being moody or reflective.

He slowly lifted his head, his eyes roving over her face and posture for a long moment as if looking for some answer to an unasked question. "Jake really bothers you, huh?" His face hung in tandem with the question—as if it couldn't move until there was an answer.

It was her turn to study her father. She tilted her head, wondering where this was coming from. "Well, yes. I think I've said that a gob of times, Papa. Why?"

Sighing as he straightened, he stretched out his arms and legs as if he'd been sitting in that position all night. "I suppose that you don't have to have him around, if that suits you. You don't need to be irritated by someone who's just trying to help."

Annabelle's eyes narrowed at him suspiciously. Leaning forward, she asked, "What are you getting at? Be straight with me."

"He gets on your nerves and so you don't have to have him around. If that's really the way you feel—well, then—I don't want him around you, either." He made to get up, but Annabelle put her hand on his shoulder to stay him.

"You're hiding something from me—don't deny it. I can read you like an open book. And you know I read *a lot* of books." By this point she was leaning toward him and piercing him with the *you-better-'fess-up* look he was so familiar with. Sometimes, it seemed as if she were the one in charge and not him. She had powers that he couldn't begin to combat.

Letting out another big sigh—a dead giveaway in Annabelle's mind—his mouth screwed up before he finally said, "Jake seems to have a tender for you."

"WHAT?"

Daniel expelled another big whoosh of air. "Last night I caught him watching us walk toward the jail. I called him out on it, and when I pressed him, he asked if he could court you."

"Whatever did you say? You didn't tell him yes, did you? Lawd, Papa! I'm telling you—" her finger was poised to point to the beat of her words, but Daniel cut those words off.

He held up his hands. "Now, honey—didn't I just tell you that if you didn't want him around I didn't want him around, either? Give me some credit, girl." He dropped his hands into his lap. Once again he made to get up.

"Just you wait a minute, please. Why now? What's going on?"

"I don't know, honey. All I know was, I was seeing red when he mentioned caring for you in a way that went beyond what he presented it to be—beyond friends helping friends. I nearly pounded him when he asked if he could court you. Not because I don't like or trust the man, but because you have such strong feelings against him. It'd never work unless you wanted it to." He shuddered as he wondered about Jake's admission and things he didn't want to mention to Annabelle.

Smoking fat and increased sizzling from the warming pan on the stove interrupted their thoughts and effectively ended their conversation. Annabelle ran to the pan and moved it slightly off the burner while putting meat into it. Glancing over her shoulder, she saw she was alone in the kitchen. Daniel had left to go get ready for the day.

He had, indeed, been sitting there all night—Annabelle belatedly noticed that the mug he was holding was from the jail. She picked it up, looking at it for a long while as if it would give her answers to the dilemma she now found herself in. The mug, however, remained silent. Sighing, she took it to the basin and began washing it out so Papa could take it back to the jail with him. She wished he could take that conversation back with him, too.

These discussions wore Daniel out. They weren't even really discussions—they were more like demands from opposing sides who weren't seeing eye to eye. He had to get out of the kitchen before Annabelle started up again. Knowing it was cowardly made doing it all the worse—lack of sleep wasn't helping his cause. It was hard raising a daughter in a rough town without family, especially with no mother to care for her. Although Lissa didn't know much about showing love and caring. She was only interested in herself.

He meant what he said about the "not loving." One couldn't love the other more—it'd never work. Even if the marriage remained intact, there were sure to be resentments. He wanted more than that for Annabelle. She was the main reason he remained strong. Lissa had blown it by running away, running back to their past back east. Nothing good could ever come of it—that was one of the few things of which he was certain. Lissa missed a chance to meet a fine young woman, a woman he was proud of even if Annabelle navigated him like a politician and was stubborn to a fault. She still had a heart of gold.

Her kind heart made him smile, which quickly turned into a scowl as he thought about Jake. He nicked himself shaving, swearing as he dabbed the trickle of blood. He still had to deal with Jake and his unholy thoughts toward his young daughter. He wanted to believe in the man's good qualities, but that desire was at war with wondering how long Jake had been thinking about Annabelle in an adult way. Swearing again for good measure, he tossed the towel into the basket and pulled on a fresh shirt.

After their unfinished conversation that morning, Annabelle decided it was time to take matters into her own hands. She didn't want to disappoint her father, but she felt trapped. While she certainly didn't want to leave him, she didn't want the alternative, either. An edgy feeling was settling inside her again. She needed freedom and independence. So what if she was supposedly free from any obligation to Jake—she still wasn't really free from him, was she? He wanted her. Papa thought he was a good man. Papa didn't say yes, she guessed, but neither did he say no. Jake didn't seem to take no for an answer, and that's the only answer she was willing to give that insufferable man. A powerful need to do something washed over her. *Best get busy, I have plenty of time…*

With the breakfast dishes finished, she moved on to tidy the bedrooms. Tomorrow was washing day, but she needed some supplies from the mercantile. More soap, thread, and some extra canned goods—foods they didn't grow in this part of the territory. They needed to stock up, as winter would eventually be on its way and deliveries would run slower. She'd have to go pick them up or at least pay for them in advance so she could slowly stock for the leaner months before the choices ran too few. Elroy had said a delivery was supposed to come earlier that week.

"Ahh!" Smacking her forehead with her palm, she spoke aloud. "It's the miners' payday—I'd better get my list together. I'm already behind!"

The night shift had probably already bought some of the newly arrived goods. Picking up a leaf of paper and a pencil, she slowly lowered herself to the table as it dawned on her: she could collect extra supplies…for herself. She propped her elbow on the table, resting her head on her open palm. Letting out a long, slow breath, she tapped the pencil on her lips while she thought more about that idea. Where did Papa say she had an aunt?

Before she knew it, well over an hour and a half had passed. She had been staring out the window thinking about the places this aunt could be, as well as the things she needed to take on a journey—she'd never been on a real trip before. Once, they rode to the next town, but only because Papa had business, which meant spending the night. He didn't want to leave her with someone else for that long.

It was her next thought about food that caused her to jump out of her reverie and run to the pantry to hurriedly collect items. Papa would be by soon, and she didn't want him to feel neglected. She also didn't want him taking too much time out of his day to wait for her. Who knew what he had to get back to? Payday always brought lots of trouble. For a couple of days afterward, it was like an explosion in an already loaded room—loud, messy, and potentially deadly. The miners seemed to lose their minds when they got paid. There was no big-city entertainment, so the whorehouse and the tavern had a steady stream of men coming and going. The mercantile got bought out and there were plenty of fights and drunkenness. Busy, busy times for the sheriff and his deputy. It was also a heavily guarded time for her. Daniel chose that moment to walk in through the back door, startling Annabelle in her rushing.

"Whoa, there! Where's the fire?" Annabelle nearly ran him over, rounding the corner. Daniel was quick, grabbing her by the elbows before she could mow him down.

"Papa! Sorry, I was making a list for the mercantile and time got away from me—I didn't want you to think that I forgot about supper."

"Never you mind about that. I'll be fine with whatever there is sitting around. You know that, darling." His eyes followed Annabelle's jerky movements around the kitchen. She'd never been like this before. She'd always been smooth and graceful, even when learning something new. He took off his hat and hung it on the peg before sitting down. He stretched his legs out and crossed his arms over his chest. He watched her in a near panic for a few more minutes to gauge her emotions.

"What's going on?" Annabelle cast a wide-eyed *Who, me?* expression over her shoulder before returning to the stove.

"Yes, you. You seem a little agitated today. Are you feeling all right?" When she didn't respond, he continued, "Do you need to go lay down or something? I can take care of myself, you know." She threw a *go on* gesture at him with her free hand as she continued to rustle up their meal with Daniel watching her.

She was nearly finished reheating leftovers and peeling oranges for them when he said, "Jake was asking about you again."

She fumbled with the plate she was loading up, almost losing it to the floor. She had to stop what she was doing to regroup. She rolled her shoulders, then straightened her posture, inclining her head. "Oh, yeah?" It sounded weak, even to her own ears. She continued filling his plate before turning around to face him. "What did he want?"

"Annabelle, you know what he wanted. What I want to know is what you want." He put his hand on top of hers. "I'll honor what you want, but I would like you to think about it before you make any big decisions." She grimaced but was cut off before she could say anything. "You're young and inexperienced. You don't know the ways of men, but you also have a dislike for how he handles you. I get that." Taking her hand in both of his, he continued, "I also get that you'd like more freedom. One way to gain more freedom would be having a husband who could take you 'round places, show you things from a husband's perspective. You'd belong to a man in a way that keeps most other men away."

"Papa, I—"

He held up a hand when she opened her mouth. "I'm not saying anything either way. What I would like you to think about is the fact that one day you'll need to be married—even if it's just for the practical reason of protection. I believe love is best, but you'll still have to work at that. Love may come easily, but it doesn't always stay—that's where the work comes in. The good kind." He whirled his arm back, indicating the town, "Look around this town. Pickin's are slim. You can hold out, but there's no guarantee. With that said, I also don't think you should go run off and marry a fellow right away, either. You have time. Use it wisely, honey. I just want to see you safe and happy. I won't be here forever. I need to see you safe."

The lump that was in Annabelle's throat grew bigger and bigger the longer he spoke. She knew what he was saying was heartfelt and pretty near to the truth. It was just that she couldn't stomach it. She wanted her papa and *just a little more* independence—some freedom to do what she needed to do without so much supervision. She wanted to walk down the street when she wanted, by herself. Would it be so terrible to feel a quarter of the independence that a man knew and took for granted? An eighth? Now she felt like she was being married off. She understood the freedoms he mentioned, but this would come with another man's schedule and a different set of rules. Papa seemed incapable of seeing it from her perspective. For a few moments of the day, she wanted to run and feel as free as the blacksmith's dog when he got loose. She knew that much freedom was asking a little much, but it'd sure be nice to experience it at least once before she had to settle down and get married.

Although Papa was reluctant to let her go, he was trying to secure her future. They both knew he could take a bullet at any time, then where would she be? If he'd died when she was little, she would have gone to the Johanssons. Now? She shrugged because she really wasn't sure where she'd go or what she'd do. Tears were begging to be let loose—like a thunderstorm brewing at the back of her eyelids. They were stinging and threatening, so she squeezed Papa's hand as she stood up. Nodding to him, she returned to the stove, packing up food and wiping things down. She brought some coffee over and filled her father's mug.

She gave him a wistful smile. "I understand, Papa. I know you love me, I do. Don't you worry about that, okay?" He returned the smile. "I love you. I promise I'll give this some more thought."

"That's the best you can do, right now. I appreciate it. I know it's a lot to take in. Jake's admission was a lot for me to take in. I never realized he felt that way. I always thought he was just being helpful. He's practically watched you grow up." A chilly silence sat between them. Annabelle shuddered; Daniel grimaced. The issue of Jake sat heavily between the two of them —Jake was a thirty-one-year-old man and Annabelle was nineteen. How long had he had these feelings?

❦ 4 ❦

Needing some time to think, Daniel didn't return to the jail right away. He found himself heading toward the opposite side of town, looking at the growing storefronts and nodding to the people out on the streets. He spent some time watching the dirt puff out from under his boots as he walked, too. He didn't feel great admitting those things to Annabelle. He felt downright underhanded, sneaky, and uncomfortable. But he was telling her the truth: her options were limited, at least right now.

What he didn't share was how torn he was about Jake. Annabelle was growing up, and he didn't know what to do about her or for her, try as he might. Even having her friend MaryAnne take her places didn't alleviate the pressure Annabelle was putting on him. She took to calling MaryAnne a "keeper." She didn't take kindly to being chaperoned everywhere—MaryAnne's agreement with him only intensified Annabelle's resistance. He knew Annabelle was yearning for a little more freedom, but right now, there wasn't much in this town for a young girl, or a woman for that matter. He'd learned that lesson from bitter experience. Daniel kicked a rock with the side of his boot; dirt went flying everywhere. He was disgusted with the whole lot of it. Shaking his head, he kept walking.

He didn't have a destination in mind but found himself in front of the bakery. He stood in the street looking at the storefront, unmoving. Finally, Mrs. Johansson came out and waved him in. "Come on, Sheriff. You look like you could do for some coffee."

Daniel had a blank look on his face but followed her in like a duckling following its mother. She indicated a seat by the door, sashaying off to get him coffee. Returning with a steaming mug freshly poured from the stove, she lowered herself into the chair across from him. After handing him the mug, she patted his hand.

"Tell me, Sheriff, what's weighing so heavily on you? I know it's not your jail because everything's been really quiet of late, and we have you to thank for it." She gave him a broad smile, making her wrinkles more pronounced, looking like someone's and everyone's grandma. Even though she had no children of her own, she was a kindly woman. She looked out for the townspeople, good and bad, and she saw both Daniel and Annabelle as her own.

Daniel twisted the mug in half turns between his fingertips, watching the back-and-forth motion. He didn't even know how to begin. He wasn't used to all this emotional nonsense, and he was thinking he was in the eye of the storm with this one.

Mrs. Johansson was a very patient woman. She sat watching the sheriff struggle with his emotions. Finally, she gave him a break. "It's okay to feel things, you know. You don't have to be the tough sheriff all the time." She waited a moment for the reply she knew wasn't coming before saying, "Annabelle is growing up and you have to let her. She has to start having choices of her own and other things to do. She's too smart and active to be cooped up in that house all day."

Daniel finally took a sip of the coffee. He looked long and hard at Mrs. Johansson. Releasing a long sigh, he shook his head. "There's not much for her to do. Her options are so limited." He shook his head as he looked at the tabletop. "I made a mistake coming here."

Her head jerked back, and she made a raspy noise of disgust from the back of the throat. "Annabelle is not *her mother*." She said it softly and as kindly as she could, barely choking out the word *mother*. "That woman never behaved like a mother, not even the day she gave birth to that beautiful girl." She shook her head. "You did what you needed to do, Daniel. Don't you forget that. That woman made her bed and now she has to lie in it. Her decisions are no fault of yours. *She* chose to be with you but didn't honor her end of the deal. We don't take kindly to that kind of disloyalty, especially where children are involved. She knew what she was getting into. More's the shame on her." Mrs. Johansson had worked herself into a lather. She was breathing hard and pointing her finger at the bewildered sheriff.

"But Annabelle never had a choice. She's here because of me. Her mom's not here because of me." The sheriff's low, sorrowful tone brought her back to the moment.

"Pfft. You know that's nonsense as well as the rest of us. She loved you, but she never was in it for the long haul. She only wanted things the way she wanted them. Sheriff, you knew that when she married you, yet you still put up with it. You deserve better than that." He looked ready to object when she stayed him with her hand. "You do. I say good riddance to the likes of her." If her husband were there, he'd have spit on the floor in agreement. She tilted her head and pursed her lips at Daniel as if to say so. "I'm sorry that you loved her because she brought nothing but pain, but that's the way it is. Annabelle's better off without her." Mrs. Johansson harrumphed. She slowly hauled herself out of her chair and went back to the kitchen. She brought back a slice of buttered bread, setting it in front of him.

"Eat up, honey. You're going to need it the way you're looking, so long in the tooth."

The sheriff did the only thing he could do at that moment. He ate the bread.

Daniel thanked Mrs. Johansson for the vittles and conversation. His subconscious must've known he needed a little chat with someone who knew of his past. He didn't like bringing it up, and he evaded it so much that people either didn't know or no longer asked. The ones who knew, really knew—like Mr. and Mrs. Johansson—kept mum.

Even Annabelle didn't know about the situation with her mother. He left it as "something happened." Something did happen—she left. Just as she had threatened all along. Why he took it so hard when he figured it would eventually come to pass, he did not know. Perhaps he thought she'd stick it out for Annabelle's sake. Maybe he was a little more attached than he'd like to admit. Now, with Annabelle on the cusp of being a woman, it was coming back to haunt him. Hell, she was already a woman; she just didn't know all the womanly stuff a mother should be teaching her daughter.

Shaking his head, he turned back toward the jail, walking slowly this time. He wasn't in a hurry for yet another conversation about Annabelle. With every step he took, his entire body became heavier and heavier. His limbs felt like they were as heavy as leg irons.

When he reached the jail, Jake was sitting at his desk, looking relaxed and self-satisfied. Daniel dropped himself into his chair, casting a glare at him. "What're you so happy 'bout? You're looking like a fucking ray of sunshine."

"And you're looking like a thundercloud. What crawled up your backside?"

"You."

Jake guffawed at that because he knew it to be true. He was planning on working Daniel until he practically gave Annabelle to him, wrapped in a bow with his blessing. If he didn't get her as a gift, he'd take her any way he could. He was tired of sleeping alone. He had a regular whore back in Adamsville, but he couldn't very well shack up with one here. He wanted a woman in his bed as well as taking care of his life for him. Besides, he'd eaten food Annabelle had made and wanted a steady diet of that—and more.

"Honestly, what're you smiling at?"

The tips of Jake's ears tinged pink getting caught thinking raunchy thoughts about Daniel's daughter. He really liked Daniel, but he was far too nice of a man. Too nice for the Wild West. Too nice, in fact, for law enforcement. He'd always wondered why Daniel was in this mining town, even if it was growing rapidly. He didn't have that hunger for riches like the others who came out west. He didn't seem to be escaping from some past, either. Questions kept rolling around in Jake's mind.

"Now what?" Daniel was not having this silence—Jake staring at him without seeing him.

Finally, Jake advanced, circling his prey. "Why'd you come to this here town?"

The day had officially gone from bad to worse. "Why are you suddenly prying into my business, Jake?" Daniel was working his lower jaw, which was a bad sign. "First my Annabelle, and now me? What're *you* up to?"

"Nothing. There's nothing to do today, and I was just sitting here wondering about the man who may someday be my future father-in-law, that's all." Jake leaned back, clasping his hands behind his head, looking pretty satisfied with himself at that one. He had the gall to smile at Daniel, feeling pretty proud of scoring one off him.

"Really?" Daniel nearly sneered. He had had it with all this talking from everyone. "Did Annabelle tell you something that she didn't tell me?" Daniel leaned over his desk at Jake. "Because, as of this morning, she wasn't too keen on the idea of marriage." He quirked his brow at him as if to say, *your turn.*

"Well, now, Sheriff, you just have to give her some time. She'll come around. Every woman eventually does."

That was the last straw for Daniel's nerves. Especially since, in his experience, not every woman "came around." His experience was telling him a very different story, and he didn't like the tone Jake was taking regarding Annabelle.

"And what sort of experience do you have with ladies? Bona fide ladies, not soiled doves from some devil's addition, that you're accustomed to being around."

It was now Jake's turn to glare. He'd lost that round. He went back to his original idea of humility. "That's a good sort of question, especially from someone I'd like to have as an in-law." He nodded as if Daniel was some sort of genius. "I don't have much experience with ladies because I've not had the pleasure of being around many, especially none as fine as your pretty and sweet little Annabelle."

Daniel knew Jake was toying with him, but he decided to drop the bait. He went to the stove and poured himself some coffee. He'd been drinking a lot of it lately. Better than drinking dynamite like his father, although his father was too sophisticated to call whiskey that. He was too highbrow to even come out and see his own mines. He always let everyone else do his dirty work. Grunting at the thought, he shook his head.

He sat down and began leafing through Wanted sketches. He kept busy for a good five or ten minutes before Jake asked him again about his past.

"Daniel, where you from, originally? You never did say when I first came."

Exasperated, Daniel didn't bother looking up at Jake. He continued to study the sketch of Van Der Kamp, even though he was already familiar with it. Cold eyes stared back at him from the poster.

"I know."

Jake's mouth dropped open a little, but he quickly recovered. "Well?"

"Well, what?" He looked up, holding Jake's eyes until Jake held out the palm of his hand, asking for more. "I don't talk about where I came from or who my people are. I'm in *law enforcement*. No one needs to know, especially if they're going to go back and threaten my people." Jake wouldn't release his eye-lock, so Daniel added, "Satisfied?" Narrowing his eyes, he tilted his head to the side, punctuating the question.

"Not really. But I hear you just fine. I won't ask any more—for a while."

Daniel snorted at that and went back to his paperwork.

5

An early-morning glow without the benefit of the sun brightened part of the boardwalk—the sun was just climbing over the mountain peaks as Daniel arrived at the jail. He wanted some peace and quiet before Jake rolled in, and he certainly didn't want to talk about Annabelle. As much as he loved the girl, she was becoming a tiring subject. The coffee was brewing, and George, the town drunk, was sleeping one off. They'd have to splash down the cell because George was becoming too much of a regular of late. It was starting to smell like a barn in there. If he had wanted to be a farmer, he would've left his family to do that. Wrinkling his nose, he opened up the tax collections books and got to work with his assessments and collections tallies. He wanted to make sure he had reports ready to send with the next expressman. He should be here any day now.

Having lost track of time, Daniel got up to get more coffee and noticed that Jake still hadn't come in. While he didn't want to have another courting conversation, or more prying into his personal life, for that matter, he was beginning to wonder where Jake was. He looked at his watch. Late—that was unusual, as well. Stretching, Daniel went to the window that looked onto the main street. The hairs on the back of his neck stood up. It was unusually quiet. Walking out the front door, he looked up and down the boardwalk. No one was walking around. He hurried home, slipping into the side door.

"Annabelle!" He waited a moment. Trying again, louder, he drew out her name, hollering, "Aaa-nnaa-belle."

When she didn't answer, he tore down the street to the mercantile. He had a feeling she'd be there. She'd been talking a lot about washing and provisions. She didn't mention her friend, MaryAnne, at all. He knew she wouldn't mention Jake. So, no chaperone, then. He raced down the middle of the street with dust flying out from under his boots until they pounded on the wooden steps of the mercantile. Still moving forward, he reached out to open the door, finding what he was looking for as well as an additional surprise.

Perfect! I'll go to the mercantile today, buy the items from my list and extra supplies for my "trip." I'm not sure where Aunt Hannah lives, but I have time to do some more investigating. I'll start slowly collecting the things I need for the trip—that way, if I'm caught off guard by Jake or Papa, I'm ready to go at a moment's notice.

Pep talk over, she nodded to herself, reassured that she was doing the right thing. Stalling, she tied and adjusted her bonnet, then took it off, before she grabbed the basket from the pantry on her way out. *Some of the other items will have to be delivered to the house later. Maybe I could persuade MaryAnne to go out with me and pick them up. I'll have to figure out a reason why everything was paid for and ready to go, however. Cross that bridge later.* Drawing in a deep, fortifying breath, she peered out the window and looked up and down the street. When she saw enough people on the streets, she decided it was time to sneak over to the mercantile—alone. Hopefully, Mrs. Johansson wouldn't see her this time.

Easing open the back door, she silently cursed the creaking sound it made when opened slowly. Once again, she peered out in either direction, straightened, then casually walked out of the house, shutting the door behind her. Thinking that she'd be back pretty quickly, she latched the door but didn't lock it. She didn't want to rouse any suspicions in case someone came by. She could always claim that she'd stepped out to check the garden or was talking to someone. Determined steps propelled her down Main Street, mingling with what little foot traffic there was, until she found herself in front of the mercantile.

Annabelle's plan to slip into the shop through the barely opened door was foiled by the chiming bell attached to the top of it. Elroy had had it installed a couple of days prior because some of the craftier miners, and the few prospectors who banded together to protect each other's claims and hadn't been run off, were trying to sneak in and steal his goods. Elroy looked up and met Annabelle's gaze, then was frantically contorting himself peering around her, the whites of his eyes betraying his shock. Clearly, he had heard the gossip about her last solo adventure and was hoping she wasn't alone.

Despite Elroy's surprise, Annabelle smiled brightly and nodded, carrying on as if being by herself was a normal occurrence. She nearly laughed when his jaw fell open, expelling air as his hands hit the counter to support himself.

She walked over to the shelves in the foodstuffs section and began picking up canned beans and other items from her list, placing them in her basket. When she was finished, she moved toward the perfumed, milled soaps. These particular bars happened to be an expensive luxury that only Mrs. Jones and some of her girls from the house just outside of town could afford regularly. Holding a bar to her nose, she inhaled deeply. Peppermint. Cradling it gently in her hands, she shook her head, returning it to the shelf. Lifting a different bar to her nose, closing her eyes, she inhaled a delicate lavender scent. Palming it, she weighed her options. Deciding that it was better to have a couple of extra bars on hand, as she might not have the time to make more, and not wanting to leave Papa in the lurch, she slowly lowered the lavender one into her basket.

As she settled it into the basket, the hairs on the back of her neck rose. She turned around slowly to find Elroy staring at her with an odd look on his face. When they locked eyes, his lips thinned as he shook his head and immediately turned toward the front window. He was behaving oddly, which made her heart pick up pace. Panicked, she swiveled her head, looking around at the few people inside before taking a couple of tentative steps toward him.

She stopped near the end of the aisle, leaning forward in his direction. A prickly feeling washed over her and the air felt charged. Being cautious, she softly asked, "Elroy?" He didn't look at her. Worried, she repeated herself, a little louder this time. "Elroy, you all right?"

Again, Elroy refused to look at her. She took a couple of tentative steps forward but stopped when the door flung open.

The bell clanged loudly before the sound was halted by the door itself. Her head whipped toward the banging sound, eyes widening at the sight of a giant man striding in. Normally, she'd have had to squint when the front door opened, because the store was poorly lit—Elroy didn't want windows smashed by thieves, so his weren't overly large. However, this man blocked nearly all the light that attempted to follow him in. Annabelle was so busy gawking at this intrusion that Elroy's odd behavior from earlier was temporarily forgotten—even though he was already pulling money out of the register and putting it on the counter. Then the tall, broad man gave Elroy his demand in a deep, even voice.

"Give me your money." Three long strides brought him to the counter. She felt as if the air had been sucked out of the room, running away with the sunshine as the door slammed shut. She couldn't see the man's face because of his hat, pulled low, and the bandana covering the rest of it. His legs were so long that he reached the counter and was sweeping money into a sack before she realized what was happening. Noticing that he didn't have a gun didn't make her feel any better; his giant hands were large enough to snap a man's neck, if need be. Elroy wasn't particularly big, either, which made the situation all the worse. While Elroy could handle most of the miners, this man was *not* a miner. She'd never seen him before. That's when the gears started turning in her head, and a moment of panic washed over her. *He's part of the gang Papa was warning me about...*

Once again the bell on the door chimed, snapping her out of her trance. This time the door opened at a moderate pace, and it was her father who was standing there, not some tall, broad-shouldered brute who blocked the light from coming in. Surprise and worry forced a gasp out of her, her hand flying to her mouth. "*Papa.*" An uncontrolled whisper of acknowledgment slipped from her mouth.

She stared at her father as the sharp chill of fear washed over her. A long, muscular arm snaked around her waist, pulling her snugly against broad warmth. She barely realized what had happened before he was speaking again. "Step aside, Sheriff." His voice was low and steady, with no hint of anger or animosity, surprising Annabelle. The sheriff didn't move, so the giant pulled her in tighter, lifting her off the floor with a little shake. The air went out of her with a whoosh, more because she wasn't prepared for such handling, not because he had hurt her.

Annabelle watched her father's eyes grow wide as the stranger manhandled her. In turn, she went wild-eyed, looking at her papa for guidance, but he ignored her, assessing the situation. His assessment was interrupted by the man's still-even tone.

"Wouldn't want your darlin' daughter to get caught in the crossfire." The sheriff's eyes were locked on the giant's while Annabelle's blood roared in her ears. Papa was still refusing to acknowledge her.

Too scared to say anything, she cooperated. She kept still, holding her breath, not wanting to anger the man holding her. For a split second she was worried about getting a scolding for being out alone. The ridiculousness of it all wasn't lost on her; neither was her fear for Papa. Finally, shaking his head, the sheriff stepped aside. Annabelle was shocked to see his face fall in momentary defeat. When Charlie walked Annabelle past him, Papa whispered, "Hang tight, Annabelle. I'll find you, no matter what."

Overwhelm consumed her, constricting her breath—making her unable to respond. She had just wanted to go to the mercantile alone—argh! She could slap herself right now. Her throat was tight and, for the first time in a long time, she was on the verge of tears—panicky tears. This strange man was so large and overpowering—he felt like a heavy blanket on an overwhelmingly hot summer's night. While his grip on her didn't necessarily hurt, it frightened her with its possessiveness. He ushered her out of the mercantile, and she somehow found her way onto his horse.

She didn't remember anything else that was said, not even the ride to the camp. It was a blur of dirt and branches until they stopped and were suddenly surrounded by a large group of scary yet curious men. It was one of those times she really wished she had heeded her papa. He was a wise man—whether she wanted to admit it or not.

6

Enough reflecting—her mind returned to her present situation. The tent provided plenty of uninterrupted time to think about the error of her ways. Watching the top of the tent ripple with the mild wind, she realized that she must've dozed off, because she was experiencing mixed feelings and sensations from moments this morning that simultaneously felt like weeks ago. Blinking and trying to stretch, she went back to talking to herself.

Yes, I could have done with a spot of listening ears, as Mary-Anne enjoys saying. Annabelle nodded to herself then shook her head. What a pickle! She leaned her head back against a crate. It was the only "furniture," so to speak, in the tent, other than a cot and two bedrolls that were neatly rolled up and placed to the side. *Whoever stayed in this tent either just arrived or is very Spartan.* Shaking her head, she knew it didn't matter. She had to get back to Papa. This was much worse than any talk of Jake. Much worse.

The past few days rolled through her mind like her history lessons, although these were personal—personal *and* painful. A big sneeze shook her. *If I ever make it back, Papa will never let me out of his sight!* She hung her head. *I suppose I deserve that, at the very least. I've been so terrible.* The thumping of her head against the crate emphasized her point. Wondering how Papa was doing, and what he was doing, lodged an already-deep groove of guilt deeper into her heart. It morphed into a physical pain in her chest, a restrictive, squeezing feeling. Unconsciously rubbing her hand over her heart, she found herself becoming short of breath.

Annabelle continued to talk to herself for the remainder of the morning and into the early afternoon. Even though it'd only been a couple of hours, no one had checked on her, and she was starting to go stir-crazy. Her entire body was numb from sitting so rigidly, coupled with the fear of drawing any attention, and she was pretty sure she needed to relieve herself. Although, as numb as she was, she could be wrong. She also thought she might be hungry. For Pete's sake, she had a poor sense of awareness, didn't she? *Thirsty, definitely thirsty.* The mere thought of a cup of water made the back of her throat tickle and brought on a spate of coughing. *Argh!* She kicked her foot out in frustration, only to be sorry after the fact. The pins and needles were unbearable.

The chattering pity party in her head started to slow down as she dropped into a doze again along with the rest of her body. That was the way Charlie found her when he came in to check on her in the early afternoon.

Charlie sat on a log that faced his tent. Annabelle had spent the remainder of the morning tied up inside it; fortunately for her, he had tied her loosely in the front and not in the back like the others wanted. He had taken care of his horse and, now, was cleaning his gun and sharpening his knives. He tried checking on her once, earlier, but she yelled and spat at him. He had to gag her and leave so she'd settle down. Not only did the gang have a variety of ideas of how to keep her prisoner, they still thought of him as being a captive and hadn't given him any weapons until he was "ready" for the heist—their fake straw-drawing that forced his hand. By the looks on their faces, they hadn't fully trusted him until today.

Looking up at the closed tent, he frowned. He had to decide what to do with Annabelle. He was so conflicted; it felt like there was a heavy weight on his chest. He felt bad for taking her, but he'd thought it was the easiest thing to do under the circumstances. He didn't want the sheriff to shoot, and he didn't want anyone to get hurt. Unfortunately, the heist had to be a success because he wouldn't allow Jimmy to get hurt again. He was just lucky that he was able to make the connection between the sheriff and his daughter so quickly. At any rate, he and Annabelle were in unfamiliar territory, so they might as well try to navigate it the best they could. Whether or not she'd cooperate was another story. Blowing out a long breath, he continued moving the whetstone up his blade.

Jimmy plunked himself beside Charlie, nodding hello. He watched Charlie for a moment, then tilted his head toward the tent. "What're ya gonna do about her?"

Charlie finished sliding the stone up the blade before stopping, continuing to stare at the blade in his hand while holding the whetstone in the other. After a moment, he finally answered. "Dunno. I feel bad about the whole thing." Shrugging, he went back to work.

They sat quietly for a few moments before Jimmy said, "Well, I'm sure whatever you decide will work out. It always does, whether you think so or not." He patted Charlie on the shoulder, got up, and dusted off his trousers before walking off.

Charlie scratched his head as he watched his younger brother leave. *That's the oddest conversation we've had yet.* He continued to watch the path long after Jimmy was gone. Jimmy was the first person he'd seen since he brought Annabelle up here. Everyone else had steered clear of Charlie, and probably Wrighty, as well. They seemed to be waiting for the inevitable showdown at dinner, which was running a little late. Deciding he'd better check on Annabelle again to see if she was okay, he set his work down and opened the tent flap.

Standing just inside the tent, he watched the jagged rise and fall of her chest, straining against her dress from the way she had fallen asleep. She refused to use the cot and was propped against the crate. She was a stubborn but attractive creature. He marveled at her strength—physically and emotionally. She didn't complain at all while she was being taken or during the ride. She'd fought Wrighty with all she had—he felt her strength and determination when he was trying to set her to rights. One thing Wrighty was correct about: she was a wildcat—one he felt an oddly fierce need to protect. He felt somewhat wrong watching her as she dozed, so he cleared his throat. Startled, her body jerked before her eyes settled on him.

Annabelle glared at Charlie; he stared back blankly at her and shrugged in return. Walking up to her, he untied the gag to find himself at the wrong end of an angry string of words.

Talking over her, Charlie said, "If you don't shut your pie hole, I'm going to put this rag *in* your mouth like the rest of the gang wanted and not around it like I did earlier. Understand?"

That shut her up pretty quickly, but it didn't stop her from glaring at him. She kicked out at him once more, but that stopped as soon as he gave her the side-eye and held up the rag as a reminder. He squatted in front of her with his elbows on his spread knees. The rag dangled from his hands in between his legs. Finally, he said, "Look, I can't say this enough, but I'm sorry. I'm especially sorry about what I'm going to have to do at dinner. It'd be best if you tried to cooperate. Believe it or not, I'm on your side." He stood up and turned toward the tent's flap.

"Are you kidding me?" She shouted after him, anger making her forget about the rag threat. "You—*you* kidnapped me! How could you possibly be on *my* side? Tell me that."

Dropping his arms, he turned around. "I didn't want anyone to get hurt. I wasn't armed, but your father was. It also seems that he and the gang already have a history of some sort."

She slammed both feet down on the hard ground. "Because you're outlaws! Why is that so hard for you to understand?"

Charlie's eyes narrowed, and his voice went very low. "I. Am. Not. An. Outlaw. Let's get that straight from the start." Extending his long arm, he pointed his finger at her, causing her to shrink back just a little. "Neither is my brother. We're here against our will. I'm just doing what I have to, to survive. Got it?" His furrowed brows and the fire in his eyes dared her to question him. When she didn't respond, he said, "I was forced to rob the mercantile. You were an unfortunate but lucky casualty."

"Lucky for you, you mean?"

"Nooo," he responded, drawing the word out slow and low. "Lucky that I won't let them do the things they want to do to you."

Still unsatisfied, she poked him, again. "What do you mean, 'forced'?"

Charlie ran his hand through his hair. She'd seen her dad do that a thousand times. Even more so recently, she realized. Hanging his head, his hands went to his hips. In a quiet voice, he said, "If I didn't rob the mercantile—they'd kill Jimmy." Lifting his head, he looked her squarely in the eyes and jabbed his index finger at her. "No more talking. Cooperating is what you're going to do. I'm trying to save us all here, and you aren't helping."

She made a displeased noise but didn't say anything more. Her lips flattened, but her eyes were wary. Her expression spoke volumes to him: she knew she'd pushed him far enough and didn't know what to make of his comments. He confused her.

Too bad for her. She confused him, too.

7

Dinnertime finally came a little bit past two o'clock, a couple hours later than normal because of the robbery and general commotion. Charlie went back into the tent to collect Annabelle. Even with his help, it was difficult for her to stand up. Grimacing, she collapsed from numbness—she was too stubborn to move around or sit on the cot. Charlie tightened his grip to help stabilize her and waited a moment before trying to help her walk. Despite the wait, she had to hold on to him for a long time before she could make any progress. Even then, Charlie had to support her with his arm. He walked them very slowly out of the tent and down the path before stopping.

"Um, do you need to—"

Annabelle turned bright red, nodding her head.

"Will you be able to—"

Her head nodded even more furiously, like she was going to combust from shame. Charlie looked around to make sure no one else was coming down the path. He thought about her running away, but she could barely walk after stubbornly refusing to use the cot and sitting with her hands tied on the cold, hard ground—even though he had tried to make the ropes loose. Besides, she wouldn't get far even if she tried.

"All right, if you think you can manage. I'm going to prop you against a tree for privacy—just don't do anything stupid. I may be big, but I can run really fast." He gave her a hard look to discourage any funny business. She returned it with her lips pressed tightly and her eyebrows knitted together, her features trying to gather in the middle of her face in a huddle of frustration. "I don't think you will, but in all fairness, I've got to warn you. Right?"

She sighed as he led the way off the path and left her to take care of things. "Holler when you're done. I'll come back for you."

As humiliating as it was, he was being extra helpful and courteous. Not what she'd expect out of such a giant brute as he was. Especially not out of a thieving gang member—*right, not a gang member*. Rolling her eyes, she took care of her business.

They finally made it to the common area. Her stomach growled as soon as she smelled food; she hadn't eaten much breakfast. She threw an embarrassed side-glance at Charlie before looking down at the ground. He smiled. "I'm pretty hungry myself, and I didn't have my day interrupted, either." She whipped her head to glare at him, but he returned her look with a sheepish one of his own.

Some of the men stopped what they were doing to watch the two of them. They looked like a couple attending a formal meal, the way Charlie was escorting her down the hill. They didn't look like a bandit and his captive. A couple of them shook their heads in disgust while the others found it amusing. Smirks and smiles crossed their faces. Two of the dirtier men snickered as they elbowed each other. Charlie didn't have much contact with women, and he was awkward in his own right. Wrighty happened to enter the clearing at about the same time.

"What the hell you doing, escorting her to a ball or something?" The men hooted and guffawed. Annabelle and Charlie both flushed. "She's our captive, for Christssake! What's wrong with you, boy?"

The teasing nature of the situation immediately deflated. Some of the men went silent. They knew Charlie and Jimmy no longer tolerated being called "boy" or any of the other derogatory nicknames they'd come up with for them over the years. In reality, they were no longer "boys," and they'd both worked hard and proven themselves in many ways. Today, especially, since Charlie's first heist had been successful—probably more successful than the rest of their first solo heists.

Charlie tensed but didn't take the bait. "Wrighty, she's practically injured from being tied up. Can't walk well. I'm not carrying her to supper." He cocked his head in the direction of a shocked Annabelle. "Besides, I don't think she wants to be carried around by the likes of me."

Before Wrighty could respond, the men started laughing and went about their business. Annabelle didn't know what to make of that after their conversation in the tent. Charlie was a paradox, if anything. Everyone was snatching plates and lining up for food or something to drink.

Charlie sat Annabelle down. "I'll grab us something to eat."

"So polite, Charlie. Your mama would've been very proud." Wrighty had sidled up behind them. Charlie tensed, ready for a fight, but Wrighty continued, "Go on, now. Go git some grub for you and the princess here. We'll be waiting for ya." He slid onto the bench beside Annabelle, straddling it so he faced her. She looked in the opposite direction, but Wrighty kept staring at her anyway. Charlie gave her a compassionate look and threw an icy glare at Wrighty, who just smiled back at him over Annabelle's shoulder. He knew Charlie wouldn't cause a scene, no matter how hard he razzed him.

Charlie walked off, but Annabelle continued to look after him, not wanting to acknowledge Wrighty. She could feel him assessing her, taking in her features with his dirty-minded eyes. While Jake looked at her in similar ways, Wrighty made her skin crawl worse than Jake ever did. She shuddered at the thought of it. Wrighty took that opening to rub his hand on her back, causing her to jump off her seat. Her body jerked away but her head swiveled toward him.

He leaned toward her to whisper in her ear, "Are you cold, darling? Let me take you back to my cabin so I can warm you up." Her eyes burned with indignation as her hand swung up to hit him. He caught her by the wrist before she could make contact. "Uh, uh, uh." He wagged his index finger at her while gripping her wrist hard. "Wouldn't do that if I were you, darling. I'm much more of a man than that youngin' Charlie is. Try something like that again with me, and you'll be flat on your back before you know what happened to you." He leaned in as he spoke, rubbing his thumb along the inside of her wrist. The look of disgust on her face made him laugh and caused others to look their direction. He made a point of kissing her temple and sliding his mouth to her ear for their audience. He whispered, "I'll be back for you. Don't you worry. I won't leave you wanting."

She gasped, furiously struggling to reclaim her arm, which caused him to laugh once again. He released her and ran his forefinger down the side of her face as he was getting up from the bench, moving before Charlie could make his way back. Two of Wrighty's men had Charlie by the arms, restraining him. He had a look of murder on his face. The men continued to hold Charlie while Wrighty sauntered over to the line, cutting in front of him. "Little filly's all yours—for now. I'd watch yourself, if I were you."

Wrighty took the plate Charlie still had clutched in his hand before Wrighty's cronies released him. He yanked his arms away and shrugged his shoulders before marching over to Annabelle to check on her. He could hear the laughter thrown his way, but all he could see was Annabelle's distressed face—his vision and senses tunneled in on her and her only.

Kneeling in front of her he asked, "Are you all right? Did he hurt you?" He brushed a lock of hair away from her face, causing her to blush.

"I'm fine, thank you. He's just trying to scare me."

"You'd be right to be scared of him—he's dangerous. Stay away from him, if you can."

Despite the fear and disgust coursing through her, she gave him an incredulous look and spread her arms wide. "Really? I think my options are limited."

"Ah, yeah." Clearing his throat awkwardly and looking around, Charlie waved his brother over. "Jimmy, will you grab yourself and Annabelle some food, then sit with her? I'll get mine when you get back." Jimmy nodded and went off.

Van Der Kamp had been off in the trees watching the entire time. He nodded with approval before joining them. Sitting directly across from Charlie, he acknowledged Annabelle with a curt nod.

"Did you make any decisions regarding our guest?" Once again everyone stopped what they were doing to listen. This hardened gang of criminals was worse than a knitting circle when it came to gossip. They were a bunch of nosey hens. Charlie shot a look of disgust at a man peering over Van Der Kamp's shoulder, but it didn't discourage him from remaining where he was.

Charlie looked at Annabelle, who wouldn't return his look. She cast her gaze at the table with her head bent slightly forward. He watched her for a moment before turning toward Van Der Kamp. "We should ransom her—and make sure she gets back to her daddy, safely."

Van Der Kamp held Charlie's gaze with cold, flat eyes that had made many a man piss his pants. He pulled in a long breath through one nostril, causing half his face to scrunch up, lifting part of his mouth and cheek. For a second, Charlie thought he was going to clear his throat and hawk phlegm on him. Van Der Kamp read the look on Charlie's face and chuckled. "Fine idea. I'm sure we can come to a reasonable agreement with the sheriff." He rose from his seat, adding, "Mighty gentlemanlike of you, too." He nodded at Annabelle before taking his leave.

Charlie released his breath in relief, causing Annabelle to finally look at him. He was about to say something when Jimmy arrived with their food. Setting a plate down in front of Annabelle, he passed the other to Charlie and held out a staying hand. "Sit. I'll go back and get some for me. That's for you."

Jimmy was off before either of them could thank him or get up. They ate in silence for a few minutes before Annabelle asked quietly, "Did you mean what you said?"

"What's that?" Charlie asked, turning his head sideways to look at her.

"About Papa—getting me back to him."

"Yes, every word. I didn't intend to take you, it just sort of worked out that way. I plan to see that you're safe." He went back to eating as if she was asking a polite question about their meal. She couldn't believe how matter-of-fact he was being. As if it were natural to take a daughter from her father. As if *borrowing her*—and then returning her—was just an everyday occurrence. She wanted to throw her hands up in the air in frustration. Instead, she watched him eat for a few minutes more, but he didn't look back up at her—she could tell he was purposely ignoring her. Sighing, she picked up a biscuit and continued her meal. It gave her a few minutes to mull over the morning's events and the few early afternoon hours that followed.

❧ 8 ❧

"It's your turn, you jackass! You're always trying to get out of work."

Orrin puffed up and pointed his finger at Horton. "Go to hell, Horton. I just had the late afternoon. I want the evening—it's my turn."

"I had late afternoon yesterday. Stop being lunk-headed, or I'll feed you my fist!"

Orrin didn't bother using words. He pushed his full body weight into Horton, who was a little shorter and much thinner than him. Horton saw Orrin's tell—he usually blinked hard before throwing himself—so Horton knew the move was coming. Orrin was as predictable as heat in summer. Fists started flying as Charlie approached.

"What the hell?" He pushed between the two men, straight-arming them apart. The men were huffing and puffing from exertion, anger, and general annoyance. "What's wrong with you two?"

Looking from one man to the other, he waited for a response. The men just glared at each other like two dogs in a fight. "What is going on? Who's on guard duty?"

"That's the problem," Horton shouted, jabbing a finger at Orrin around Charlie's broad frame. "*He* doesn't do anything around here. *He's* always trying to get out of work."

The scuffling started again, and Charlie had to keep Horton away because he was the angrier of the two. It was easily done with a shove of his arm. A surprised Horton stumbled back, wide-eyed. Charlie glowered at Orrin. "Why *aren't* you taking your shift? I know that Horton took the afternoon yesterday. I'm sure there wasn't any trading, *was there?*" He quirked his brow at Orrin as he towered over him. There was a time when Charlie wouldn't dare stand up to these two men, or any of them, for that matter. Not even Jaems, who was much shorter and weaker than him, even two years ago when Charlie was still growing. This robbery had changed him. The kidnapping even more.

Orrin tensed under the scrutiny. He wasn't used to Charlie taking such a decisive and physical stand against him. Horton was glaring at him from behind Charlie's back. Orrin finally relaxed and admitted what he wouldn't before.

"Annabelle is just too much. I get tired of her lip. She makes my head want to burst—it's pounding by the time I'm off duty. And I certainly don't want to have to fight a woman, neither." He crossed his arms and glowered back at them.

Charlie heaved a sigh, slouching his shoulders. "For the love of Pete, what are you guys? You act like a bunch of women around here. You," pointing directly at Orrin, "are taking the afternoon. You'll do it politely, no matter what she throws at you. Keep yourself under control. Why do you let her get to you?"

Orrin looked ready to protest, but Charlie straightened to his full six feet four inches, which widened his naturally broad shoulders, and so Orrin thought better of it.

"Fine." He kicked the dirt like a petulant three-year-old. "I'm not happy about this, Charlie. Someone needs to do something about her—soon."

Orrin stalked off to the tent and threw himself on the ground, purposefully giving them his back. Sending the message that he didn't want to talk to them and neither did he fear them. Doubly insulting. Hmph.

Charlie looked at Horton. "Are you two done being babies?" He put his hands on his belt, tilting his head forward.

"Charlie, she's a wildcat. No joke. Someone needs to put her in her place. She's nice to you; you do it. It'll make life 'round here easier." Charlie just looked at him.

"Hell, I never thought I'd say this about a woman, especially one as pretty as she is, but the sooner she goes, the happier I'll be." Horton shook his head. "Damn."

Horton walked off, leaving Charlie wondering why Annabelle was such a problem for the rest of them. She'd turned a bunch of hardened criminals into sissies. It was his turn to shake his head, because Jimmy and Charlie had been afraid of these men for years, yet this little slip of a woman had *nearly* everyone cowering.

Communication, if you could even call it that, didn't improve, and the following days were difficult for everyone. Nerves were jumped on and patience was frayed. At the center of this turmoil was a small woman, just shy of five feet three inches tall. The problem was, they didn't know what to do with such an outspoken piece of calico. Much smaller than the men in the camp, she fought them tooth and nail. She was fairly strong for her size, and her words were more powerful than the blasts of dynamite from the mines. None of them dared use force because she was now a "guest," and Van Der Kamp had made it clear—*do not hurt her*. Some of them thought a good slap was in order, but they didn't dare try that, either. She elicited a range of reactions from the men, from outright refusal to take watch to wanting to give her a good lacing.

It was the desires in between the two extremes that had Charlie in knots. He was constantly on edge because he couldn't watch her the entire time—that would indicate he was interested in her. It would set off Wrighty, who already made it clear that he wanted her. From the get-go, Wrighty had shown too much interest in Annabelle, which made Charlie nervous. Fortunately, Wrighty wasn't taking any shifts because he was so high in the pecking order, but he did have loyal kiss-asses who were willing to do his bidding.

Charlie was pacing outside the tent for an afternoon shift—the most dreaded shift, because that's when Annabelle was the orneriest. She was tired, bored, and then, eventually, hungry for supper. He had just returned Annabelle to the tent post-dinner. Goat greeted him with a raised hand and moved slowly toward him.

"Hip bothering you, today, Goat?"

"Yup." Goat rubbed it for good measure. "I sure could use some help with the meals."

"I'd help you, but I really need to keep watch."

"Mind if I sit a spell with you? You look like you could take a load off your feet."

"I suppose I could, but just for a bit."

"What? You need to wear a deeper groove in the dirt?" He pointed to the spot where Charlie had been pacing. "You look like you've already been real busy-like." Goat made a snorting noise as he sat down. Charlie watched him slowly lower himself before he joined the older man. Goat had taken a lead plumb to his back, which affected his left hip. If he worked too long, he became overly stiff and walked slowly, sometimes even hobbled. Van Der Kamp went easy on him—Goat was the only one who didn't suffer from his ire.

Goat sighed with such satisfaction it made Charlie smile. At times, he was such a simple man. Charlie settled in, all the while keeping an eye on the tent.

"She ain't goin' nowhere." Goat bobbed his head toward the tent.

Charlie's gaze didn't waver. "That's not the point. She's not safe here."

"So, she's causing a stir. She's angry and bored." Goat turned to look at Charlie. "Can you blame her? She's been sitting in that damn hot tent for the past three days with nothin' to do. I'd want to kick some ass if I was forced to sit around like that—tied up and all." He shrugged, reaching in his pocket for his tobacco pouch. He laboriously shook out some tobacco into a paper, spreading it out evenly. Charlie watched him because he knew a moral would be following his deliberate actions.

"You know what I'd do?" He licked the edge of the paper before rolling it. He ran the freshly rolled cigarette under his nose, inhaling deeply. "Aaah. Love me some fresh tabacky." Striking a match, he put the cig in his mouth and lit it. He took a long pull on it, making the end glow brighter as the flame died down. His eyes closed while he took in a drag and then opened after he blew out a long spiral of smoke. His startling blue eyes met with Charlie's speckled brown ones. "I'd give her a job to do, maybe a series of tasks—keep her occupied. She keeps busy and gets work done—she's too tired to be trouble, then everyone can all simmer on down. Yer like a pot fixin' to boil over. Can't have that, especially if you want to ransom her. There won't be a ransom if things boil over." He offered the cigarette to Charlie, who shook his head.

"What kind of jobs would you have her do?"

"She can do the wash. We all hate that job. Mend. Y'all stink at that. She can help me serve food. No one wants to do that either, but y'all want to eat." Goat took another pull on the cigarette while watching Charlie's face. He could see the wheels turning in Charlie's head, which was what he had planned with his exaggerated hip pains.

Annabelle was like a lone hen trapped in a fox's den—if her situation didn't get settled soon, there was going to be a lot of trouble. Charlie was fortunate that he was so large and powerful—he also had Van Der Kamp on his side with this heist, otherwise someone would've attacked or at least tried something with Annabelle by now. As it stood, no one was quite sure what to do with the young man now that he'd finally proven himself. He was a gentle giant, but also not one to be messed with—he had a strong sense of fairness and could hold back others without much effort because of his size. Now, he wasn't afraid to use brute force to keep peace. The pecking order had been disrupted by this—depending on which way you saw it—brave or foolish robbery and kidnapping. The girl had spunk, and he'd hate to see something happen to her, especially since it'd send Charlie into a tailspin. He was always looking out for everyone, even those who didn't need looking out for. He heard that Charlie had defended Horton and shut down the shift tango the men kept doing with each other. *Hell, he was always worried about my damn hip, so that was evidence enough of his caring and protective nature.*

Charlie interrupted Goat's inner monologue with his own reflections.

"I suppose I can talk to her at supper about behaving and getting out of the tent some more." He rolled his neck, trying to alleviate some tension. Then he sat up straighter and stretched his shoulders back as far as he could. These were the longest couple of days he could remember. "I could do with some clean laundry." He grinned at Goat, beginning to feel the first inklings of hope he had in a long while. Goat continued to smoke until his cigarette burned his fingers. He threw it in the dirt and ground the toe of his boot on it. He grunted as he got up, patting Charlie on the shoulder.

"I'll gather some of my clothes, too. It won't take long for word to get out. The others will just start dumping it on her." He cackled as he walked off to tend to the stew he had already bubbling over the fire.

❧ 9 ❧

Annabelle had had it with the long, boring hours alone in the tent. Charlie had insisted that they leave her untied, but some of them still kept her tied up even though she hadn't tried to escape, not once. Where in the world would she go? She'd barely ever been alone outside of her house, and they had no need to leave town. None of their family lived nearby, so they didn't go visiting. This was the furthest out she'd been. She could barely remember the ride out here, let alone which direction they rode. If she ran she wouldn't even know which way to go. At this point, she'd probably make matters worse. She slumped at the thought. Better to wait it out and form a plan. That's if she didn't go crazy in the meantime.

She shifted for what felt like the millionth time, grunting and panting to find a comfortable position—comfortable being a relative term. *Bored. Bored. Bored.* Wanting to scream, she was inwardly railing at these bullies for keeping her while simultaneously hoping Papa would find her. *He's a great tracker, I know he'll find me, but the gang he's up against is large. He might not have enough men; it'd take time to round up help.*

I suppose I should try to be good, so they'll all leave me untied. Being untied will be helpful when Papa arrives.

She was beginning to think this was the way of her life for a long while, all things considered. Shaking her head, she agreed with the gang that, on some level, she deserved to be constrained—not initially, mind you, but afterward. *Yes, in all fairness, I did bite that towheaded guy who came too close to me. I didn't want "just a little peck"*—she shook her head, scrunching up her face—*especially from someone who smelled like the bottom of a whiskey barrel.* Her whole body shuddered in disgust. Oddly, a smirk stole across her face. Rubbing her forehead, she thought about the one with the unruly beard. *He came too close and got what he deserved, as well.* That one made her chuckle. The look on his face when she nearly knocked him on his backside with her head! He still hadn't forgiven her. He was one of the men who refused to take a turn at guard duty—she heard him arguing outside the tent afterward. The impact made her see white light and sparks. The thrumming in her head refused to go away for an entire day, but it was worth it, especially since he refused to look at her during meals. She was still smiling when the tent flap opened up, letting bright sunlight in. The tent's darkness kept her from seeing who it was—it was shaded by a large tree. The bright light forced her to squint and duck her head to avoid the searing pain in her eyes. But that was after the man entering caught her smile.

"Glad you like your accommodations, darlin'. Is that what the smile is all about or were you anticipating my arrival?"

Her head jerked up. She was looking directly at Wrighty's piercing blue eyes. Annabelle stiffened at the sight of him. He had a way of looking at her that chilled her entire back with one glance. At times, it was as if he were looking through her and not at her. This was one of those times. If she could've backed away, she would have. He sauntered closer, making her heart beat wildly. He was the one person whose actions she could not anticipate. He seemed to alternate between wanting to fondle her or throttle her—sometimes they seemed one and the same. It was unnerving. Stilling, she waited for him to make his move.

He squatted down in front of her; his cold eyes remained locked with hers. Despite the chill, she refused to break eye contact, not wanting to look weak. It took a lot of willpower not to dodge his hand when he raised it to cup her face. His thumb rubbed her cheek gently. It was like a lover's caress, only she wasn't fooled. As little familiarity as she had with the opposite sex, she knew enough to know that men like him didn't truly love—they only took. She had seen that with a couple of the men in town. They didn't stay in town for very long, either.

"That's it, darlin'. I can make it real good for you. All you have to do is cooperate." He leaned in, pulling her head toward him, burrowing his nose in her hair and breathing in deeply. Like an animal caught in a predator's sights, she held very still, afraid to move. However, when he shifted his face, nuzzling her neck, she jerked, tensing. His lips travelled her neck, placing kisses down the column before grabbing her breast. Her heart thumped wildly and her stomach churned. Annabelle was already struggling to move away from the kisses, but when he grabbed her breast, she panicked and lashed out with her leg, catching him between his. He yanked her head back by the hair and pulled hard. Her eyes watered as she gasped in pain.

Her head was cranked back at a hard angle. He was looking down at her wide eyes, nose to nose, when he growled, "*Not* a good idea, darlin'." He pulled her hair again for good measure before releasing it. Grabbing her by the shoulders, he yanked her to standing, shaking her. "Don't make a noise or I'll make you real sorry you did."

His lips latched to hers as he kept trying to make her open her mouth to him. She clamped her mouth tight and tried to turn her head as her hands pushed at his chest, but his lips wouldn't release hers, and he held her shoulders tight. He had her backed against the tent pole, which was causing the tent to lean. Alarmed, one of his men came busting in.

"Boss! You okay?" The words came out before he realized what was going on. Wrighty glared over his shoulder at the man. "Oh, sorry. The tent's about to fall down, Wrighty. You're pushing hard on the pole." He indicated their position—everyone looked up at the top of the tent. Wrighty backed up, easing off the pole, before turning back to his man.

"Cover for a few more minutes, Moris."

Wrighty turned back toward Annabelle. Shaking his finger to punctuate his words, he said, "No one hits me and gets away with it. Not even a pretty little petticoat like yourself. Charlie may have found you, but make no mistake—I get what I want—you're mine." With one last hard shake, he threw her to the ground and leaned over her. "You need a real man to teach you about real life." Grabbing hard, he pulled her toward him by her leg, making her skirts ride up. She frantically tried to scramble away from him, using her hands to propel herself backward, but he pressed his boot against her leg to pin her. He unbuckled his belt and began unbuttoning his trousers when his man interrupted his sex's liberation.

"Boss!"

"What?" He growled over his shoulder. "Can't you see—"

"*Van Der Kamp's on his way.*"

"Fuck." He quickly pulled his belt free and whipped Annabelle across the exposed part of her leg causing it to redden and welt immediately. He struck her again for good measure. The crack of the belt against her pale skin made Moris wince. Even Wrighty knew better than to openly mess with Van Der Kamp. "I don't have time to finish this right now—your lesson or my plans," Wrighty threaded his belt, buckling it. He didn't bother re-buttoning his trousers' top two buttons. "There's more of that coming to you, whether you cooperate or not. It'll be far worse if you don't."

Wrighty turned on his heel, walking past his man who stood there gawking at Annabelle. Wrighty threw the last words out over his shoulder, "Even though Van Der Kamp's a gimp, he moves quickly. Don't think you're getting off the hook." She was biting her lip to hold back the tears. However, despite her best efforts, fat tears were rolling down her face and her body shook uncontrollably. Her dress had ridden up high on her thigh, so the belt struck a good portion of her flesh. Wrighty had hit her so hard, her skin was already discoloring and swelling. Panting shallowly, Annabelle turned away from Wrighty's retreating back, realizing his man was staring. Her face flushed as she scooted backward until her dress shifted, covering her leg. Her movement and tiny whimper caused Moris to snap out of his shock. Finally realizing her embarrassment, he looked away in shame. Moris knew she was fixing to cry, so he left her alone for a spell. He slowly backed out of the tent, not wanting to be a part of this when Van Der Kamp arrived.

As soon as Moris left the tent, Annabelle curled over herself as best she could and let out heaving sobs. She tried hard to keep as quiet as she could, but she'd never encountered such violence or threats before. She didn't want any more of this or of Wrighty. She certainly didn't want this to get any worse, God help her! This was frightening enough. The thought made her shudder and cry even harder. Dirt from her unwashed face mixed with her tears and made a mess of her face and her clothing.

Just outside the tent, Moris could hear her trying to muffle her sobs—which embarrassed him—but he was also embarrassed by what he had witnessed. He knew Wrighty wanted the girl, but he also didn't think he'd resort to raping a captive. Even for the amount of sass she had, everyone could tell that she was an innocent. She had no idea what Wrighty would do to her. Hell, even most painted ladies had no idea what was coming to them when Wrighty got a hold of them. He'd heard stories—stories he didn't repeat. He could hear Annabelle in the tent trying to be quiet and brave and was stumped as to what to do with her, so he just stood there for a long while doing nothing. Dewit happened to walk by about thirty minutes later.

"Whatchya doin'? Your turn to guard?" Dewit threw his thumb back at the tent.

"Yeah."

Dewit looked at Moris for a long minute before saying, "You don't look so good. What'd she do to you?"

"Nothing."

"Go on—you can tell me. Wrighty'll get her good if she hurts one of us."

"She didn't do nothin', and Wrighty got to her, anyway."

Dewit's face fell. "Really?" Their heads swiveled toward the tent then back facing each other.

"He wanted time alone with her, so I was guarding. Thing is, Van Der Kamp was supposed to be on his way. I ran in to tell him, and he had her on the ground unbuckling his belt."

"Shit."

"When I told him, he was furious for the interruption and for Van Der Kamp. He whipped her with the belt. It bruised before he even left the tent. That girl is in for it. I actually kinda feel sorry for her." They were quiet for a minute before Moris added, "I let her cry for a good spell. I knew she wanted to but was embarrassed. Will you go get some water and a rag? I'll stay here. Van Der Kamp can't know she's upset—I don't know where he went."

"Be right back."

When Dewit brought the water and the rag, Moris took them. Dewit watched for Van Der Kamp. He couldn't know that someone hurt her or there'd be hell to pay.

When Moris opened the flap, Annabelle tried to jerk into an upright position, but couldn't. Between her injury and lying on her side, she'd gone numb. She was also exhausted from all the sobbing and fear running through her.

"Don't." Was all she could muster, her head dropping back to the ground.

"I'm not gonna hurt you, girly. But you got to get cleaned up. If Van Der Kamp sees you like this, someone's gonna get it."

"Yes, Wrighty."

Moris leaned over Annabelle. "No, not Wrighty. Didn't you *hear* him? You'll wish you were dead if you double-cross him. You have no idea what he's capable of. None. You've led such a sheltered life, I don't even think you're aware of the dangers of any man, let alone a man like Wrighty." He gently pulled her upright by her shoulders and held onto them for a minute so she wouldn't slump back over.

"I'm gonna clean you up, and you're gonna forget this ever happened. You tell on Wrighty, and you can kiss your life goodbye, but not before he makes you feel pain you've never felt before. He'll take you to the edge of death and bring you back again just to do it all over. He's like that, you know."

The blood drained from her face, but she braved the next words, "I didn't cry in front of him when he whipped me. I'm strong." She tilted her chin upward as best she could.

Moris shook his head at her. "You're tough, but you're no match for the likes of him." He wetted the rag with water and began dabbing at her face. When she jerked away, he growled, "Hold still. I'm trying to help you. Stop being so mulish." She held still while he cleaned her as gently as he could. His hands were shaking thinking about the ways in which Wrighty would kill both of them if something went wrong. They were quiet in their own thoughts for a few moments before he continued, "He'll hit, kick, and strangle you. He'll choke you until you turn blue and think you've died before letting go. He'll kick you while you're on the ground, desperate for breath. Women, well, with women he always pulls their hair. He has a hair fetish—loves to smell it, and pull it. Loves the feel of it in his hands and how he can control them with it."

Annabelle gasped, especially at the hair portion. She remembered him smelling her hair and later pulling her with it. She hated it, and he loved it. She was shrinking into herself, but Moris was lost in memories. "He cuts, too. Likes to tie women up to the bed and slice at their skin." He shuddered at the thought. "I'm sure you aren't familiar in the ways of men, but he's rough when doing that, too." His eyes looked glazed over before he shook it off, refocusing on Annabelle. "Do you get the picture? That's just some of what he's done— who knows what else he does or is capable of. I, for one, don't want to think about it. I'd hate to see you in that position. You'd best cooperate."

Forcing bravado, she shot him an incredulous look.

"You've been warned."

He suddenly got up and left her there, frightened out of her mind. These things she had just heard—they were beyond her imagination. A river of sweat ran between her shoulder blades and breasts. Her hairline was damp. She felt flushed and chilled, and couldn't stop shaking. Bile rose in her throat. Mean people said terrible things—sometimes they stole, and sometimes they killed each other. Men got in fights, but they eventually stopped or were stopped. No one prolonged another's pain, certainly not for pleasure. Annabelle was left shivering, cowering, and staring off into nothingness until suppertime. Moris was the one who came to take her to the clearing.

She didn't acknowledge him, and he didn't say much, either. What was there to say? Reaching down, the daily ritual occurred. Even though she wasn't tied up this time, she was still pulled to standing and held by the shoulders until her feet and legs regained sensation. This time, she had difficulties standing because of the giant bruise on her leg. She winced when he pulled her to her feet, and her left foot and knee gave. Moris held her tighter.

"You can't say anything. Nothin', you hear?" He shook her to make her respond. She nodded, still favoring her left side.

"I don't think I can make it to supper. I can't make that walk."

"I'll carry you."

"NO!"

"What am I gonna say to them? You were fine this morning, Annabelle. They're gonna know something's up."

"They're going to know anyway with the way I'm walking."

Moris nodded, realizing the error in his thinking. He waited for her to come up with an idea. He was too busy worrying about managing Wrighty.

"Let me think." Turning pink, she made an awful sound in the back of her throat. "If they ask," she swallowed, whispering, "tell them my courses came." Her face flamed with embarrassment, but she held his eyes. It was the only excuse she could think of. There was no way she could walk down the hill by herself, and she wasn't about to let herself be carried and show even more weakness to Wrighty.

Moris looked like he swallowed a frog. "I'm not telling them that! You tell 'em."

She looked at him with raised brows and pursed lips.

"All right. I'll holler for Dewit to bring us something. I'm staying here. I don't want no trouble. There's been enough today."

"Pfft. You're telling me," she said under her breath. Moris didn't hear the words, but could catch the meaning well enough. He shook his head. *Still with the sass, that one.*

10

Everyone was sitting around the benches, some were eating and drinking, and others were wondering where Annabelle and Moris were. Finally, Dewit came barreling down the hill, running directly toward Van Der Kamp. He spoke in low tones and waited until Van Der Kamp nodded. He went off to get two plates, filled them, then quickly left. No one said a word, but they watched him the entire time. Wrighty was the only one who seemed unbothered by the turn of events. He continued to eat without looking up.

Charlie looked over at Goat, who just lifted one shoulder briefly before going back to work at the fire. Knots were forming in his stomach, and the food soured before it even reached its destination. Jimmy was watching Charlie. "What're you thinking?"

Charlie wasn't thinking—he was worried. He'd had the morning shift, and everything was fine until Moris took over. In fact, Moris came earlier than usual. "I'm not."

"You are. Don't do anything stupid. Wrighty is over there looking pleased with himself, so he must be up to something, or at least he knows what's going on."

Jimmy and Charlie looked over to see Wrighty looking at them. He nodded, taking a long pull from his drink.

"Yup. He's up to something. Watch out, Charlie. I don't want anything bad to happen."

Charlie nodded, but couldn't get the words to come out of his mouth. His throat was too tight. He was looking forward but not at anything in particular. In the corner of his eye, a shadow crossed the table. He knew it was Wrighty without having to turn. He sat up straighter but continued to look ahead.

"That Annabelle sure is a fine woman, wouldn't you reckon?" Wrighty had a loose stance, but his hand was on his gun belt, resting there for good measure. Wrighty had many subtle, and not so subtle, ways of reminding people who he thought was in charge, even though it was really Van Der Kamp's gang.

Charlie wouldn't take the bait because he didn't know if Annabelle was in some sort of trouble or if this was the usual goading Wrighty liked to give him. The stakes had been raised since her arrival—for everyone, whether they wanted her or not. The jackals were waiting to see how Charlie was going to respond and if they'd get to see a fight tonight. They were in a holding pattern and, with the addition of Annabelle, all the pent-up energy had them pushing up against each other, raring for a fight even more so than usual.

"I suppose. I also suppose it's time she was put to work, don't you think?" Charlie turned around to look at Wrighty.

Guessing by the silence, he'd caught him off guard. But, slowly, a sly grin spread across his face. "I can think of a lot of ways to put that woman to work." Everyone laughed at the innuendo, especially when Wrighty thrust his hips forward.

Charlie's jaw clenched, but he clarified what he had meant by "work."

"She can do laundry and mending for starters, maybe help Goat with supper in the evenings."

Van Der Kamp had been watching the exchange between the rivals and decided now was a good time to interject. "That's a mighty fine idea there. We could use an extra pair of hands around here, especially since I've just sent out some scouts this morning."

Wrighty and Charlie snapped their heads toward Van Der Kamp, disbelief on their faces. "Sit down, Wrighty. You're not in charge of Annabelle, anyway." Wrighty looked ready to murder but sat down, nonetheless. "Charlie, you get on Annabelle about doing some chores. The guard duty can remain the same—they'll just trail her while she does chores." Van Der Kamp looked around at the lot of them before adding, "If she needs any help with lifting and carrying and such, you're to help. Understood?" He quirked a brow. The men murmured and some replied with clear yeses, but it didn't matter. If Van Der Kamp said it was to be done, it was done. He got up from the bench and slowly made his way back to his cabin.

Wrighty watched him limp away, muttering to Seth, "Damn him, anyway. He barely does anything around here, and they all do what he says."

Seth had the smarts not to answer. He knew Wrighty wanted to eventually take over the gang, feeling that it was just a matter of time before Van Der Kamp took some lead himself or, perhaps, found himself swinging from the leafless tree. He was with Wrighty *and* Van Der Kamp, he just didn't want either to know it. He didn't talk much, so he didn't have to reveal much. Worked best that way.

11

Her lie was a good one. No one seemed to suspect, and they definitely didn't question her. Because of her leg, it took longer for her to relieve herself, and she moved with such stiffness that her symptoms could be attributed to her "womanly situation," as the men took to calling it. To hide the pain in her leg, she clutched the left side of her stomach whenever they untied her, at least, for the one or two who still did. Mostly, they left her untied and had to help her up anyway because she looked so pale and unwell. No one was willing to question the gameness in her leg—they just assumed she had "it" bad. They also tended to steer clear of her, both out of embarrassment and memories of women from their pasts, and their afflictions when they had "this" going on. Superstitious cowards that they were, they'd shudder and run in the other direction. Only Wrighty, Moris, and Dewit knew the truth of it. Moris brought her what she needed, and Wrighty stayed away. Her seclusion and silence was all he needed from her right now. He'd collect the rest, later.

Moris also managed to take extra shifts without Charlie catching wind of it. He was a natural choice anyway, because he was one of the few who'd had a wife before joining the gang. Moris's wife had died in childbirth. He refused to talk about her. The extra time he spent in Annabelle's tent, as well as carrying her to the forest, didn't seem too unusual. Moris would come by a half an hour or an hour into the others' shifts and then offer to take over or have some excuse that sent the guard on duty away to do things that only they could take care of. Naturally, he'd offer to take watch for them.

The injury to Annabelle's leg was fairly severe. It was bruised to the bone and took a couple of days to heal. None of them wanted any suspicions cast on her situation, so Moris was extra careful when inserting himself. Besides, the more they kept her culled from the rest of the gang, the more control they felt they had over her situation. Truth be told, they had the right of it. She was scared and wasn't fighting anyone these days. It was the talk of the camp. They'd never met a woman who was nicer and more docile during that time of the month than she was. They could almost live with her like this, was the running joke.

Moris didn't bother binding her after the whipping, and the other men soon followed suit—the others reasoned it was on account of her *delicate situation*. If she was ever bound, it was really just for show and for the fact that some of them wouldn't go near her unless she was bound. At least not after the biting and head-butting incidents. If forced to bind her, Moris took to loosely tying her arms in front of her and laying her on the cot so she'd keep off her bad leg. He just wanted her to heal faster and get on with the chores so he didn't have to hide this secret any longer. If anyone thought it was odd, they didn't say. She tended to lie on her side, curled up, facing away from the flap so it looked like she wasn't feeling well. In reality, she didn't. Nearly her entire leg throbbed with shooting pain up the length of it, and her stomach churned with anxiety, but she kept silent about it. The pain drained her of any energy she may have had, and the lack of food didn't help. She barely ate and was becoming listless. She was slowly losing the spirit she showed up with those first few days. The third day of her "situation" rolled around—she was still feeling pain, but felt well enough to move about on her own. It was also the day that Charlie finally popped his head into the tent. He'd been watching nights and had no reason to check in on her. He wanted to make sure that no one tried to sneak into the tent. He slept outside, and Jimmy slept in Goat's quarters to give Annabelle privacy and attempt to preserve her modesty. Today, he assigned himself a day shift because he wanted to see her.

"How're you feeling?"

"Much better, thanks."

"Here, let me help you up. I have some water." He reached down and gently brought her to sitting. He held her upright for a minute longer than necessary because she was looking wan and had lost the spunk she had the last time he saw her. He cocked his head, taking in her appearance as he squatted in front of her.

"Do you need anything? Do you—ah—need the necessary?"

Annabelle blushed to the roots of her hair. "Um, no. But, ah, thanks."

Annabelle started to lower herself, grimacing. Charlie leaned forward, slipping his arm around her, lowering her to the cot. She let out a heavy sigh. Watching her for a moment, he stepped away from the cot and nodded, looking down at his feet before looking back up at her. She could feel him staring at her through closed eyes.

"Is there something else, Charlie?"

He looked startled, but said, "Oh, uh, yeah. Van Der Kamp thought it'd be a good idea that you get out of the tent and start helping around with chores and such. I didn't tell you earlier because that was the day you, um. Well, ah—didn't come to supper."

He fidgeted with his hat in his hands, and the tips of his ears were burning red. He was one of the few who took off his hat when he came inside.

"Right. Well, you haven't been at meals, so I couldn't let you know. This is the first day shift I've had, too. Wrighty had me doing all sorts of chores and such around camp, so I couldn't come by earlier."

What little color she had drained from her, which made Charlie stride back toward the cot. He reached out and touched her forehead.

"Are you sure you're all right? You blanched all quick-like. Do you need some more water or something?"

"Sorry, I'm fine. Really. It'll be nice to get out of the tent. See some actual sunlight for longer than ten minutes at a time." She gave him a lopsided smile.

"Right. Yes, it would." He continued to observe her before saying. "Perhaps you can start with the washing tomorrow? Are you up for that? Maybe, start with a small basket of it. If you get too tired, you can let Conrad know. He'll be taking you down where the washing's done. Van Der Kamp also made it clear that if you needed help with anything—lifting, carrying and such, that you're to let your guard know. He keeps thinking that you're a delicate woman—little does he know."

Charlie winked at her and she blushed, both out of embarrassment for what had happened as well as the teasing. Despite his size, Charlie was really pretty adorable when he was being shy and polite. He was like an overgrown puppy, except he'd be some giant mastiff or wolfhound puppy or something. Maybe the colt of a draft horse. She snorted, and they both looked at each other, surprised.

"See, very delicate." He laughed, turning back for the tent's flap. "Let me know if you need anything or don't feel well. I'll be right outside. I'm not going anywhere."

He was still chuckling at his little jokes. Little did he know that she had jokes of her own. Smiling, she lay back down and closed her eyes. For the first time in three days, she was finally able to relax.

12

Charlie watched as Conrad leaned back against a tree, leering at Annabelle's backside swaying in rhythm with her scrubbing. Charlie's jaw went tight at the expression on Conrad's face—he looked like he had won a big hand, smirk spread wide. The man was mesmerized by Annabelle doing housework, practically drooling. Then again, he knew Conrad had never been around a woman as delicate as Annabelle. It was her first day of doing anything other than sitting in a tent, which was making everyone crazy. None of the men liked sitting around, unless it was sitting around and drinking. He heard what they were saying—*might as well put her to good use, although they could think of better ones than this.* It chapped his backside to hear them talking about a lady like that. They wouldn't talk about her around him, but he heard them, nonetheless. He lifted his hat off of his head, fanning his face. It was a scorcher. He could feel the heat coming off the ground, even in the shade. It wasn't at all close to evening, either. Even proper Miss Annabelle was relaxed in her dress. Her shirtsleeves were rolled above her elbows, and the front of her dress was slightly unbuttoned—it was blazing hot out. Good thing it wasn't unbuttoned further, otherwise she'd show some cleavage, especially when she bent over. When she turned to pick something up, he caught glimpses of her pale collarbone. Her neck was slender and long. He could see the sheen on her skin and was embarrassed by the tightening in his groin. He was pulled away from his observation by Conrad pushing off the tree and moving quietly toward her.

Annabelle bent down, grabbing another shirt off the pile, plunging it deep into the tub. Swirling it around several times, giving it a good soaking, she reached for the soap. Instead of touching soap, her hand met with a man's hand, causing her to recoil.

"Looking for this, little missy?" Conrad had the soap in his opposite hand, rotating his wrist, taunting her with flashes of soap. She reached for it, but he stepped away from her. He held up a finger to stop her. "What will you give me for the soap?" He leaned forward, moving his face closer to hers.

Annabelle broke eye contact, moving back a step. Ignoring him, she looked at the pile of dirty clothes by her feet and picked up another shirt for a good soak. Conrad grabbed her wrist, yanking her closer to him.

"I asked you a question, missy. It isn't polite to ignore a man," his voice dropped lower, "*or didn't the sheriff teach you good manners?*" He waited a moment for the insult to settle. "I know it's hard for a man to teach a girly like you all the things a woman should know, with your mother running off and all—"

Annabelle's face went pale then bright red. Her fists clenched. She opened her mouth to say something, but held out her hand for the soap instead. Conrad continued to look at her, smirking. He was waiting for his prize.

"I'm sorry, I have nothing to give. Soap—please." She shook her still-outstretched hand for the soap.

Conrad came closer to her, dangling the soap in front her. "Oh, little missy—I think you do," he drawled.

Charlie had watched the interaction between Conrad and Annabelle long enough. For a normally fiery woman, she broke eye contact and was far too submissive. She was also shrinking when Conrad entered her space. *What the hell, Annabelle?* Seeing more than he wanted, Charlie got up from the log and walked over to the pair. The laundry would never get done at this rate. Besides, Conrad was supposed to be guarding her, not harassing her at every turn.

Conrad looked like he was about to kiss Annabelle when Charlie asked, "What're you all doing here, then?"

Annabelle jumped back, the palm of her hand slapping her chest. She looked from Conrad to Charlie, leaning away but not moving her feet. Conrad smiled, but it didn't brighten his face.

"Why Charlie, Miss Annabelle and I were just conversing—getting to know each other better. Weren't we, Annabelle?" He turned to Annabelle, holding up the soap.

Annabelle looked a little wild-eyed, but said, "I—I dropped the soap. Conrad picked it up for me." Turning toward Conrad she said, "I need it, now. I have a lot of wash to do." She waved her hand over the pile of laundry as the three of them looked down at it.

"You sure do, Annabelle." Charlie crossed his arms over his chest. "Conrad, hand over the soap—no funny business. You're supposed to be guarding her so she doesn't run away, not harassing her and making her job difficult."

Conrad's face twisted into a mask of rage. "Who do you think you are, Charlie? You're just some snot-nose we picked up—Van Der Kamp should've let Wrighty kill you and Jimmy. Just because you found her doesn't mean you get to keep her."

He tossed the soap at Charlie, storming off, forgetting that it was his job to guard Annabelle.

Charlie handed Annabelle the soap, watching her carefully guarded expression. She turned toward the tub, dunking and lathering the soap. Charlie waited for her to say something. When she started scrubbing the shirt, he gently asked her, "What happened?" She looked surprised at the question, so he added, "I don't mean right now, because I was watching for a while. What happened before?" Watching her initially alarmed, then shuttered expression, he added, "Did something happen to you while you were in the tent?"

Annabelle's face flushed pink, then deepened to a shade of red. She looked down, shaking her head, resuming scrubbing. Charlie gently put his hand on her arm to stop her. When she looked up at him, there was a shimmer of tears, but she didn't cry or talk. She looked back at the tub and resumed scrubbing. Sighing, he said, "I was watching you. You aren't the same girl I dragged to this camp, fighting and kicking. You aren't the same girl who's been tied up in a tent for the past few days, either."

He looked down, kicked the dirt, then began tracing a rhythmic line in it with the toe of his boot—back and forth, back and forth. As Charlie watched his foot, Annabelle covertly watched him, the scrubbing slowing to a halt as she watched him out of the corner of her eye.

"The past couple of years around here, I've learned that you don't break eye contact. Ever. It's a sign of submission or an admission of guilt, whether you think it is or not. They do, and that's all that matters." Charlie nodded at the washing. "You better get on with that or Wrighty might—" Her face went pale when he mentioned Wrighty's name. It strangled the remaining words in his mouth, nearly choking him. Grabbing her shoulders and angling her so she couldn't avoid eye contact, his voice went low and slow when he asked, "What did he do?"

He was so angry that he didn't realize he was squeezing her shoulders and clenching his jaw. Her squeak made him relax. He rubbed his hands up and down where he had gripped her to ease the pain. "I'm sorry. I'm so sorry—this is all my fault. Wrighty isn't to be trusted. I should've guarded you more carefully." His hands had moved down her arms, grasping her small hands in his large ones. He held them gently, bouncing them slightly to the beat of his words. "Tell me, what did he do?" Tears trickled down her face. She tried hiding them but didn't turn away fast enough. His voice hoarse, he asked, "Did he touch you?"

She shook her head vigorously, but it still took her a minute to find her voice. Waiting a moment, she slowly moved her head, inhaling a shaky breath. On the stuttering exhale, she answered, "No, but he said he'd be back for me. That I'd enjoy what he had planned." She hung her head in shame. She had no idea what, exactly, to expect, but she was pretty sure she wouldn't enjoy it. Her skin crawled when he was around. Her leg throbbed from the recent whipping and her heart beat wildly at every thought and mention of him. Whenever his name came up, her heart felt like it stopped beating for a moment or two before galloping away.

"Annabelle, listen to me. You have no reason to trust me, but I promise I'll protect you. No matter what. I didn't plan to kidnap you—it just happened. But I will not let any more harm come to you, especially from the likes of Wrighty. Don't let these men bully you or show that you're afraid. You didn't when you got here; don't do it now."

"But—"

"No, buts. I'll figure this out. The only problem is, I can't be with you all the time."

"Charlie—I—"

Snapping his finger, "I know—I'll get Jimmy to watch over you when I can't. He's my younger brother. You'll like him. He brought us food the other day." He smiled brightly, and Annabelle lost her train of thought. She was trying to tell him something, but Charlie was problem-solving right over her protests and words. She let him, because his smile dazzled her, along with the way his eyes sparkled when he spoke. "Here," he picked up another washboard, placing it on the opposite side of the huge tub, "I'll help you. Conrad wasted a lot of our time."

Shocked, Annabelle watched Charlie pick up the second shirt in the tub and scrub vigorously. He didn't seem to think anything of it, working away. Everything seemed resolved for him. Slowly inching back toward the tub as she watched him, she picked up the other soaking shirt and followed suit.

13

"**Y**ou want me to do what?" Charlie caught Jimmy off guard, doubly so—both by sneaking up behind him while he was cleaning the horses' hooves and with his request. Jimmy tended to go within while he was with the horses; they gave him peace that he couldn't find elsewhere. That also meant that, occasionally, someone got one up on him, which he hated. He was on the defensive with Charlie from the get-go.

"I want you to be around Annabelle whenever I can't be."

"That's crazy! Wrighty's already scheduled guards for her, including her working schedule. I heard him during dinner. Why would you go against his word? You're already a burr under his saddle." Jimmy snorted, shaking his head.

"Wrighty's threatened her. She's terrified of him. You should've seen her face when I mentioned him. She went pale as a sheet. Didn't want to talk about it."

"Maybe you should've just let it go, then."

"No can do, brother. She can't defend herself against any of them, and I'm responsible for her. I dragged her into this to begin with."

"You're not responsible for everyone, you know." Jimmy spat out the words as if they were something bitter in his mouth. They often went back and forth over Charlie's need to protect and manage things.

"I'm not. I'm responsible for *her*, however."

"Fine. You better make this right with Van Der Kamp, though. I don't want any more trouble with Wrighty—we've had enough."

"I'll go talk to him now. Besides, he already said that Annabelle was my responsibility, not Wrighty's. Just have a wander down by the provisions, will ya? I think she might be helping out with dinner."

Charlie and Jimmy walked in opposite directions. Charlie was on the hunt for Van Der Kamp so he could get Annabelle settled. However, he had no idea what he was going to say to him.

He walked down the path and was about to turn toward Van Der Kamp's cabin when he heard footfall behind him. Turning around, he saw Goat. He nodded, getting ready to move on, when Goat called out, "I have a suggestion for you."

"What?"

"A suggestion. For you."

"About what? I'm kind of in a hurry—I need to find Van Der Kamp."

"That's just it. Walk with me and I'll tell you."

"Goat, I know you mean well, but—"

"Walk with me. I need to chop some wood."

Charlie rolled his eyes, but did what he was told. Goat had always been good to him and Jimmy, and he didn't have a malicious bone in his body, aside from the fact that he was part of this gang. Mentally, Charlie shrugged. Despite that, his shoulders tightened up. It wasn't something he could shake off at the moment. They had walked down the wooded path and turned toward a small clearing where a tree stump was. Goat picked up an axe and handed it to Charlie.

"You chop. I talk."

Charlie looked at the axe and then at Goat before taking it, picking up a log, then setting it on the stump. Just as he was swinging the axe, Goat said from behind, "You should claim Annabelle for yourself." The axe slipped from Charlie's grip, landing on the ground a couple of feet in front him with a loud thud. His mouth fell open as he continued to stare at Goat as if he'd grown another head.

Goat held up his hand, "Now hear me out, young man. She's in trouble here. I see the way the men are eyeing her, hell, I've been there before, myself." Charlie tensed, shifting as if readying to punch Goat, so Goat quickly added, "Not now, mind you—*before*." Charlie's body relaxed as Goat continued to eye him. "You already feel responsible for her, don't you?"

Charlie was surprised by the observation, but tried to cover it. "Why do you ask?"

"Lookie here." Goat raised his index finger at Charlie, "I've helped you out for a couple of years now. Haven't I?" Charlie nodded. "I haven't let you or Jimmy down, am I right? You're the one who needs to protect her from the others—in your mind you already are. The only way you can do that is by claiming her for yourself. Or someone else will. At the very least, one of them will take what's not theirs to have, if you get my drift, son."

Bile rose in Charlie's throat at the thought of someone harming Annabelle. Especially since it was his carelessness that brought her here in the first place. "How do you expect me to do that? I didn't bring her here to harm her."

"How you do that is up to you, but you and Annabelle have to convince the others that *you're* in charge of her, and no one else." Goat was now pointing his finger at Charlie as he spoke.

"I was going to talk to Van Der Kamp about her, anyway. She's really afraid of something, which isn't who she is."

"Wrighty." They nodded in unison. "He's been sniffing after her skirts since she got here. I'm sure he's still sore about her rejection since he first tried to grab her. Although I'd say I wouldn't cotton to someone yanking me off my horse, either."

"She said he didn't hurt her in that way, but I'm sure he threatened her. She won't tell me what happened. I was watching her do the wash. Conrad was supposed to be guarding her, but he spent more time ogling her and trying to get her to kiss him than anything." Goat watched Charlie's hands curl into fists, then he looked him straight in the eye.

"Son, you go talk to Van Der Kamp right now. Tell him that you want Annabelle for yourself. You claim her, and if he agrees, then no one can touch her."

"I've asked Jimmy to go find her and watch after her when I'm not around."

Goat chuckled, slapping Charlie on the back. "Good job, sonny. I knew you had it in you."

"What?" Charlie looked truly perplexed.

"You're a natural leader. One of the many reasons Wrighty can't stand you." Goat was cackling like a hen, which brought a small smile to Charlie's face. Wrighty didn't have a lot of fans in the gang, but he was efficient and good at what he was told to do. Those who did support him were fierce.

"Don't you worry. I'm watching from afar. Go on, git."

Charlie walked off, looking more purposeful and hopeful than he had earlier.

❧ 14 ❧

Charlie felt a weight lifted off him. He rolled his shoulders as if to confirm it. Still unsure of what he'd say to Van Der Kamp, he was sure in his knowing that he had to do everything necessary to protect Annabelle. He was surprised and surprisingly angry that the fire had left her. Her pain was an unintentional burden on him, the guilt lacing him. She was so vibrant and alive, and now she was like a trampled bloom. *Wrighty.* Charlie ground his teeth, walking faster. Practically stomping his feet as he trudged up the hill, he thought about how he'd get her back to her father as soon as he could. That thought made it easier to talk to Van Der Kamp—he had a direct mission, now. Knocking on the door, he heard boots sliding off of wood before hitting the floor.

"Come in."

Charlie stepped into the darkness. Van Der Kamp wasn't a bright and cheerful man, preferring darkness and silence. That's why he stayed in the cabin by himself most of the time—for physical and emotional reasons. The war had taken a toll on him, headaches being the most prevalent symptom. Silence and darkness helped calm him. They eased the migraines and mental turmoil. He took meals with the men to keep his eyes on them and an ear to the ground. A leader needed to have some sort of presence. Taking a quick look around, Charlie squared up to Van Der Kamp.

"What do you want, son? Is everything going okay with our guest?"

"Well, that's what I came to talk to you about, sir." Van Der Kamp held back a smirk. He'd been waiting for Charlie to come. Something had to give when a woman was concerned, whether or not a man wanted her.

"Go on." He dipped his head then back up again, matching the slow pace of his words.

"You see, like I said before, we should ransom her."

"But?"

"But I want her." Charlie cleared his throat. "I want her for myself." Van Der Kamp kept his appraising eyes on Charlie, forcing him to fidget, just a little. "I think I should have her because I found her." Charlie stopped shifting his feet like a small child and looked him right in the eye like a man with his last words. He waited for Van Der Kamp to respond. Van Der Kamp made the pause feel like forever. He shifted forward in his seat, leaned his elbows on the table, as his eyebrows knitted together.

"Why?"

"I'm sorry?"

"Why do you think you deserve her? Why should I give her to you? Wrighty has been after her since you rode in with her. He's my second. Why shouldn't I give her to him?" Charlie stiffened at the last question, his nostrils flaring.

"She's a prize—the sheriff's daughter. I managed to capture her without a gun, without hurting anyone. Hell, the mercantile man was packing up our money before I even asked. I'm not so sure they can really get us for robbery on this one—no gun."

Van Der Kamp quirked his brow when Charlie mentioned not using a gun, but otherwise, his face remained blank. He was pushing Charlie, and Charlie knew it.

He went on. "We can get money for her, you said so. Besides, it hurts the sheriff and everyone seems to have it out for him—I don't think it's just because he's the law, either."

"You're a smart one, Charlie. I like you, even though I didn't think we should've kept you alive." Van Der Kamp said that in a matter-of-fact sort of way. Had it come from Wrighty, the words would've been a threat. He inhaled deeply, exhaling as he leaned back in his chair. "She's a real looker, too. Isn't she?"

Charlie blushed to the roots of his hair, not really sure what to say. He knew she was pretty. He'd watched her for many hours, from afar at least. She felt good in his arms, too. At least, when she wasn't fighting him. "Cat got your tongue, son?" Charlie was brought out of his thoughts to see Van Der Kamp smirking at him. He didn't show much expression, so it caught him off guard.

"Ah, um…"

"Yup. A pretty face'll do that to a man." He chuckled, further surprising Charlie. Van Der Kamp shook his head. "Tell you what. You can have the little filly for yourself, but it's up to you to protect her. Anything happens to our prize, you're done for, you hear? I'm still not sure if we'll give the girl back to her father yet, or not, but I don't want any harm coming to her, either. You're in charge. Don't disappoint me." His face had returned to its natural sternness, which always put Charlie a little on edge, despite the fact Van Der Kamp had always protected him from the others.

"Yes, sir. Don't worry, I'll protect her. I'll get on it right away." Charlie turned and practically ran for the door before stopping and turning back to Van Der Kamp, "Sir?" Van Der

Kamp's eyebrows lifted slightly, his eyes answered with a *yes?* "Thank you, sir. Thank you very much." With that, he ran out the door and down the path. He had business to take care of. Urgent business.

Wrighty was at the end of the path, heading out for his check-in with Van Der Kamp, when he saw Charlie enter Van Der Kamp's cabin. This was something worth waiting out. It looked like Mr. White Knight was springing into action. He stepped behind some trees, waiting Charlie out. He remained still while his eyes tracked Charlie down the path. Aside from the toothpick rolling around in his mouth, Wrighty's body remained motionless as he leaned against the tree. Charlie wasn't in the cabin for long. He came bounding out, jogging down the path. When he rounded the bend in the path, Wrighty pushed off the tree and strolled toward the cabin. Time to find out what that was all about. He banged on the front door.

"Come in."

Wrighty entered the cabin, throwing himself into a chair opposite Van Der Kamp, who hadn't moved since Charlie dashed out the door. He was trying for nonchalance, but Van Der Kamp was too astute for that nonsense. "Come to see what that was all about?"

Wrighty whipped his head toward Van Der Kamp, which made the man guffaw. "Son, yer about as predictable as that young buck you hate so much. Like clockwork, the two of you."

"Actually, I was coming to talk to you about the prisoner—"

"Too late."

"What?"

"Yer too late. Charlie beat you to it." Choking on his rage, Wrighty was rendered speechless. The corner of Van Der Kamp's lip quirked upward, "Meaning, Charlie's in charge of the sweet young thing, and you're going to keep your hands and all other body parts off of her. In fact, you should probably stay away altogether."

"What the hell? Why you rewarding him with a prize like that?" A large vein in his neck protruded as he worked his jaw tighter.

"He came first." Van Der Kamp shrugged his shoulders as if it were obvious. Wrighty's face went red and looked as if he were coming unglued. Before he could say something he'd regret, Van Der Kamp interrupted him, "The kid deserves a little break. He's smarter than you give him credit for, and he's been working hard. Besides, that little filly is more his speed than yours. I don't want you scaring her or breaking her. We can't have that—I'm still not sure what role she'll play."

"Haven't I been faithful to the gang? Haven't I done everything you've asked?"

"A little too gleefully, I'm afraid."

"What's that supposed to mean?"

"It means, you take a little too much pleasure in the killing and destruction. I'm in it for the message our robbing sends, not for the other things you take pleasure from. Seen plenty of that during the war. No more—not if I can help it."

"That's why you hired me—because you can't stomach the killing." Wrighty's voice was getting louder and taking on a sharp edge. No one naysaid Van Der Kamp—he was deadly when he wanted to be.

Van Der Kamp didn't move a muscle. In a low tone he said, "I can stomach what I have to do to get things done. I don't take joy or pleasure in it. *You*—you go out of your way to do those things. That's your choice, not mine. Watch where you put the blame, son, or the next place you'll be resting is at the bottom of a ravine. Got it?"

Wrighty knew he'd crossed a line, but he was getting tired of this, all of it. Van Der Kamp was becoming weak, and he was letting Charlie get away with more and more. There was always a reason—now it was Charlie this and Charlie that. Even some of the other men were softening on that damn whelp, Charlie. That wouldn't do. Right now, however, he had to make peace with Van Der Kamp, or he would be dumped somewhere with a broken neck or a bullet between his eyes. Van Der Kamp was still strong as a beast, with a deadly aim. He also didn't brook dissension or disorder amongst the ranks. He worked them like he did his men during his military days. They continued staring at each other, waiting for the other to back down. Finally, Wrighty nodded but remained silent.

"I'm glad you came to your senses. Hate to lose you, Wrighty. Is there something else you came for?"

Wrighty shook his head painfully slow before using his hands to press himself to standing. His lips were drawn tight into a seam and his facial features stretched taut across his face. He got up and started walking out. Just as his hand reached for the door latch, Van Der Kamp said, "Don't do anything stupid, now, you hear? You're a valuable member of the gang, even if I didn't give you what you wanted."

Wrighty's hand clenched the latch and flung the door open. He had to leave before he really did do something he'd regret. He even decided to steer clear of Charlie and his prize for the time being. He wanted to live another day.

When Charlie finally stopped running, he arrived at the main part of camp where the provisions hut as well as several outdoor benches and tables were. He looked around, noticing the door to the hut open. Moving into the doorway, he watched Jimmy and Annabelle going through the supplies and pulling items for supper. Annabelle was bent over a box, handing things back to Jimmy, who was fumbling with several cans when Charlie walked in on them. Charlie nodded his thanks to Jimmy before grabbing Annabelle's hand to help her to stand.

"Now, Charlie, whatever are you doing?" She brushed her hands off and then smoothed her skirt down. "We're trying to work here. It'll be dinnertime before we know it. I've got to get started on this." She flung her arm toward the stacks of cans and other provisions.

"I know. It's just, I'm trying my best, you know?"

Annabelle tilted her head to the side, watching Charlie's face. "I'm sure you are." She started to turn, but Charlie grabbed her upper arm. She tilted her head forward in question.

"I have to protect you. I feel bad for dragging you into this—I—" Charlie was struggling; he didn't want the fight that was sure to follow his explanation.

Jimmy's interception saved him. "Annabelle, Charlie went to talk to Van Der Kamp. I'm sure he has something to say about that. *Right, Charlie?*" Jimmy shot Charlie a wide-eyed look over Annabelle's head as if to say *get on with it* as he fumbled with an armful of cans. His head jerked forward, angling at Annabelle, when Charlie didn't start talking immediately.

Clearing his throat, he tore his eyes from Jimmy to look down at Annabelle. "Ah, yes. I, well…"

"Charlie, get on with it. I have to start fixing dinner. I don't want men grousing when they return." Annabelle's hands went to her hips. Charlie's eyes widened slightly. Not a good female sign. He remembered the days when his mom did that to his dad. Although, this also meant his desert wildflower had returned—and that was a good sign.

"Right." He let out a breath. "I have to stake a claim."

Annabelle looked at him and shrugged. Once again she turned her back on him, returning to her task.

"On you."

She whirled around so fast that Charlie took a quick step back. Her voice went to a scary low pitch that he also remembered his mom using on his dad. Every word was enunciated, "What. Do. You. *Mean?*" She was leaning forward by the time she was finished.

"Well, to protect you, I need to claim you." His hands spread wide in a placating manner, as if that was supposed to make complete sense to her.

Her mouth fell open, and he could feel the litany building. Holding his hands up, pumping them back and forth, he said, "Wait now, let me explain. I don't want the others hassling you anymore. I need to protect you—I'm responsible for you, and I want to do right." She leaned away from him and paused, before a string of words flew out of her mouth.

"I don't need protecting, Charlie!" She stamped her foot. "I am capable. I am smart. You!" She pointed her finger at him, lowering her voice to a deadly tone. "*You.*" Then shook her fist, raising her voice. "You!" She growled out the word *you*, pointing her finger at him again before throwing up her arms in disgust. She didn't even know the man, and here he was trying to control her. "I can handle it." Her stomach dropped for a moment as Wrighty jumped into her mind. She must've paled because Charlie reached his hand out to steady her. She let him, but only for a moment. *I'll be fine as long as I do what he tells me to do. I'll be fine. I can handle it. I'll be fine.* She shook off his help, but was still breathing hard.

Charlie and Jimmy exchanged concerned looks because Annabelle went somewhere in her mind where they weren't.

They were staring at her when she finally stopped ranting, but Charlie wasn't going to back down. "Really?" Charlie quirked a brow at her. "Like you were handling Conrad?" Annabelle's jaw dropped open, looking as if it had broken a hinge in the process. She turned beet-red and sucked in a breath as if to start yelling at him again, when Charlie interrupted her.

"I'm sorry. That was admittedly low." He put his hands on his hips. "You're cantankerous and prickly. Something happened back there," he threw his arm behind him, pointing back up the hill, "and you aren't telling me. You changed after a few days in the tent. You weren't standing up for yourself. You're too fiery to be broke that way, Wildflower. I saw the way Conrad was with you and it wasn't okay."

Jimmy darted his eyes at Charlie with his use of an endearment. It surprised and confused him. Charlie didn't notice Jimmy's look or pick up on his thoughts, like they normally did with each other. He was too busy staring at Annabelle, willing her cooperation.

Annabelle huffed but didn't deny anything. Jimmy's lips turned down as his eyes widened, nodding his head and taking it all in. Her pause caused him to throw another look at Charlie. Charlie shook his head.

Waiting another moment, he said, "I can help. I want to help. At least let me try to make it up to you."

Her arms were crossed, but she looked like she was taking what he said into consideration. Taking her break in yelling as a *yes*, he grabbed her arm and pulled her out of the provisions hut. She gasped, stumbling slightly, then hurried along after Charlie as he was explaining what he was up to. She couldn't hear much because she was pulled behind him like a toddler's toy.

Charlie marched her across the common area toward one of the smaller paths. She caught up to him, peppering him with questions. Finally freeing her hand from his sweaty mitt-sized one, she stopped.

"Who is Goat? What is going on?" Annabelle leaned toward Charlie, hands on hips, and her brow furrowed. "If this is some kind of joke, you can just think again, Charlie—I—argh! Charlie-I-don't-even-know-your-last-name—Charlie."

Charlie was incredulous. His eyes opened wide before he calmly said, "Stapleton."

Sighing heavily, he turned to walk away. Annabelle scurried after him like a hen chasing after her chicks. "Don't you walk away from me." Charlie kept his steady pace, stopping when he approached an older man mending a pair of britches.

He turned back toward Annabelle, sweeping his arm, hand palm up, toward the man. "*This* is Goat. You weren't introduced. Meals aren't exactly a *social event*." Charlie pushed his hat back and scratched his forehead. "He's the one who's going to save your bacon, *ma'am*."

Goat threw his head back, guffawing at poor Annabelle, who stood there with her mouth gaping open.

"I take it you told her yer claiming her?"

Annabelle flushed as she exchanged an angry look for a shocked one. She still wasn't used to such crudeness.

Charlie gave Annabelle a sheepish look.

"Yeah, in a way. Clearly, she didn't take it well." He tossed his head in Annabelle's direction, making Goat cackle again.

"Looky here, girlie. Our young Charlie is doing you and hisself a favor by staking his claim on you. If he doesn't, some other man will, or there'll be fights over you—I promise it'll get real ugly before it gets better. You're in a den of wolves, in case you hadn't noticed." Annabelle's sharp intake of breath blended with Goat's next words. "Besides, the last man you want staking a claim on you is Wrighty."

With that, Annabelle went completely pale and started to sway. Charlie jumped forward and wrapped his arm around her shoulders to steady her. He frowned, thinking that every mention of Wrighty elicited some form of visible fear in Annabelle.

"He," Goat went on, indicating Charlie with the hand holding the needle, "has to make a big announcement so that everyone hears his claim—I'll help with that, but you have to play along or the others won't believe it. Besides, you're not exactly the most cooperative of people. This is probably going to be tricky."

Goat looked at Annabelle for confirmation that she understood. She nodded, swallowing visibly.

"Good—we'll do it at dinner. Everyone'll be there. Once we get this over with, Charlie can go back to his regular chores instead of following you around all the time with his eyes."

This time it was both Charlie and Annabelle who jerked back in surprise. Charlie still had his arm around Annabelle as they dashed a quick look at each other before looking back at Goat. Goat shook his head.

"Son, I don't care how you two eventually arrange it between yourselves, but you have to carry her off after the big announcement, make it look real-like. Understand? You have to somehow *be* together, share a tent, so to speak." Goat leaned forward, this time waiting for Charlie to respond. Charlie nodded his head curtly before grabbing Annabelle's hand to drag her back to the provisions hut.

They could hear Goat's laughter chasing after them.

~ **16** ~

Annabelle and Jimmy were in charge of dinner that evening. Goat had other things to do that afternoon, which was another reason why Annabelle hadn't clued in to who he was. Jimmy cut up bits of meat while Annabelle ladled beans and added biscuits before bringing them to the table. Emboldened by her recent docile behavior, two of the men made grabby hands at her that she didn't successfully dodge. Partially because the bruised bone in her leg was still healing, slowing her down, but also because men starved of the company of women can be real quick when they want to be. She batted at them with her free hand, making them laugh. She was tiny, and her swats made no difference to them. They only stopped when they saw Charlie make like he was coming over. Others made rude comments too low to be heard well, or undressed her with their eyes. It didn't matter what the men did—all the while, Charlie's ears burned red at the tips, and his fists clenched under the table. His eyes followed Annabelle's every move. Luckily, there were enough men who knew better than to mess with her, because nothing had been settled about her fate.

There seemed to be two general camps—those who were polite and thanked her for the meal, and those who grunted an acknowledgment. Either way, Charlie was thankful that the outliers were few. For whatever reason, he felt a fight brewing up in him, and, generally, he wasn't the fighting type. His leg started bouncing up and down before he noticed Van Der Kamp and Wrighty were both watching him intently. Blowing out a breath, he looked over at Jimmy and tried to find some patience. Annabelle brought Charlie and herself a plate before sitting down next to him. Their eyes locked, and her face burned as she lowered herself onto the bench. She quickly turned her head away when her bottom hit the wood plank.

Finally, everyone had been served, but Charlie's nerves still hadn't settled. The few bites he managed to take felt like sod in his mouth. He had to chew a bunch of times before he could finally swallow it. The food was choking him, and he desperately wanted to spit it out. Everyone else was engrossed in their meals or conversation. An occasional laugh or curse bubbled over a few murmuring conversations. Grabbing his cup, he furiously chugged water, slamming it on the table before shooting up to stand. Between the jarring sound of his tin cup breaking the silence, and Charlie's broad form jumping up like a plank that someone accidentally stepped on, everyone stopped what they were doing to stare at him.

He gently rested his hand on Annabelle's shoulder, squeezing it before stating, loudly, "Annabelle here is *mine*—all mine. I claim her for myself, and I don't want interference from the rest of you."

His voice was resonant and commanding, unlike his usual deference and politeness. He looked around to make sure everyone understood that he meant business. And he really did. He didn't realize how much so until that very moment. He knew that something monumental was happening, and there was no going back. He was claiming her, all right. He just didn't know how far this would go.

He looked directly at the two who had groped her. "No touching, and no looking. I brought her here, and I get to keep her."

He jabbed his thumb to his chest. Everyone was silenced by his words, looking around at each other before looking in the direction of Van Der Kamp and Wrighty. Annabelle was the only one who wasn't looking around. She stared directly at Charlie with complete disbelief. This didn't seem like a ruse to her—this seemed real. Her mouth hung open looking at him. She snapped it shut when she saw how angry Wrighty was. The man looked like he was ready to murder Charlie, but Van Der Kamp was his usual relaxed self. It was as if polite conversation had been taking place, not a throw-down by his second-most-docile gang member. Van Der Kamp nodded his approval and continued to eat. Slowly, everyone else went back to eating. Goat was smiling down at his plate while shaking his head in mirth. It was as if he had instinctively known that Charlie wouldn't be able to wait and that he'd handle it himself, in his own way.

Charlie sat back down but still couldn't eat. He whispered for Annabelle to eat, nudging her with his shoulder, then lifting his chin toward her plate. She nodded demurely, looking back down at her plate because she didn't want to attract any more of Wrighty's attention. After a few minutes, he got up. Annabelle looked at him in question. He helped her out of her seat and led her away from the tables. Someone had dared to catcall, causing Charlie to turn around and glare at the offender. When he turned back around, he scooped up Annabelle and threw her over his shoulder. She hollered in protest, beating his back and then made all sorts of demands that were lost to their ears as he hauled her toward the forest, far away from the others.

The men broke out into laughter, making off-color re-marks and suggestions while joking about *that boy*, when Van Der Kamp silenced them. "*That boy* means business. You all best be taking him seriously, you hear? That's his girl, whether or not he fully realizes how much so."

Jimmy and Wrighty were the only ones who took those last words to heart. That's when Jimmy realized Van Der Kamp wasn't talking about Charlie's usual extra-protective behav-ior or his strong sense of responsibility—Charlie was actually falling in love with the sheriff's daughter, which could only mean trouble. He had a shocked expression on his face when he looked up, realizing that Van Der Kamp had been watching him come to this realization. Van Der Kamp inclined his head toward Jimmy, then continued to eat.

"**C**harlie! Charlie! Put me down. Right this instant. *Charlie.*" Annabelle continued to ineffectually beat on Charlie's back. Even though she wasn't hurting him, he still wouldn't have noticed. His actions felt like they were someone else's. Charlie gripped Annabelle's legs tighter, not wanting to drop her. He walked far away from the cooking area, off into the forest. He wasn't sure what he was doing, but he had to get away from the gang before he started some fights he couldn't finish. They were down by the stream when he finally released her legs and let her slide down the front of his body. He held her steady by the shoulders for a moment so the blood would start circulating in her legs again. She grasped his forearms for balance and caught her breath from all the yelling, free to breathe now that her chest was not being pressed against and bounced around on Charlie's solid frame.

"What is going on?" She beat her fist one last time against his chest. Charlie pushed her back by the shoulders, his head tilted down, and looked deeply at her face with a furrowed brow before pulling her hard to his chest. Wrapping his arms around her back, he held her tightly without speaking. Cocooned in physical and emotional warmth, she initially tensed, then relaxed into him. Her head rested comfortably, square in the middle of his chest. Charlie eventually calmed his breath and his nerves before placing a kiss on top of her head.

"I don't know." He rocked her like a mother would rock a child in need of comforting. "I don't know."

They stood holding each other for a few more moments before Charlie interrupted the peaceful silence. "I knew Goat was going to help us—I trust him. But it was taking so long to pass out the meals—and then Seth and Gabe kept grabbing at you, saying things—I felt like I was going to combust. My muscles were tense, and I didn't know what to do with myself—I had to hold myself back. I was near losing control." Breathing deeply, he said, "I actually wanted to leap over the table and punch those idiots more than once, but I couldn't. They're Wrighty's cronies and that wouldn't go over well, even with Van Der Kamp's approval."

He let out a big sigh and rubbed his hands on her back without realizing he was doing it. "Annabelle, these men are dangerous. Jimmy and I tried to escape once—" He stopped talking because he hated those memories, even though he'd never forget them. The pain Jimmy endured, and his inability to save his brother from Wrighty or from this God-awful fate, dogged Charlie like his shadow.

Annabelle waited for Charlie to finish. When he didn't, she gently nudged him by rubbing her face like a contented kitten against his broad chest. "Go on."

He shuddered from the friction her face made, the rubbing of his shirt against his skin, and the heat she created doing it. He made an anguished sound, squeezing her tighter before releasing her. Holding her forearms, he bent down to her height, so they were face to face.

"I can't. I can't let anything like that happen again. I won't let Wrighty get the best of us. He keeps fighting me, but he's not going to best me this time."

Wrighty's name caused Annabelle to tense in his arms. Suddenly, her leg made its presence known. It started throbbing—and not because Charlie had manhandled her earlier. The pain in her leg throbbed in time with the misery of her breaking heart. Charlie's untold anguish mingled with her physical pain and fear. None of them were there because they chose to be, and they all suffered because of the gang, specifically because of Wrighty.

Annabelle's hand slid up to Charlie's upper arm. She gently squeezed him, placing her head back on his chest.

"Charlie, what happened?" she asked him very quietly.

She didn't realize that tears were streaming down her face—his emotions felt as if they were seeping into her skin and into her very being. She felt the horror, sadness, and regret he was feeling. He just wasn't saying the words that she was feeling.

The dampness of her tears soaking his shirt sent him back to the early days when Jimmy cried himself to sleep but was embarrassed by his behavior. Jimmy was afraid of being beaten again, but was also afraid of getting Charlie in trouble. He constantly struggled with not being "man enough." For a long time the men called him "girlie" or "wee one"—especially when he was first able to walk after the beating. At least, that was until he shot up to 6 feet tall one summer. He continued to grow taller—definitely broader and stronger—so then the name-calling stopped pretty quickly. Jimmy was as broad as Charlie, although a couple of inches shorter. Charlie was "as broad as a barn" as Van Der Kamp liked to say. One of the many reasons it was "okay" that he "allowed them to live."

Charlie worked as hard as an ox and was built like one. Shaking off the memories, he stroked the back of her head, making a soft *sshh* sound like a mother would to comfort her child.

"It's okay, Annabelle. I won't let them harm you. Don't worry, little wildflower. We'll find a way. Just know, we're not them—we'll find a way out of here."

All Annabelle could do was nod her head and cling to Charlie. Everything wasn't what it seemed, and she no longer knew what to think. Charlie opened his mouth to say more when he heard Jimmy's voice down the path, calling out to them.

He hollered back, "Up here," waiting for Jimmy's appearance.

He released Annabelle, but not before placing a gentle kiss on her forehead and brushing the tears from her cheeks with his thumbs.

Jimmy was breathing hard when he rounded the bend and had to stop to catch his breath. He bent over with his hands on his knees, breathing loudly for a minute, before he panted out, "Van Der Kamp wants you two to return. He says you had enough time *claiming* your woman. She needs to come back and clean up supper."

Charlie rolled his eyes at Jimmy. Annabelle ducked her head but not before they saw she had turned bright red.

Jimmy took a look at Annabelle's tear-stained face before looking at Charlie, "Charlie, what did you do to poor Annabelle?" He stood up straighter, tensing as if he was going to lunge at Charlie.

Charlie made a low sound in the back of his throat. "Nothing, you idiot. We're trying to figure out how to handle this all. Don't be such a dolt."

Charlie reached for Annabelle's hand, holding it with both of his.

"There's nothing to be embarrassed about. They'll think what they think, and it doesn't matter—as long as it keeps them away from you. Understand? I won't force you—that isn't what this is about, no matter what they say or call it."

An odd look passed Charlie's face. Jimmy, however, could already see for himself that Van Der Kamp was right. Charlie was lying to both himself and Annabelle.

✤ 18 ✤

"Say, Charlie—how was your ride yesterday? Saddle-sore?" Lafayette guffawed, slapping Orrin on the back, who, in turn, nudged him with his elbow. Their big grins made them look even more foolish than they were. Charlie had had worse, but he worried about Annabelle's sensibilities. His head swiveled around, looking for her. This is exactly what she was worried about—the public shaming.

The razzing the men gave Charlie was bad enough. Lewd jokes, elbowing, smirks. He could handle it because the men had said all kinds of things to him and Jimmy before. It just happened that this time the content was sexual and involved Annabelle. It made his blood boil thinking about Annabelle's sensibilities, but not wanting their sham uncovered won out— he didn't confirm or deny anything. As long as the rest of them stayed away from her and didn't touch, he told her that he could put up with their shenanigans.

Returning from pulling up the dry laundry, Annabelle carried a folded stack of mending. Jimmy was slightly ahead of her, carrying one of the larger baskets as they passed a pair of men chopping wood. They continued to chop until Annabelle walked by—one of them held out his axe, pretending he was riding it, and the other grunted, thrusting his hips at her, causing her neck to cramp in response. She was holding it so stiffly she thought it might snap. Jimmy was unaware because he generally ignored the others and was too far ahead to see—he wasn't used to her short legs, and she had trouble keeping up. It'd been like that the remainder of yesterday and into today. The men would wait until Jimmy or Charlie, whoever happened to be with her, wasn't looking, and make sexual gestures, rude sounds, or crude remarks to her.

It was like running the gauntlet returning to the tent last night—someone in the shadows made moaning noises at her, someone else called out that there was room in his tent for her when she was done with Charlie. Words, sounds, and laughter followed her all the way to Charlie's tent. Luckily it was dark, as she could feel her face flaming the whole way. When Charlie rounded the corner, all sounds and movement ceased, so he couldn't catch anything specific.

This was nearly unbearable for her, and it had been less than twenty-four hours. Annabelle was feeling like an unwilling horse caught on the too-tight end of a tether. Her entire body was stiff from keeping herself ramrod straight. She managed to ignore them as best she could, although her face felt like it was constantly on fire, and her body was sore from tensing up at the indignity of it all. She braced herself for the worst. In some ways, things had become worse after Charlie made his big announcement. At least before, they were steering clear of her. However, she knew that was most likely short-lived, given her so-called "delicate situation" was a monthly thing, not something permanent. She groaned thinking about it.

Things finally came to a head, and it was poor Charlie who took the brunt of her ire. All of the men had taken to calling her "sweet Annabelle," which she could tolerate, for the most part. It was when certain men used that moniker that it became an issue for her—more specifically, Wrighty and

Conrad. Wrighty was a given—anything he did was an issue for her. She still felt wary around Conrad after his attempt to bribe a kiss out of her. Both men gave her bad feelings that she couldn't shake, so she avoided them at all costs. Conrad seemed to sense that, so he made it a point to call out to her with a "sweet Annabelle" and then leer at her when she looked his way. If she didn't look at him, he'd say vulgar things, but only when Charlie was out of earshot.

At supper, Annabelle and Goat were working at a frantic pace. Scouts had returned early and hungry. She was too busy ladling beans to notice that Conrad had horned his way to the front of the line. Then she smelt the alcohol…too late.

He leaned forward and whispered, "Hello, sweet Annabelle. You got something special for me tonight?"

Behind him, she could hear Lafayette chuckling and snorting as her face warmed. Aggressively tipping the handle of her ladle, she slopped beans onto Conrad's plate, splashing some on his hand. He wasn't too drunk to feel the burn of hot beans.

He jumped back and yelled. "You stupid bitch! You burned me."

Her voice and the ladle rose in response. "I'm so sorry. Perhaps you shouldn't stand so close to me, Conrad."

The ladle went back into the kettle for another scoop of beans, but Conrad refused to move away. Annabelle raised her brows and asked, "You wanting some more beans, Conrad?"

They now had an audience, with Conrad attempting to keep up his bravado.

"You know what I'd rather have, sweet Annabelle."

The men guffawed but quickly quit when the sound of Annabelle's palm striking Conrad's face cut through their laughter. Everyone went silent with surprise as they watched Annabelle drop the ladle into the kettle and push her way through the men. She continued to march up the hill to where the cabins and tents were located. Charlie glared at Conrad as he sprinted after her.

He finally reached her at the top of the hill and grabbed her by the arm. "Are you okay?"

"No, I'm not okay, Charlie." She threw her arms up in exasperation then pushed against his chest. "I'm trapped with a bunch of criminals who keep saying awful things to me. I feel—violated."

"Has anyone—"

"How could they possibly? You and Jimmy are always around me—no, no one's touched me. That isn't the point. The words are *nearly* as bad, Charlie. The way some of them look at me is *nearly* as bad."

Charlie ran his hand through his hair while looking down at the ground. Drawing in an extended breath, he looked at Annabelle for a few moments. "I'll take care of this, right now."

Turning on his heel, he marched back down the hill. The men had been watching them while they talked but couldn't hear what they were saying. By the look on Charlie's face, it wasn't good. Everyone marked Charlie's progress as he marched directly up to Conrad and punched him square in the nose. Conrad's head whipped back before he could utter a sound, blood spraying the two of them, and his nose breaking loud and clear. He landed flat on his back and looked up at Charlie's angry face.

Charlie jabbed a finger at Conrad, getting right in his face. "I told you not to mess with Annabelle. I won't be asking politely if you come near her, again. She's not to be bothered."

With that, Charlie shook out his fist and marched back up the hill toward Annabelle, her mouth hanging open. He gently took her by the arm and steered her back toward their tent.

Despite Charlie's threat, she was still watched constantly. However, only Charlie, Jimmy, or Goat did the watching since Charlie claimed her. She wasn't left alone with the others for any length of time. The message was sent after Conrad was laid flat, so most of the gang fell in line. After a brief reprieve, there were the occasional comments or looks, but nothing terrible or out of the ordinary. It was usually when Jimmy was around, but there were no volatile actions accompanying them. Jimmy was a quiet man. He was like a lockbox with his words and emotions. If Annabelle railed about something or complained, he'd pick up the pieces and keep moving. He didn't want to chase her out, nor did he get angry with her. He pretty much ignored her intermittent pettiness. He didn't have anything to say to the men because he knew from experience there was nothing to say to them—they had to get it out of their immature systems. Any interference would come back on him. They might've been older than both Annabelle and Jimmy, but Jimmy was an old soul when it came to good behavior. Besides, once he saw the harsh realities of his new existence, he grew up in a hardened sort of way. He stopped crying and he stopped feeling anything, for preservation's sake. He protected Charlie in his own way, which included helping with Annabelle. It also meant keeping his mouth shut, which he wished Annabelle would learn to do.

❧ 19 ❧

Annabelle persuaded Jimmy to let her help with the horses when she wasn't washing or mending. It gave her a break from worry about her father, her fear of Wrighty, and boredom. She also had someone to talk to other than Goat when they were cooking together. Charlie was too busy glowering at the other men and shielding her to talk much.

Jimmy walked with her up the hill after breakfast so they could do their chores. She enjoyed Goat, as he was off-color and entertaining, but Jimmy had a calming presence about him. It wasn't because he was so quiet, either. At his core, he was a gentle, peaceful young man. The animals sensed that and loved him.

"How old are you, Jimmy?"

"Eighteen, just turned."

"Hm."

Initially, it was difficult to tell because he looked older than he was. It could've been his serious and mature nature or just being part of a gang. It also could've been that he was six foot two and as big as a bull. Annabelle cast a side-look at him as they were nearing the temporary corral area. He was built nearly as large as Charlie. His height was less impressive only because his sheer size was the most notable thing about him. If he entered a room, he blocked out all of the light. She had to make him stand to the side in the provisions shelter because it was already dark in there, and it turned nearly pitch-black when he helped.

Charlie blocked out light in a similar way. She remembered the light brightening the mercantile for a flash, then disappearing right before the first time she saw him. Even then, she knew there was something magnifying about Charlie, despite being scared stiff and unable to see his face. Yes, they both filled doorways. However, unlike Charlie, Jimmy didn't make the air crackle when he entered an area. Charlie and Jimmy were both calm and collected, but Jimmy was like a placid lake—his turmoil was kept under deep waters. Charlie was more like the explosives the miners used to blast. When he was ignited or even near a flame, it didn't take much for the destruction to be swift and powerful. However, he used his explosive moments strategically, like a miner. Oddly enough, she always felt safe around him—both brothers, for that matter.

They walked in companionable silence the rest of the way before Jimmy grabbed a brush and tossed it to her.

"You get to brush down some horses today. Some of the men are riding out to hunt, and they need their rides in tip-top shape. Whaddya say?" He smirked at her. "Up for the task?"

That was the other thing about Jimmy—he teased Annabelle in a way he didn't with others. He was playful and had a good sense of humor, when they were alone or with Charlie. He was like a brother she never had.

Her eyes lit up at the challenge.

"The better question is, are the mounts ready? They'll never want anyone else after I lay my hands on them." She vigorously rubbed her hands together, scrunching them, then poofed them out, like a stage magician.

Jimmy's eyes lit up at her theatrics.

"I'm pretty sure that sentiment could apply to more than the horses." He gave her a wry look, because good-natured Gabe had been at it, again. He was smitten with Annabelle, despite Charlie's warnings and glowering. Jimmy screwed up his face, then burst out laughing, which stopped her from yelling at him. After a minute, she couldn't hold back the laughter, either. Tears were rolling out of her eyes from the expression on the normally stoic Jimmy's face.

"He's not too bright, that one, is he?" She shook her head as they approached the horse pen. Charlie had made things between her and the gang much smoother, after reinforcing his point with Conrad's nose. Gabe was harmless—he admired Annabelle from afar and was never rude. He was truly a simple man.

"He just doesn't know when to quit." They stood looking at the horses for a minute before she asked, "Which one first?"

They watched the horses milling around until a pinto came trotting over, nudging Jimmy's hand, looking for a treat. Jimmy smoothed his hand over his muzzle before scratching him behind his ear. The horse snuffled Annabelle to see if she had any treats.

"Payson, this here is Annabelle. She's going to be grooming you today. I'll get your hooves after she brushes you." The horse nibbled on her sleeve, causing Annabelle to giggle.

"Oh, your lips are ticklish!" He nickered in response, nudging the hand holding the brush.

"Looks like Payson's ready for you. I'll bring him out and hitch him to the post over there." They stepped back as Jimmy opened the gate, grabbing the pinto by his harness. He led him over to the post, securing him.

"Here you go. Why don't you hand me the brush and I'll show you how to do it, then you can take over after he's comfortable with both of us here."

She handed him the brush and Jimmy set to work. He fell into an easy rhythm, seeming to forget that she was there. He started crooning to the horse, whose eyes took on a sleepy look. The pair looked contented, so much so that she hated to interrupt. But they were burning daylight, and after a while, she cleared her throat.

"Ah, sorry. It's easy to get lost in work out here. The men only come up here when they're coming or going—I've pretty much taken over these responsibilities." He looked up to speak, quickly dipping his chin in embarrassment.

Annabelle put a hand on his arm. "It's nothing to be embarrassed about. You're really good with the animals—they love you." It looked like his face caught fire, turning bright red. Annabelle smiled at his shyness, remembering he was much younger than he looked. "Should I have a try, now?" She canted her head toward Payson.

Jimmy nodded and handed her the brush. The pause in grooming had Payson turning his head toward them, tossing them a disdainful look. When Annabelle patted his hindquarter, taking up where Jimmy left off, Payson snorted his approval and relaxed. Jimmy watched her for a few minutes. Seeing she had the hang of it, he went to fill the feeders and returned later with a file, pick, and brush for Payson's hooves.

"I'm not going to ask you to do this, but in case there's a need, you might as well learn." Holding up the pick and the file, he showed her what the tools looked like, then pulled up a stool, getting to work.

"You can just watch. You're a quick learn, and like I said, you won't have to do this." She watched him work on the first hoof before wandering off to sit in the shade. The day was growing hot. She fanned herself for a bit, watching Jimmy in deep concentration.

They sat quietly, Jimmy working and Annabelle fanning herself, while Payson occasionally nickered. Annabelle watched some of the other horses come and go from the fence. They were curious to see what they were about.

Finally, she said, "Gabe doesn't bother me so much, although he's a nuisance."

Jimmy stopped what he was doing to look at her. "Oh, yeah?"

"Yeah. I think he just doesn't know how to behave around me."

"You're being mighty generous if I say so, myself." Jimmy went back to picking at the next hoof.

"No. I mean, I'd rather he left me alone, but he's not one who worries me."

She couldn't help it. She knew she wasn't supposed to be talking about what happened, but she felt a great urge to unburden herself about Wrighty. He terrified her. He hadn't been around her alone since he beat her, but he sent her looks during meals that made her stomach turn sour and her hands shake. She knew that he was never far away, either. Just as sure as the sun rose every morning and set every evening, she knew he was waiting for her to mess up so he could come punish her. The anxiety of watching for him in the shadows or anticipating him coming up behind her was wearing her down. She was sure he took more pleasure in that than anything else. Despite the heat, a chill went down her spine, making her shudder.

"You okay? Do you need to go back to the tent?"

"I'm okay, thanks."

"You're suddenly looking a little pale."

"No, I'm good." She waved him off.

"Charlie won't let me hear the end of it if you get sick on my watch, although I sure do seem to be getting stuck on a lot of watches these days." He cracked a smile.

"Oh, no—he can't blame you!"

"Yes, he can. He takes responsibilities very seriously. Haven't you noticed?" He quirked a brow at her.

"Ah, yes. I suppose he is very conscientious." They were quiet for a moment. She mulled over Charlie's behavior, which was so contradictory to the bandit she'd thought he was. "He's certainly apologized to me—a lot—about the kidnapping. He can't seem to get over that."

Jimmy blew out a breath before releasing Payson's hoof. If anyone, he understood Charlie's guilt on that score. He also understood why he did it, but neither of those things made the situation any better. He sat up on the stool, stretching and dwarfing it even more when he stretched to his full sitting height. He thought about what he could share, because this was really Charlie's tale to tell, not his.

"Yeah, Charlie has a lot of hang-ups about what he thinks are his responsibilities and those he feels he needs to protect." Jimmy was looking intently at something.

Annabelle craned her head to see what he was looking at, which was nothing in particular. She'd never be able to see the memories in his mind. Realizing this, she turned back toward him, anticipating more details about this enigma, Charlie. Jimmy turned his head and studied her for a long moment. Annabelle was leaning forward, nodding in a *go on, go on* manner.

With a loud intake of breath, Jimmy stood. Patting Payson on the rump, he walked around to untie him.

"Let's get another horse and keep moving. We don't want to be caught unprepared." He mumbled under his breath, "Or we'll have Hell to pay."

His last words had Annabelle springing up so quickly that she nearly stumbled as she rushed forward to help. Jimmy paused, looking at her oddly, before leading Payson back to the makeshift corral.

The remainder of the morning passed in a similar manner. Jimmy and Annabelle worked well together. They didn't need a lot of words, especially after Annabelle picked up what Jimmy wanted her to do. They were working on the fourth horse when Wrighty and his cohorts came lumbering down the path. They could hear them before they saw them—loud talking and razzing, Seth and Dewit pushing at each other.

"Woohee—hel-lo, darling!" Chortling and snorting followed.

Annabelle nearly dropped her brush, fumbling with it before she looked nervously between the group of men and Jimmy. Jimmy kept working, aware she was nervous.

Without looking at her, he said, "Ignore them—keep working. They just want to rile you."

Annabelle's head ducked back to the horse's flank as Wrighty rounded the hitching post.

"Well, well, well. Lookee here, boys. Isn't this cozy?" Wrighty walked right up behind Annabelle and watched with satisfaction as her shoulders tensed when he moved into her space. His legs bumped against her skirts as she felt his hot breath on the back of her already over-heated neck. He stroked the back of her head, grabbing the curly ends, repeating this motion. He bobbed his head from one side of hers around to the other, trying to get her to look at him. Taking Jimmy's words to the extreme, she ignored him as best she could, continuing to brush the horse with shaky hands. It was becoming difficult to keep hold of the brush because her hands were sweating, and the brush was getting slippery. The horse started to shift nervously with the tension until Jimmy laid a hand on the mare.

Leaning his head in, Wrighty said, "If I didn't know better, I'd think something was going on between the two of you, given how quiet you were when we showed up." When neither of them answered, he said, "Have you two been busy working or have you been getting busy?"

Annabelle's sharp intake of breath gave her discomfort away, and the men hooted with laughter.

"Come on, sweet Annabelle. You can admit you like variety. Spice of life, you know." Lafayette winked at Jimmy.

"Ain't so tough as you try to make yourself out to be, huh?" Seth called out.

Moris shot him a look. He still felt bad for Annabelle, especially since she was out of her league with such hardened and experienced men. He noticed that she still blushed when one of the brothers looked at her like she was special or when they paid her a compliment, and they were benign as far as men went—still wet behind the ears.

"Are you all going? We have four horses ready—we can have two more ready in thirty."

Wrighty snarled at Jimmy. "Wasn't talking to you."

Jimmy stood to his full height and breadth, inhaling and exhaling loudly, which served to make him seem even larger. "You asked for horses. I'm assuming you've come for them. Don't you have work to do?"

The air stopped moving around them, as did all activity. The horse tucked its ears back and let out a long snort, punctuating Jimmy's remark. Annabelle let out a soft cry when Wrighty pulled hard on her curls before releasing her, walking around the horse to face off with Jimmy. They stared at each other for a long moment before Wrighty nodded.

"Only four of us are going, and we're going right now. Orrin and Lafayette are making the rounds. They're here to make sure work is getting done." He jerked his head to the side, and three of them went to get their horses while the other two looked around the area to make sure chores had been completed. "Van Der Kamp gives you too much freedom." He flicked his hand at Jimmy before turning around facing Annabelle. "Sorry you're missing the chance to stroke me like you're stroking my horse." He toyed with her hair once again. He had a serious fetish with her curls and with hair in general. "I'll be back later, darling."

He laughed uproariously as he sauntered off to get the tack for his horse. Annabelle moved away from the upset mare, still holding the brush. The men saddled up the freshly groomed and watered horses and moved out. She remained rooted to her spot the entire time, with her shoulders folded in on herself and her hands clasped in front of her.

When the last of them left, Jimmy went up to Annabelle and hugged her. She was shaking so hard that he held her for a few moments before releasing her. Walking her to the stool, he sat her down.

"It's going to be okay, you know that, right? We won't let them do anything to you. Now that Charlie's laid claim, they can talk all they want, but they can't touch. Van Der Kamp laid down the law, and they know better than to go against him, no matter what Wrighty says."

Annabelle nodded but didn't say anything. She was still folded in on herself. Her breathing was shallow, so they sat quietly for a few more moments so she could catch her breath.

Jimmy observed the complete change in her demeanor, weighing his words before speaking.

"What did he do to you?" Jimmy said it so softly that Annabelle almost mistook hearing him say it.

He rubbed her arm a few moments before sitting on the ground in front of her. They watched each other for a few minutes before Jimmy blew out a breath. He ran his hand through his hair, dropping his head and his arm.

He spoke without lifting his head. "We tried to escape, once."

Annabelle jerked her head up, her eyes wide.

"We had planned for weeks. Charlie saved bits of his dinner and what he could sneak from Goat when he was helping with meals." He swallowed hard, the movement of his throat visible from the side. "But I was scared. Really scared. They killed our parents, and I didn't want to die. I didn't want Charlie to die." He shook his head. "Charlie insisted we could do it. He was methodical—he picked the dark of the moon to run. We had run for miles but got a slow start because I was holding Charlie back with my fear. He stopped to reassure me—I was crying, shaking. I was so scared I could barely make my body cooperate. I tripped and didn't get up right away—I…I didn't know what to do. I didn't know where we were going but didn't want to stay there, either. I couldn't stop trembling. When Charlie finally persuaded me to get up and start running again, it was too late—we heard 'em."

Annabelle gasped. Her hand flew out, grabbing Jimmy's arm. Like the old soul he was, he patted it.

"We didn't cover our trail well enough and my fall really did us in. Wrighty caught me—lifted me right onto his horse. It was humiliating. They hooted and hollered, taunting us. He told Charlie that he'd skin me alive if he didn't cooperate. Charlie held up his hands, and Seth and Conrad grabbed him." He audibly swallowed this time before continuing. "We cooperated and knew we'd get punished. The thing is, Van Der Kamp let Wrighty decide the punishment…He beat me so badly I couldn't walk for days. I could barely see, my eyes were so swollen and my head throbbed. I was in so much pain that I wished I'd died."

He twisted his head toward Annabelle. "Do you know the worst part of it?"

She shook her head, lips pressed tight. She was ready to pass out from fear because he uttered the same words Moris did—"When Wrighty gets done with you, *you'll wish you died*."

"Charlie begged to take the punishment—*begged*. Wrighty refused. He said if we ever ran away again, he would skin us *both* alive, and we better toe the line or he'd start breaking limbs—one by one. Charlie was so torn up that I got the beating and that there wasn't a damn thing he could do about it. Not a thing." Annabelle's tears were flowing freely at this point, her hand covering her mouth, body shaking.

"Wrighty still uses me over Charlie. If Charlie didn't rob the mercantile that day, Wrighty was going to kill me. He said he'd be *nice* and just put a bullet between my eyes because he was feeling generous." Jimmy chuffed, mouth turned downward, looking sour.

Annabelle couldn't take it any longer. She folded over herself, putting her face on her knees, covering herself with her arms. She heaved loud, heavy sobs. Jimmy rubbed her back the way his mom used to do when he was hurting or upset. He felt awkward at first, but when she began to quiet, it gave him a sense of peace he hadn't felt in a long while.

"How'd you come to be with the gang in the first place?" The question came out in a whispery whoosh of air, then she snorted in her snot in an unladylike manner, wiping her face with her sleeve.

"They kidnapped us."

"What?"

"They took us after they robbed the stagecoach we were on—they killed our parents and the driver. It was actually Goat's idea; otherwise they would've killed us, too. Wrighty was so angry because he had Charlie by the hair and was ready to shoot him. He'd already been beatin' him. They made us watch while they taunted the others and beat them. Goat interrupted, saying they could use us for tasks and chores. That got Van Der Kamp's attention, so Goat quickly added that eventually we'd be big enough to go hunting and do jobs on our own. Wrighty was hopping mad, so they beat us real good so we couldn't run or rebel. He kicked us extra, just because."

"Oooh. Now I see."

"Yup."

They sat in silence, the horses nickering sweetly to them. Annabelle was calming down a little bit more, but her breath still came in erratic sniffles and stuttered in-breaths. Jimmy stood, brushed off his backside, then stretched. "We better get a move-on. We can do about three more horses, and then I should get you back to Goat."

✦ **20** ✦

Annabelle's mind was still reeling from what Jimmy had shared. He didn't take her with him after dinner clean-up, so she had a minute to rest at the tables before she realized that she was being watched. It wasn't a fearful sensation of being watched, oddly enough. Slowly turning on the bench brought her nearly eye to eye with a little white burro. She jumped, gasping, and the burro answered her with loud braying and grunting.

"Arghh! Oh, shush, shush. Shussh." Annabelle made patting motions in the air trying to quiet the beast. Finally, she got up and the burro followed her. She fed it a biscuit while cooing to it. Eventually, it nuzzled her hand for more. Looking around, making sure she wasn't being watched, she handed it another biscuit and stroked him between his ears. He made contented little grunting sounds before trotting off when he realized the feeding was over.

Goat had watched the little burro trot off and saw that Annabelle was watching it as well. "Be careful none of the others see you feed that one."

Annabelle nearly jumped out of her skin a second time. Her hand flew to her chest as her feet left the ground. "Goat! You're going to be the end of me—please, don't sneak up on me like that."

Goat cackled and sat down. He flipped his hand in the direction the burro went.

"I used to feed more of them burros, that is, before Wrighty got it into his head to try to ride one when he was filled with gut warmer. He was so drunk, he could barely walk but thought it was a good idea to try to ride that little white one." He was shaking his head, smiling at the memory. "He nearly got on it when it kicked but good." Hooting, he slapped his thigh, rolling back and forth on his backside. He laughed so hard, he wiped a tear from his eye. "He was dusted by a burro!" More laughter and tears poured out of him. "Serves the sum o' bitch right." He nodded for emphasis.

Annabelle was horrified to be discussing Wrighty, not only twice in one day, but also in a less-than-flattering way. She tossed a quick look over either shoulder and then around them, making sure no one heard. Her mouth hung open and her eyebrows raised high—like a wide-open barn.

"Don't you worry. Everyone knows the story and agrees. The only thing we don't agree on is the damned burros. Belonged to some miner who took a fall. He had a pair of them, and they wander around from time to time."

"Where is he now?"

"I suppose six feet under."

She made an "O" shape with her mouth, but no sound escaped. "Is this…"

"You asking if this is his land? Part of it. We ran the others off when we found out about him. No one else will come up here, see? 'Haunted.' Bad luck. No silver. No gold."

Annabelle pursed her lips, but nodded, then shook her head. She didn't know what to think. Prospectors jumped each other's claims, often. Sometimes, they became very violent on the rare occasions they came into town.

"Them burros come 'round once in a while looking for scraps. If Wrighty catches either of them, he'll kill 'em. Probably do them a whole mess of harm, first."

Annabelle swallowed hard but, Wrighty aside, she was used to schooling her face. She had a couple of years' practice with the deputy—she didn't want to hurt his feelings with her discomfort. Since she had already fallen apart this morning, some of the anxiety had been released, allowing her to regain control. At least those previous annoyances were being put to good use.

Goat interrupted Annabelle while she was trying to look on the bright side of things. "You know, Charlie is a lot like them burros."

Her eyebrows drew together, but she didn't say anything.

"Yup. He pretty much keeps to hisself and does what he needs to do, but he crossed paths wrongly with Wrighty and now Wrighty's forever out to git him."

Annabelle clearly looked like she was thinking that one through, so Goat kept going.

"I saw you feed that burro. You were so sweet and gentle with it." He smiled. "But you were scared when he first showed up. Am I right?"

She nodded slowly. *Does everyone spy on me?*

"I heard you hollerin' and then that burro talkin' back to you."

His broad smile made her feel a little less foolish. *Well, at least he's not a mind reader.*

"Goat, what're you getting at?"

"You were scared, but you still did the right thing—you fed it. But I saw you lookin' 'round to see if anyone was watching. It's as if you knew you weren't supposed to feed it, but still wanted to. The burro wanted you to feed it, too. You *listened* to a damn burro."

"All right, but—"

"Charlie, he's scared, too. He just feels like he isn't allowed to be scared—it's not just him but him and his brother that he's got to watch out for. But he always does the right thing, even if it seems like the wrong thing. Like you—he took you, but he's also taking good care of you, despite Wrighty trying to keep the two of you apart."

"What?"

"Charlie's been watching over you as much as he can. That's 'cepting when Wrighty sends him off on bum chores and errands because he doesn't want the two of you 'round each other. He's jealous, that one. Wishes he found you for hisself."

Annabelle's eyes widened slightly at that. She knew the latter to be true and had the scars to prove it. Wrighty all but told her that. However, Goat mistook her expression for wondering about Charlie.

"That boy's trying hard to do right by you. It wouldn't hurt to give him a biscuit, too, if you know what I mean."

Goat was done talking. He got off, tipped his hat, and walked away whistling an off-key tune. That was about the time Charlie strolled into the clearing. He smiled brightly at her, and she returned his smile with a bemused look.

"I saw Goat. He said you were all done."

Charlie looked at Annabelle. She was looking at him but didn't seem to be seeing him.

"Annabelle? You all right?"

He waved his hand in front of her face. She blinked, jerking her head before focusing on Charlie.

Her hand flew to her chest. "Oh, Charlie. I'm sorry. Goat says the oddest things at times. I was just trying to figure out what he meant."

A smile broke Charlie's face in half, like the sun was bursting out of an egg. "What'd he say?"

"Um—well, I fed a little white burro and—"

Charlie's face fell. "No one saw you, did they?"

He looked around just like Annabelle had earlier. It would've made her laugh if she weren't so torn and confused.

"No. Funny you should ask. I made sure no one did, and I didn't really know why." She shook her head, her eyes scrunching up. "Goat told me not to let anyone catch me doing it, either."

Charlie's chest and shoulders visibly relaxed. "Thank God. Wrighty and that little guy have a history—not a good one, either. It's best left alone."

Annabelle nodded.

"If you ask me, though, I think that little whitey will beat Wrighty at his own game."

The play on words made them smile at each other and relax. Annabelle thought the same thing about the little burro that Goat likened to Charlie—they both were going to beat Wrighty at his own game. She just hoped it'd be sooner than later.

Taking her by the arm, Charlie led her up the path.

"So, what chores do you have left to do?"

21

Annabelle woke to the whistling winds nearly tearing the tent off its poles. Charlie and Jimmy had learned to sleep through the winds and the rains, but Annabelle was still getting used to sleeping in a tent, and with men, no less. She hadn't really been treated like a prisoner since she became Charlie's so-called woman, but that also meant she had to share the cot with Charlie, both for appearances' sake as well as assurance that she wouldn't try to escape. After the initial awkwardness of being in such close proximity to so much *maleness*, she grew to like it. They started every night sleeping back to back. He'd sleep closest to the flap, and she'd face the tent itself. If she tried to run, she'd have to climb over Charlie's mountainous body and make sure she didn't step on Jimmy on her way out. Then, sometime during the night they'd turn toward each other and he'd wrap his giant arms around her, holding her in a protective cocoon that made her forget, momentarily, that she was a prisoner. Come morning he'd have released her, thinking that she didn't know he ever held her.

Tonight, however, everything felt off. Everyone was restless all evening. When they went to bed, both Charlie and Jimmy were tossing and turning all night. Sometime in the early hours of the morning, Annabelle decided that she'd go check on the horses. They hated this kind of weather—it stirred them up. She was able to navigate the bodies and tent easily. Charlie had finally settled; he was flipped on his side facing the tent flap. She scooted to the end of the cot and easily avoided Jimmy because the lightning was brightening the tent, providing her flashes of visibility. She barely lifted the bottom of the flap, slipping out.

Once out of the tent, she stretched her arms in the air, bending herself backward. Looking around and seeing everything was quiet, she walked the path to the stables. The wind was picking up and, on the more open parts of the path, gusts would sweep down from between the trees and shrubbery. If she wasn't fighting against the wind, walking, she was fighting her skirts tangling between her legs and her hair blinding her. Despite the impediments, she continued at a slow crawl, finally reaching the nervous animals. She went inside, patting muzzles and speaking sweet words of reassurance to the beasts.

There was one horse, however, who wasn't having it. He was the horse Wrighty had stolen from a traveler he shot in cold blood. He was a beautiful horse with a glistening, dark brown coat. A sleek, proud creature who didn't take kindly to Wrighty. In turn, Wrighty didn't take kindly to the horse's disgust of him, and took to beating the beautiful beast. The horse was losing his spark and beauty, when he wasn't roaring with anger at Wrighty, and now was pitching a fit—stamping his hooves and shaking his head.

Annabelle went into his stall, hugging him around his neck. He slowly calmed when she arrived. She was the only one who could get close. Not even Jimmy could do as much with this horse as she could. After hugging and stroking the horse, she checked his wounds. Wrighty had taken his whip to him and opened several places on his back and hindquarters. Fortunately, she had been able to tend to him, and the wounds were starting to close up.

Feeding him a carrot, she made her decision. Slowly opening the gate, she led him out of the barn and into the open. His jitters returned, shuffling his feet and bobbing his head, but Annabelle continued reassuring him with soft touches, leaning close to him. Moving in front of him, she stood looking into his eyes for a long time, silently communicating with him. The wind was blowing her hair and dress wildly between them, roaring and whistling in the treetops while her heartbeat pounded in her ears. Finally, she put her face to his, whispering something that was lost to the wind, and released his halter. He shifted, looking at her with his ears pricked forward, before raising his head and rearing on his hind legs, letting out a loud whinny. He landed, then bobbed his head at her, dashing off into the forest.

Tears were streaming down her face. She didn't want to release him in such a storm, but it was the only way to save the poor horse from Wrighty. At some point, either he'd kill the horse or kill its spirit. Whatever the outcome, it would be a death for the horse. It was a terrible shame that such a beautiful creature, who seemed to have been well loved and cared for before Wrighty got his dirty hands on him, should be forced to die a slow, painful death. She shook her head at the thought. *Not on my watch.* The horse was long gone when she turned to head back. A scream caught in her throat as she turned around; Charlie was standing a few yards away, watching her. They stood facing each other as the storm picked up, swirling dirt and tree bits around them. They remained rooted, their eyes locked.

It was Charlie who moved before she realized it. Hurrying forward, he grabbed Annabelle by the arm, pulling her to him. He rocked her like the day he claimed her, a soothing motion meant to comfort. This time she wasn't sure who he was comforting. The wind started to die down enough so they could hear each other without shouting. There were so many things Charlie wanted to say and ask, but they caught in his throat, like things often did when he was around her. In the end, he managed to ask the more important logistical question.

"Did you leave the stall door open?"

Annabelle leaned back, looking at him in question. "Yes."

"Good. Perhaps you didn't latch it well enough and the horse was able to push it and escape?" He cocked his head so that they didn't have to actually *lie* about what happened.

"Charlie, I—"

He grabbed her head and pulled her in for a deep kiss. She kissed him back, dazed and surprised—she was expecting to get in trouble, not this—when he broke it off.

"Shh. I know." His large, calloused hands framed her face, his thumbs stroking her cheeks "You did the right thing. Someone will find the horse, and it'll be better off wherever it goes. Maybe your father will find it."

She opened her mouth, but he didn't give her a chance to respond to that. Grabbing her hand, he tugged her down the path. "We have to hurry. We need to get back before anyone misses us. *We were never here.*" He gave her hand a little downward pull to emphasize that. She nodded, and they rushed down the path, trying to stay one step ahead of the deluge.

❧ **22** ❧

The path was slippery, and they narrowly missed getting caught on their return. The rain started to fall in large, splatting drops, here and there, before steadily increasing to a downpour. One minute they were dodging giant drops, then ten minutes later the sky opened up and dumped buckets. When they arrived, Jaems ran out of his tent, grabbing buckets to catch leaks, while Lafayette was hammering a piece of wood on the window of one of the huts to keep the sideways rain out. They were too busy to notice that Charlie and Annabelle had come down from the hill and not out of their tent when they saw them. Jimmy was moving sandbags around the edges of their tent. Charlie and Annabelle picked up sandbags on their way over to help, as well as pieces of wood to create a barrier. Jaems had given up on the leak in his tent, coming over to help them dig a trench and, later, stay with them until the storm passed over. It was a long night, fighting heavy winds and rain.

Fortunately, the rains didn't last long, so they were able to finish reinforcing for future storms and get some rest. Monsoons in the desert were unpredictable, and since they were staying longer than originally anticipated, they needed to secure their living quarters. They hadn't planned on being here during the monsoons, but this storm was an early one. Annabelle swept the rain out of the tent while others brought more materials for later reinforcements. Finally, everyone lay down for a couple of hours.

Morning broke to a tired, grumpy group of people. Goat had started the morning meal, and the others slowly made their way down to the eating area. It was waterlogged and muddy, but they all sat down to eat. Even though Wrighty had a secure shack to stay in, he looked fit to be tied with all the mud and water around. Lafayette wasn't having any of Wrighty that morning.

"What're you belly-aching about? You didn't have to get up and sweep out water or board up a window because it was like the ocean was coming in."

He jabbed his fork into some bacon and shoved it into his mouth with such force, no one would've been surprised if the fork came out the back of his head. Hunched over his plate, his eyes narrowed into slits while glaring at Wrighty.

Wrighty knew Lafayette had him on that—there were two tents and that unfortunate shack that Lafayette was saddled with, but the others had pretty sturdy cabins and shelters. While the noise of the wind and rain might have bothered them or woke them up, they didn't have to labor to keep a roof over their heads. He snorted in a long breath of phlegm and did what he did best—deflected and made it someone else's fault.

"If it weren't for the greenhorn, we'd be outta here by now."

Everyone threw a look at Charlie, who had his fork halfway to his mouth. His brows drew together, but he didn't say anything and continued putting the fork in his mouth, slowly chewing his food.

"We sent a newbie in to do a *man's* job—and he came back with *her*"—he threw his head in Annabelle's direction— "and now we have to wait. And what in the hell are we waiting for, anyway?"

Van Der Kamp chose that moment to speak up. He didn't want Wrighty to climb too far up on his soapbox this morning. He didn't get good sleep either, with all the pounding rain, and he wasn't in the mood. He was scowling at Wrighty, as if to remind him.

"We're waiting for Travis to catch up with us." Van Der Kamp's voice was its usual low and slow, but there was an unmistakable edge to it.

Wrighty's jaw worked, making the muscles on the sides of his face flex. He threw himself into a seat and tucked into his meal. Everyone was quiet for a few moments, but Wrighty couldn't help himself. He kept darting glances around at the men between bites. Van Der Kamp eyed Wrighty and could practically hear the wheels moving in his head. That man needed to keep moving or fighting. Right now, fighting was his only option.

"We wouldn't have waited if it weren't for our hostage."

"We would've. This is a perfect place to regroup and redirect. No one suspects we're up here because they're too superstitious. Besides, it's dangerous with all the open shafts around here."

Van Der Kamp tossed Wrighty a look reminding him that he could end up at the bottom of a mine at a moment's notice. Wrighty huffed, acknowledging their earlier conversation. He jabbed at his eggs, which kept slipping off his fork, angering him. Finally, he threw down the fork and pointed at Charlie.

"And when in the hell are we going to ransom her? You two keep playin' house, and I don't like it."

"You don't get a choice in that, Wrighty." Van Der Kamp cut in. He finished cutting his food before looking up. He used his fork to point at Charlie. "Charlie's going to negotiate with the sheriff—any of the rest of us try, we'll get shot on sight. I don't think the sheriff has connected Charlie with us; at least he couldn't be positive about it if he did. Charlie's not wanted, either."

"What are we waiting for, then? Send him on out, Van Der Kamp." Wrighty's tone was nearing a shriek.

Van Der Kamp was done with this disobedience. He slid the bite into his mouth and slowly lowered his fork to the table. He lifted his head and looked directly at Wrighty.

"You, *son,* need to learn some patience and some manners. Annabelle here has been real helpful with the chores and meals—she's a *guest*, understand? A *valuable* guest."

He waited to see if Wrighty would object yet again. Happy with the silence that met him, he continued talking in his slow, deep-voiced manner.

"Travis is going to meet us here and update us on Mack as well as the big mine further west. He also heard word of a gold delivery by the army that we may want to check out, seeming's how it's on the way."

He chuckled at his own joke. It was deep and warm, unlike his usual icy demeanor. That put the men on edge—they weren't sure which Van Der Kamp they liked better. And *like* was a relative word for them.

"I don't see how you think we can move anyway. That botched robbery is too fresh. If you hadn't been so greedy for that damn horse that hates you, you wouldn't have had to kill those witnesses."

"He had it coming to him, and that horse doesn't hate me—it just needs to learn some manners."

Van Der Kamp quirked his brow at that. "Kind of like its new owner? Take a look around you, Wrighty." His arm swept the area they were sitting in. "Do you think we can travel in this muck? We're better off staying here with good shelter and protection. If we're ambushed, we'd have the advantage—we're on the higher ground with the hills to our back. There's no rush." He finished eating and stood up. "Don't be so stupid."

With that, he sauntered off, leaving an infuriated Wrighty at the center of everyone's grouchy attention. No one was in the mood for his funny business or temper tantrums that morning. Even those who weren't working through the night didn't like trudging through the monsoon's leavings. The sun was beginning to crest, and soon it'd create a hot, steamy sensation as the dew evaporated off of everything, mud quickly turning to dust, once again.

"I'm checking on my horse." With that, Wrighty stalked away in attempts to save what was left of his dignity.

Annabelle looked at Charlie, but he wouldn't return the panicked look she gave him.

Instead, he deflected by asking, "What chores do you have today?"

That had become the running joke between the men because she was much more efficient as a "guest" than they were as part of the gang. She was a little general in her own right and had begun bossing the men because she knew she was safe when she was with Charlie. She'd thought she was, before the kiss. But now she really knew.

23

Boots squishing into the path, Wrighty stomped off, talking to himself. *If anyone's being stupid, it's Van Der Kamp. Putting too much trust in Charlie, and swayed by that bitch, Annabelle, too.* Wrighty was fit to be tied, deciding that a good round with the new horse would be just thing to blow off some steam. *I'll get that horse to turn around.* His hands clenched, thinking about it. *I'll just get Annabelle to spend less time coddling the thing. She ruins everything—she spoils and coddles. I wonder what she's doing for Van Der Kamp to get him to go soft.* That gave him some pause as he finished the final steps toward the boarding area. *She must be spreading her legs for him, too.* He blew out a sound of disgust. *I'll learn her—when I have her, she'll realize there's no going back. I'm the real man she needs, and I'll tame that bossy little nature of hers, too, while I'm at it.* He grinned thinking about it. *It'll be real—*

His lascivious thoughts were stopped in their tracks, as were his feet. His mouth dropped open when he nearly came eye to eye with a horse looking down at him. There were a couple of the horses meandering in the yard, loose. *No!* He ran inside the stable to the last stall. He didn't really need to, but his feet took him there anyway. The stall door was wide open. Stopping in front of it, he looked in, as if he could will the horse's appearance. Empty. As he knew it'd be. He slammed the door shut repeatedly, and it kept flying back at him, taunting him with its emptiness. Although he knew the horse would run if given a chance, he went outside and frantically looked around. Confirming what he already knew, he stomped back down the path—he would've run, but didn't want to slip and add insult to injury.

When he got to the dining area, he marched right up to Annabelle and pointed a finger at her.

"*You!*" His voice went deadly low.

Annabelle leaned back, eyes widening, trying to get away from him but having nowhere to go.

"You did this, didn't you?"

She was pale with fright because she knew what he was talking about but tried hard to play dumb.

"What, Wrighty?"

"The horse. *The horse!*" His voice became louder and louder, making her cringe.

"What about it?"

"*It's gone.*"

She just looked at him. She couldn't get the words to come out of her mouth to deny him nor could she falsely explain. She was quivering uncontrollably, her body remembering the undeserved beating she got in the tent as well as the beatings he gave the poor horse.

Charlie came to her rescue. "Which horse, Wrighty?"

Wrighty spun on the ball of his foot, whirling around to face his nemesis. "Don't play stupid with me, boy."

Charlie's jaw clenched. *Fighting words.*

"You know God damned well which horse—mine!"

"I told you, repeatedly, I'm not a boy." He quirked a brow at him. "Did you look in its stall?"

"Of course I did!"

Wrighty was all but shouting at this point, and everyone was coming back in hopes of seeing a fight. They'd been spoiling to see those two go at it. Secretly, some of them had been placing bets, including Wrighty's cronies.

"There were horses wandering around. What have you and Jimmy been doing up there, all this while? It's as if the horses have taken over." He was pointing up the hill and leaned forward as words spewed out of his mouth. *"And you let my goddamned horse go!* What the hell," he spat.

He turned, lunging for Annabelle, who had now stood up, but Charlie stepped in front of him. The men closed up the circle they had already formed around this show.

"What do you think you're doing?"

"I'm going to teach your woman a lesson she won't forget. If Van Der Kamp had just given her over to me, we wouldn't be in this mess. She's making you all weak."

He tried reaching around Charlie, but Charlie was too broad. That's when he started pushing, which Charlie didn't take kindly to.

Nor did Charlie budge, but he returned the pushing with his own punishing shove, causing Wrighty to slip in the mud. Wrighty lost his grip on Charlie as his hands slipped down Charlie's chest. Charlie made a sweeping motion with his arms. They went around then under Wrighty's arms, hitting them and pushing them out to either side. Wrighty lost all balance and fell forward. Charlie stepped back and watched Wrighty fall face-forward in the mud. The gang hooted and hollered. Some of them had been waiting years for Charlie to man up and get the best of Wrighty, but Charlie would never fight. It seemed to them that he had something more to fight for these days.

Wrighty roared as he pulled himself off the ground and went for Charlie's legs. Charlie's boot shot out, connecting with Wrighty's shoulder—he didn't want to kick a man on the ground, but Wrighty gave him no choice. Unfortunately, he wasn't quick enough to retract it and landed hard on his ass when Wrighty caught his foot. The men cheered—it didn't matter to them who did it; they were itching for this particular fight. Charlie twisted his body and threw himself on top of Wrighty as the man was pulling Charlie toward him. Wrighty didn't stand a chance; Charlie had a good twenty pounds of muscle on him from all the work he did as well as his natural, broad build. Wrighty had rolled over, but he was stuck with Charlie sitting on top of him.

"You sonofabitch! Get off me!"

"You apologize to Annabelle. She doesn't deserve to hear the things you say to her. She doesn't deserve those accusations, either."

Wrighty remained tight-lipped in his anger, so Charlie lifted him and smashed him into the earth, hard.

Raising his voice, he repeated, "Apologize. Now."

Charlie called over his shoulder, "Annabelle, come here." She cautiously stepped closer, not wanting to get in the middle of all that.

"Yes, Charlie?"

"Wrighty here is gonna apologize to you real nice and *sincere*—without touching you. Would you please step closer so he can look you in the eye and do it?"

She took another couple of steps so that she was behind Charlie but could see Wrighty's face from her vantage.

"That's my Wildflower," he said in a soft voice before hardening it for Wrighty. "Go ahead, Wrighty." He shook him so his head thudded in the mud again. "Time for your sincerest apologies."

Wrighty spit to the side before he looked Annabelle in the eye. "Annabelle, I'm sorry you had to hear all that."

Annabelle blinked but didn't say anything.

Charlie gave him the stink eye but knew that was the best she was going to get unless he beat him into a pulp, and he didn't want to do that. That'd cause more trouble than it was worth. Wrighty was lying through his teeth, because that wasn't an apology. It was an admission that he was sorry he got caught thinking out loud in front of the wrong person—Charlie. Annabelle quickly nodded before backing away. She gave them space to get off the ground and out of the mud pile they'd made worse with their fighting. Goat grabbed her shoulder, steering her clear of the crowd that was also moving backwards to give them more room.

Wrighty got up, spitting at Charlie's feet. He jabbed a finger at him. "This ain't over, son, and you know it."

Charlie nodded. "I know. It isn't." Wiping mud from his brow, he added, "And I ain't your son."

The crowd slowly dispersed as Wrighty stormed off, and Charlie pulled Annabelle off to the side. He lowered his voice more than normal.

"Are you all right?" He crouched, looking her in the eye while making a quick assessment of her facial expression and emotional state. He stood up, lowering his forehead to the crown of her head.

Annabelle let out a stuttered breath but nodded. Charlie pressed his lips to her forehead, his lips lingering. Straightening, he put his arm around her, pulling her close before leading her away.

Humiliating. Fists clenching and unclenching, Wrighty grunted as he stormed off to Van Der Kamp's cabin. Banging on the door and shifting his feet, he had trouble restraining the anger bubbling up inside him. He'd outright kill Charlie if his consequences weren't so dire. Everyone liked him. He was "useful." He was "strong." Wrighty banged on the door again, growling.

"Van Der Kamp—you in there?"

He heard a grunt and decided that was close enough to "come in." He threw open the door, stomping into the little kitchen area where Van Der Kamp was standing.

"Don't think I asked you in." Van Der Kamp didn't bother turning around, nor did he stop what he was doing.

"I heard you grunt, thought it was enough."

"That's your problem, Wrighty."

"My problem is Charlie and that Annabelle."

"What now? You jealous you aren't getting some?"

He waited for Wrighty's growl before turning around, mug in hand. He leaned against the crude counter, waiting for Wrighty's comeback. He knew it'd be a comeback and not a reasonable response. That's how Wrighty rode—hard and dirty.

Pointing his finger at Van Der Kamp, he raised his voice. "These things wouldn't be happening if you just let me have her. You gave her to that greenhorn, and everyone's gone sweet on her. She runs this camp like it's hers—she's a woman, for Christ's sake, and a prisoner. I—"

Van Der Kamp held up his hand. "You'll kindly remember that the sheriff's dear Annabelle is a *guest* with us and will be treated accordingly. The *greenhorn* is the perfect host for that— *he* has *manners*." He gave Wrighty a pointed look. "Besides, he's the one who caught her, and he should be the one to keep her. You know the rules, or are you trying to change them?"

His eyes went flinty, warning Wrighty that he always had his ear to the ground and knew more than he let on.

Wrighty looked as if he were going to bust a blood vessel but huffed at Van Der Kamp instead. "That woman let my horse loose." He threw up his arms in frustration as well as to keep from taking a swing at Van Der Kamp, knowing full well he'd not fare well if he tried that. Age be damned—there was something steely about Van Der Kamp that made him one step quicker and just a touch stronger than everyone else. It was if he was playing opossum, with his slow talking and slow walking, so he could kick ass when he really needed to.

Van Der Kamp shook his head and let out a guffaw. "What're you talking about? You can't mean old Lane? He's not goin' anywhere. You beat that poor horse something fierce. He's got no spirit left in him." He made a disgusted sound in the back of his throat. "You're making up stories like an old woman."

Lifting the mug to his lips, he took a sip but continued watching him over the rim.

"I'm not making up stories!" He nearly stamped his foot but caught himself in time. He didn't want to prove Van Der Kamp right. Unfortunately, he wasn't quick enough, because Van Der Kamp smirked when he saw the tell. "I went up to check on my horse, and he wasn't there. She let the new one go—the gate was wide open and *no horse*."

"Oh, *that horse*. Not really yours."

Wrighty suddenly went calm, lowering his voice. "Why is it that Charlie finds Annabelle and gets to keep her, and I find this horse, and it's not mine?"

The rational part of his brain finally kicked in, and he'd used Van Der Kamp's logic back at him. He even stopped huffing and puffing long enough to ask the question civilly.

"We didn't need another horse, and we didn't gain anything good by you killing that gambler for it, either."

"He was being stupid."

"Why? Because he wouldn't hand over his stallion? What kind of man worth his salt does that?"

"People who know better—people who don't want to cross me."

Van Der Kamp snorted over that. "Seems to me you're thinking you're entitled to a lot more than you really are."

"What do you mean?"

"Just what I said."

"Hmmph. What are you going to do about her letting that horse loose?"

"Nothing."

"What? She needs a lesson taught to her and I'm the one to give it."

"You'll do no such thing. Guest, remember?"

"Guests don't run around mucking things up and losing valuable property. I doubt the sheriff has enough to give in return for her anyway. She's cost us more than she's going to bring. We should wring the value out of her."

"Enough. The only thing you're going to do is dip yourself in the river. You're a mess and making a mess of my cabin. Get out and clean up." He watched Wrighty look down at himself then back at him. "Come back and sweep this out when you're done." Van Der Kamp swept his arm through the air, indicating all the mud and dirt Wrighty had tracked in as well as what was cracking off of his clothing as it dried.

Wrighty turned on the ball of his foot to leave. When his hand touched the doorknob, Van Der Kamp called out, "Which one of the youngins did that to you, Wrighty? Charlie or Annabelle?"

Wrighty slammed the door. He could hear Van Der Kamp's laughter taunting him clear down the path.

Van Der Kamp stood against the counter for a few more minutes, sipping his coffee. The corners of his mouth turned up. For the first time in a long time, the half-smile reached his eyes. The lines surrounding them just barely crinkled, but it was the light in them that gave him away. It was going to be a good day. He put down the mug, stretching. His leg was stiffening from the rains. Deciding it was about time to walk out the leg and check on the troops, he made his way out of the cabin and down the path to see what he would find.

Walking the last stretch of the path, it didn't surprise him to see Charlie hovering over Annabelle. He slowed down to take it in, chuckling, shaking his head at the sight. Van Der Kamp knew that kid was sweet on her, but did Charlie realize it, yet? Who wouldn't? She was a little firecracker who brought life into this camp with her bossiness and kindness. Even Lafayette and Seth had let bygones be bygones—and she'd bitten Lafayette and head-butted Seth. Van Der Kamp grinned. Neither did it hurt that she was pretty *and* irritated Wrighty like nothing else. She irritated him even more than Charlie did, because she didn't fall all over him like other women. That man thought he was God's gift and then some. He'd soon learn a harsh lesson that he might not recover from. A harsher one than being rejected by a pretty girl or even being dusted by a little burro. That made Van Der Kamp's face light up like a cannon on a dark night and put a spring in his creaky step.

He slowed, watching them for a few more moments as Charlie bent over, clasping Annabelle's shoulder and looking her in the eye while she sat on a box after some serious pacing.

"It's going to be all right."

Eyes flaring and lips pressed together, she gave him a pointed look, indicating that she didn't agree. Her eyes were welling up since all the men had scattered, and she'd finished cleaning up after breakfast. She sniffed hard, making a snorting sound, then wrinkled her nose after realizing what she'd done, frowning. That just made Charlie smile brightly at her.

He ran his hand down her arm. "You're going to be okay, Wildflower. Will you at least trust me?"

She searched his face as if trying to discern the truth of his words before nodding yes. He smiled back at her, kissing her nose. His lips brushed hers, then he heard someone coming.

"I'd trust him, if I were you," Van Der Kamp said, just as Charlie turned around.

He nodded at a pair of astonished faces, throwing himself onto the bench closest to them, sighing as he stretched out.

"I heard there was a little tussle this morning."

Annabelle and Charlie glanced at each other before slowly turning back to Van Der Kamp.

Annabelle dutifully nodded at Van Der Kamp while Charlie explained.

"Wrighty accused Annabelle of releasing that horse he's been beating, even though there were other horses loose, wandering around. He also accused her of not doing any work."

Van Der Kamp watched Charlie, waiting patiently for the story in its entirety. When Charlie realized Van Der Kamp wasn't finished listening, he went on.

"He said she was making us all soft, and that he should have her, not me. He wanted to teach her a lesson. That's when he lunged at her, and I stepped in, making sure he apologized."

Van Der Kamp smirked. "What sort of apology did he make?"

"An insufficient one."

It was Van Der Kamp's turn to snort.

"So who dusted him, this time?"

Charlie nearly barked out laughter because that was the joke among everyone but Wrighty—the dusting the white burro gave him. He schooled his features before responding.

"I suppose I did. I had to pin him down to get him to give Annabelle his half-assed apology. Figure it was better than nothing, especially since it sent him on his way. I'm a little tired of him being in my face all the time. If not that, then it's Annabelle's skirts he's too close to."

They turned to look at Annabelle, who flushed scarlet, suddenly busying herself with brushing dirt off her skirt. She was easily embarrassed still—this added to Van Der Kamp's suspicions that Charlie was continuing to do right by Annabelle. Most men would've made good on their word and actually taken her. He knew that Charlie was being honorable with that stunt. How he managed to keep his hands off of her was anyone's guess. All the more reason she needed him in her life—he'd make a good man for her. As soon as he figured out that he really did like her and wasn't *just* protecting her.

Van Der Kamp pulled a deep one-nostril breath, nodding his head.

"I agree with you. Don't worry about him, either of you."

He looked at Annabelle to make sure she understood. She seemed overly hysterical about this, which got him wondering. He looked hard at her.

"Annabelle," he drew out her name. "Wrighty didn't try anything on you, did he?"

He could see Charlie tense up out of the corner of his eye. Annabelle's eyes went wide, and the flush she'd had earlier was replaced by a ghostly pallor.

"No." Annabelle's voice was barely above a whisper, but the men could see her body trembling, and her eyes took on a slight glaze.

Charlie was enraged and started toward her, ready to ask her more questions, when Van Der Kamp stopped him with a look.

He continued to watch Annabelle but spoke to Charlie. "I think that you should be the one who handles the negotiations with the sheriff. Are you willing?"

"Yes, sir. Annabelle needs to be far away from Wrighty." He turned back toward Annabelle. "Annabelle—"

"Charlie, we're going to leave the Wrighty issue, for now. We'll get this all settled. I'm not liking what I'm hearing."

He narrowed his eyes at Annabelle, causing her to shrink back. Now, he really knew she was lying. Whatever Wrighty did to her, he was going to pay. He had been told to leave her alone, and Van Der Kamp meant it. Annabelle wasn't for the likes of him. Besides, he knew that, even though Charlie didn't want to be in the gang, he'd been loyal. That counted far more than the so-called loyalty Wrighty was doling out. Wrighty had crossed the line too many times and needed to be taught a lesson. Van Der Kamp would make sure that Charlie was going to be the one to deliver it. That way, it'd be even more painful for Wrighty.

"I'll figure out the details; it's about time. Wrighty's been told to leave you two alone. Besides, that horse wasn't even his.

Damn thing hated him." He raised his brows at Annabelle, tipping his head forward.

That seemed to reassure her, just a little. Her breathing returned closer to normal, and her shoulders relaxed. Van Der Kamp sat up, slapping his palms onto his thighs as he did so. He took in a deep breath. "Well, you two do whatever it is you were going to do. I'll organize a messenger and a meet and let you know the details later." He stood, but Charlie and Annabelle made no move to leave. He waved them off. "Go on, git. Daylight's a burnin'." He slowly made his way back up the hill. This time his leg didn't seem to be bothering him as much.

Wrighty did take his dip in the stream and felt better for it, no thanks to Van Der Kamp. *That man has no sense of loyalty. I've been working hard for him and bringing in the loot, keeping order—at least until Annabelle showed up. She's a little too attached to that whelp and his damn brother, too. Made themselves right at home, even though this isn't home to any of us.* Wrighty headed back to his cabin to think about how he was going to get them to let their defenses down enough around him. Their eyes were too busy following each other around the camp, but when they were together, they were watchful of everyone else around them, especially him. He snorted. He would figure his way out of this one.

24

Everyone was sitting around the campfire, drinking and laughing. Two different sets of scouts had returned, and everyone was relaxed and catching up. Even Van Der Kamp had joined them for longer than usual. The night allowed little light, as the moon was in its dark phase, and the stars were obscured by clouds. The flickering light of the campfire illuminated their faces but shadowed anyone beyond the periphery.

Annabelle was by the cooking fire, stirring a pot and serving some of the scouts who had just arrived. Some just glanced at her oddly, but some of them really gave her the once-over. She smiled politely while ladling stew into their bowls. Eventually, they all nodded their thanks, moving to take a seat around the giant fire.

Annabelle stepped away from the pot to stretch her back. She'd been tending the stew and mending all day, so her back and neck were cramped up. Rolling her neck a few times, then twisting her back, she caught a glimpse of Wrighty standing slightly off from the trees, in the dark. She might not have seen him at all, but the flask he was holding caught the firelight. He had his back to everyone else, but it looked like he was pouring some whisky into a cup. She started to shrug it off as Wrighty not wanting to share, but just as she was turning away from him, he pulled out a small bottle. He darted quick, stealthy glances around before shaking it three times over the cup. He slipped the small bottle back into his pocket once again, looking around. He stood up straighter, holding the larger whisky bottle and the cup, and walked in Charlie's direction as he began making an announcement.

"Everyone, I propose a toast." The talking died down and everyone looked at Wrighty with expectation and curiosity. He was smiling and holding the bottle aloft. "I say we drink to Charlie and his recent successes." His toast was met with silence. "C'mon, guys. None of us thought he'd make it this far, certainly not robbery *and* kidnapping." A few of the men nodded and chuckled. "He's not as yellow-bellied as we thought." He guffawed. Elwood started to get up, hand on his holster. Wrighty flapped his arms for him to sit back down. "Sit. I'm giving the boy a hard time." Charlie gritted his teeth at *boy*. "Honestly. I was out of line yesterday, grouchy from the rain and angry there's a hard-won horse lost. But I'm making peace. I'm looking forward to seeing how much more Charlie can bring in."

Conrad and Jaems shrugged, and Goat pulled a face, but eventually everyone cheered as Wrighty lifted the tin in salute, then held it out to Charlie. Charlie started to get up to take it, but Annabelle pushed through the crowd, gripping an empty tin. She bustled past Charlie, then tripped, flying into Wrighty and knocking the tin and the bottle out of his hands. The tin dumped its contents down the front of Annabelle's dress before she landed on Wrighty. Charlie was over there in a flash, pulling her off, but not before Wrighty roared his displeasure at her clumsiness.

"What the hell is wrong with you, woman? You did this on purpose! Now, you've wasted good whiskey." He stood up, brushed himself off, and glared at the pair of them, who stood staring back.

"Oh, Wrighty. I'm so sorry. I was bringing a tin for you. I'm just so happy that you're wanting to be nice to Charlie—I was so excited that I tripped hurrying over here." The men laughed at that, diffusing the tension that Wrighty usually brought with him. He looked crossways at her, so she rubbed her lower back. "Besides, my lower back was really aching from all the mending you hard-working men create."

Conrad, remembering her bent over laundry on a hot day, called out, "Come on, Wrighty. The woman works hard. Give her a break, she slipped."

"It's not like she dusted you or anything!" Thigh-slapping and roaring laughter broke out with a few mentions of the "desert canary" and "Wrighty's white burro." Wrighty's face twisted into a mask of fury. He glared at her, hard. His jaw clenched and his eyes bored into her. As angry as he was, he wasn't sure if she was onto him or not, so he decided to play it off. "Well, if you wanted me, you should've just said something, woman. You didn't have to throw yourself at me."

Charlie's eyes flashed in anger, but Wrighty held up his hands. "Just having some fun, since the whisky's spilt."

"C'mon, Charlie. Don't spoil the good mood Wrighty's in—we don't get to see that very often." Goat guffawed at that, and Van Der Kamp was leaning back, smirking.

Charlie backed off, good-naturedly but not before shooting a glare at Wrighty. Wrighty grinned back at him, pretending he was in a good mood. Lafayette grabbed the bottle that was dropped and took a long pull from it before Orrin grabbed it from his hands. As soon as everyone went back to drinking, Wrighty turned away, a scowl crossing his face as his hands clenched. He started to stalk away, but Van Der Kamp raised his normally low voice. "Where you going there?"

Wrighty tensed, slowly turning around. He glowered at Van Der Kamp. "I have to go find some more whisky for the celebration."

"Hurry on back, then. Wouldn't want you to miss anything."

Wrighty walked off toward his cabin while Charlie pulled Annabelle away from everyone, handing her a wet rag to sponge the whisky out of her clothes. He held her by the shoulders and looked down at her with concern.

"Are you okay? You didn't hurt yourself in the fall, did you?"

Annabelle finished scrubbing at her bodice and brushed at the dirt on her skirt. She looked up at him, then leaned close and whispered, "Wrighty put something in that cup. I saw him."

"Whisky. I can smell it on you, you smell like a saloon." Charlie cracked a smile.

"No," she hissed becoming exasperated, then frustrated. She blew out a breath. "Yes, whisky first, then three shakes from some bottle he had in his pocket. At first, I didn't see that he was standing in the shadows, until I saw the glint from the metal flask. And I didn't think much of it until he pulled out the bottle and added something into the cup." She leaned away from him so she could look up into his eyes. From afar, it looked as if they were about to kiss, yet undecided—holding on to each other, yet pulling back—gazing deeply into each other's eyes. That lingering moment just before bodies embrace and lips connect.

Moris suspected something was going on between them. He also suspected that Annabelle's alleged fall was a ruse. So he hollered out, "Go to your tent!"

More laughter burst out into the night as the fire crackled and popped. Multiple conversations went around, as did the whisky bottles. Charlie looked toward Van Der Kamp, who nodded. He nodded back before taking Annabelle's arm, guiding her back up the path to their tent.

From the depth of the trees, Wrighty watched Charlie and Annabelle walking away from the campfire to hoots and hollering. His eyes narrowed. The corners of his mouth turned down in disgust. He'd thought he had a foolproof alternative to shooting Charlie, but now he'd have to start over. He'd also have to watch Annabelle a lot closer, or give her another warning—she was a lot smarter than he gave her credit for. He was pretty sure this evening's mishap was all an act, because she wouldn't come near him voluntarily like that. She was always hiding behind Charlie when he came around. His mouth twisted as he thought back some more—sometimes she did that to Moris, too. His hand went to his chin. When he was sure they were gone, he returned to the campfire, but only because he wanted to get rip-roaring drunk.

He'd talk to Moris tomorrow.

"Why do you think he was trying to poison me?"

"I have no idea. All I know is what I saw, Charlie. You have to believe me."

"I do believe you, Wildflower. The problem isn't whether I believe you, it's that I don't know why he's trying to do it now. If he wanted to kill me, he's had plenty of opportunity before."

"Do you think it's because he's heard that you're negotiating my return?"

"Maybe Van Der Kamp said something to him first. I don't know. I've never had to think about these kinds of things before. I just do what I'm told."

"Like rob a mercantile?" Her face twisted into a smirk, her eyes bright.

Charlie's face lit up. "Yeah, like rob a mercantile, only with my own special twist."

They were lying on the cot in the tent, wrapped in each others' arms. Charlie was growing very accustomed to this routine and, as much as he wanted to see Annabelle safely home, there was a growing part of him that wanted to keep her for himself. He smiled as she sighed in her sleep and shifted closer to him. Her body instinctively knew that he'd keep her safe, even when there were times she fought him on that. He tucked the blanket around her shoulder, smoothing it over her arm. He was surprised that she had thrown herself at Wrighty, considering how frightened she was of him. She went to great lengths to avoid the man and still hadn't told him why, exactly—what had Wrighty done to her? Goat hadn't got it out of her, either. He hadn't directly asked Jimmy, yet, because he'd been tight-lipped about Annabelle. He still didn't know if that was because he didn't let anyone close to him or because he had some reservations about her. Jimmy was the one who told him that he couldn't save everyone and to let her be. Charlie wondered if he still felt that way after working so closely with her. They seemed to work really well together. Annabelle had mentioned that she liked Jimmy…

No, Jimmy's likable—he's funny and compassionate. She couldn't have feelings for him, could she? Did he have feelings for her? The thought gave him a sour feeling in his stomach, kind of like when Goat tried to pass off rancid meat by making stew, over-salting it and cooking for an extra-long time.

He pulled a face at that memory. He'd been sick for days and spent a lot of time out in the bushes. His shuddering woke Annabelle.

"Huh?"

"Ssshhh. It's okay. Go back to sleep." He stroked her head, and she quickly fell back into a deep sleep. She had worked hard today, extra, considering the campfire, and the scouts returning so late for dinner. Plus, the panic of Wrighty's attempted poisoning had really worked her up. He was pretty sure that he was a little worked up, too.

25

"No. Absolutely not."

"Why not? I thought you were in."

"I am."

"Well?"

"Van Der Kamp says no, and no means no with him. You cross him. I don't want to."

"The way I see it, you're already crossing him."

"Arggh. Fine. Don't expect miracles. She barely lets me get around her, and he makes it a point to always be around. I don't expect this'll work."

"Just do as I say, for once."

Moris's eyes screwed into little crescents. "I do, and look where it's got me. I spent nearly a week cleaning up your mess—"

"That wasn't my fault. You said Van Der Kamp was coming."

"He was! I don't know what happened to him. What kind of lookout would I be if I didn't warn you? You would've been caught with your pants down doing what you were told not to do. You're the one who didn't have to go and do that to the poor girl."

Wrighty growled at Moris. "Poor girl?" He asked, getting in Moris's face. "Remember who she's related to, then we'll talk."

Moris wasn't buying Wrighty's bluster this time. "This has nothing to do with the sheriff. You just want her because you can't have her. There's plenty of women who throw themselves at you. Why can't you be content with them?" He put his hands on his gun belt, broadening his shoulders.

Wrighty was too hung over to be having this conversation, and even he knew that he was sounding like an impetuous two-year-old who didn't get a sweet he wanted. He waved off Moris's comment as he walked away.

Moris spit on the ground. Wrighty was becoming too tiresome, and his schemes had been rapidly failing the past few months. He drank too much and couldn't keep his temper or his cock under control. Wrighty's violence was appalling for even him. He walked off in search of his quarry but was hoping he didn't find her. He didn't plan on looking too hard.

Annabelle woke feeling refreshed, rested, and the most comfortable she had felt since she got here. They had talked late into the night until she finally fell asleep mid-conversation. Stretching, she rolled to her side, looking around the tent and seeing it empty. This sense of inner peace that she was feeling was odd. Despite all the hard work, she'd finally started to relax and find a rhythm to her days. She felt safe with Charlie, Jimmy, and Goat watching over her. They made for good company, too. It made her feel both guilty and confused. For the first time in her life, she felt useful and independent, even though she was a hostage. She was never a hostage in her father's home, but she didn't necessarily feel independent there, either. Her father was always so worried. Worried she'd wander off and get hurt or accosted, and they lived in a tiny mining town. Granted, there were dangers for a lone woman, but he behaved as if something else was going to happen—all the time.

Here, everyone had grown less diligent about watching her. They knew she wouldn't run—not only because she had no idea where she was or which way to go, but also because she was Charlie's. Warmth spread through her at the thought of being his, even though, technically, she wasn't.

Sitting up and straightening herself out, she wondered what it would be like to *be* Charlie's. To wake up every day in his arms, to have more kisses, kisses that really meant something—to have him all the time, caring for and loving her. Lost in her daydream, she had wrapped her arms around herself, leaning forward on the edge of the cot. Shaking off mixed thoughts of dread and want—dread that she was becoming dependent on someone else, and wanting so bad that she considered throwing herself at Charlie—she stood and stretched. She didn't want his so-called claiming to be a sham. She wanted whatever everyone thought it was—and more.

It wasn't technically washing day, but she'd washed everyone's clothes but her own. She felt gritty and uncomfortable, especially after the brawl, and she was pretty sure she was starting to smell as bad as Elwood. He smelled like the barn, but he didn't work with horses. *A good dunk is what I need—no more sponge or rain baths.* She looked around the tent for dirty clothes and a clean shirt of Charlie's to wear while her clothes dried. Picking one up, she decided it definitely would be long enough to keep her modesty while she waited. She could roll the sleeves and continue to do some work before gathering everything up. She wouldn't be missed because Jimmy was working the horses, and Charlie was supposed to meet with Van Der Kamp—it was early enough that some of the men would still be sleeping off their drink. She clapped her hands with glee as she searched Jimmy and Charlie's things for some soap and a drying cloth to add to her collection.

Peering out of the tent to make sure no one was looking, she casually made her way down to the creek. If anyone questioned her, she had laundry. Most of them had stopped caring about her schedule, anyway. Luck would have it that her path was clear—she looked skyward to thank God. *Is that a thankable thing? Doesn't matter—I'm thankful.*

Dropping the laundry near the table, she removed her boots and stockings, tucking the stockings into her boots. Picking up the soap, drying cloth, and Charlie's spare shirt, she headed toward the river. She veered to the left so that the overhanging trees would shield her from anyone who came down the path, but she could still see the washing station. Scanning the area, she made sure no one was around before she quickly shucked her clothing. When she was finished, there was a neat pile of all but her chemise, which she kept on, just in case. She could work around that, then take it off when she grabbed the drying cloth. It would dry the quickest, anyway.

Initially taking tentative steps into the water because it was a little chilly, she remembered where she was and what she was doing and moved more quickly because she was afraid of getting caught. The chill wore off, turning into relief. *Ah! It feels so good to wash away the grit.* Even though the downpour had rinsed her clean the other night, the dust returned, and some soap was much appreciated. She took the plunge, submersing herself and thoroughly soaking her thick mane of hair. Her hands kept getting caught in the tangles, but it didn't deter her. The curls were hard to soap up and rinse out, so she got to work. She was so busy concentrating that she didn't hear Charlie and Goat come down the path, despite their loud banter and laughter.

"It looks like she's here. There's a small pile of clothes—looky, here, and sum boots, too."

Charlie's eyes about popped out of his head when Goat held up Annabelle's boots. The rolled stockings were neatly peeking out the tops of them.

"They're lookin' a little like girlie boots to me." He held them closer to his face, nodding to them before holding them back out to Charlie—as if he didn't recognize her boots, or Goat wanted some sort of confirmation.

Charlie pivoted, looking around him. He started down toward the water, and that's when he heard talking. *Annabelle's talking*. She was having a full-on conversation with someone, but he didn't know who. His blood ran cold with fear as he picked up his pace, skidding to halt when he saw her. Her back was to him, arms raised. She had her hands in her hair, a tangled mess of soap, curls, and splashing water. She was struggling to wash the mop on her head and was arguing with herself as she tried pulling her hand through the beautiful tangle of curls.

"You have *got* to hurry up, Annabelle. Hurry! Someone might come and then what'll you do?" She grunted at a particularly difficult knot, huffing as she tugged on it. She hadn't seen a brush, personally, in days. Frustrated, she dunked herself under the water again, and this time she stood up taller than the last. Both hands came away from her head in opposite directions. "Come. On. Argh!"

Goat had chosen that moment to saunter down the path to the river and got an eyeful of Annabelle before Charlie whirled around on him using a slicing motion with his arm.

Goat made a strangled sound before Charlie said, "Go. Away. NOW."

Annabelle gasped, spinning around. She was too busy arguing with herself to hear them before Goat's choking reached her ears. Her hands were still stuck in her hair, and her breasts were exposed. The wet chemise did more to highlight her breasts than they did to hide them. Her dusky nipples shone through the clinging, wet material, two pointed peaks from the cold. Charlie and Goat's eyes went wide before she plunged into the water up to her neck with a squeak. Goat turned around and high-tailed it back to main part of camp without another word.

Charlie watched his retreat, partially to make sure Goat went far away and partially because he wasn't sure what to do with his eyes. He was pretty sure he wanted a better look but forced himself to resist.

Finally, he spoke up. "He's gone. Are you covered?" Swallowing hard, he asked, "May I turn around now?" He waited a moment before slowly turning around.

Annabelle was still up to her neck in water but had managed to liberate her hands. She kept her arms crossed in front of her as she glared at him.

"What are you looking at me like that for? You're the one in your birthday suit. And while we're at it—why are you naked??"

"I'm bathing." Annabelle answered as if it were as simple as that.

"I can see." He widened his eyes at her, tipping his head forward. She responded to his dry response with thinned lips.

"Well?"

"I should be asking you that question. What the hell you doing in the river, bathing?" She started to respond and he held up his hand and added, "Alone."

"I couldn't very well ask you to join me, could I?"

Her snide remark stoked something inside him; his body suddenly felt afire. His nostrils flared and his eyes burned brighter. Annabelle didn't know what to do with the intensity of his stare, so she turned her head away. Charlie took some calming breaths before he could respond without feeling choked.

"No, I don't suppose you could. What you could've done was ask me to watch your back." Her eyes widened. Before indignation could really set in, Charlie went on quickly. "Not your actual back, Annabelle—keep a lookout. Shoot." He kicked the ground, watching a puff of dirt spray out from his boot. "You know it's not safe—besides, you're so…so, exposed." He waved a hand at her, clearly exasperated.

She snorted, surprising him. He lifted his head back up and met a fiery glare of her own.

"You weren't around. Jimmy wasn't around. I felt filthy, and my clothes needed washing. I've been wearing the same clothes for nearly two weeks and I am unaccustomed to doing so. Do you hear? I've been washing all of your clothes and none of mine. Not that I have any spare clothes, mind you."

"You kind of forget this isn't a pleasure trip you're on, don't you?"

"And whose fault is that?" Annabelle nearly screamed with frustration. He just wasn't getting it.

"Look here, I'm sorry about that. I feel bad. I've told you that. We're a little stuck right now, and you need to learn to make the best of it."

"You—" Annabelle drug out the word like a curse. She stood up, pointing her finger at him, totally disregarding her state of dress. "You are so self-righteous." She jabbed her finger toward him, again. "You—you—pig-headed lunkhead! Why I ought to—"

Her words were cut off as Charlie splashed into the river, grabbing a furious Annabelle and hauling her over his shoulder.

"What are you doing? Charlie, put me down this instant!" Instead, he swatted her backside, causing her to utter a shriek.

He carried her to the river's edge. "Charlie—" her protest was cut off when he dropped himself on a rock, pulling her over his knee. "You are not my fa—ooowww!"

His hand made connection with her backside as she howled and yelled. She twisted and kicked, trying to break free, but his arms were like a vise. His grip on her was strong as he continued to smack her bottom a few more times until she quieted down. Charlie wasn't hitting her hard—it was the humiliation of it all. She was being punished like a wayward child. When she was finally quiet but still gulping for air because she'd made herself so upset, Charlie shifted her so she was seated in his lap. He rubbed a soothing hand down her back, the other wrapped around her waist. In that moment, she felt so small and protected sitting there.

"Annabelle, when are you going to learn? I'm not your enemy. I'm trying to protect you and you make it extremely difficult." His voice was soft and full of concern. Oddly enough, she knew he cared—and in turn, she felt cared for.

She hadn't been comforted like this since she was a little girl. Charlie's embrace and comforting gestures—well, aside from the spanking—were melting her resolve. She melted even more when he pulled her closer to him, nuzzling her wet hair.

"Annabelle. Talk to me, Wildflower."

She sat up a little straighter and sniffled. Exhaling deeply, she asked, "Charlie, why do you call me Wildflower?"

He chuckled at that, shaking his head a little, but returned to nuzzling her hair as he spoke. "Jimmy was curious about that nickname, too. You, my dear, are like a desert wildflower. You're strong, resilient, and beautiful. You continue to stand even when the rains come down like a flood, and then the sun dries everything up, scorching the earth, turning things to dust—even when you are under the hooves, you stand tall. It's something to behold." He was looking out into the distance as he spoke.

"When did you decide that?"

"The day I kidnapped you—when you kicked Wrighty as he was trying to grab your ankle." Annabelle's mouth dropped open. "You didn't complain the whole way here. It was dusty, long, and hot. I'd taken you and you didn't know what was going to happen, but you didn't say a word. You were brave through it all. You fought Wrighty like the wildcat that he called you." He grinned momentarily but continued looking out over the water. "You know your daddy loves you, don't you?"

Annabelle started to cry, in earnest this time. He held her close and didn't say anything. He didn't have to. This was the first time Annabelle had broken down in front of him—she'd been so brave and strong the entire time she was there. It just wasn't fair that he had taken her—it especially wasn't fair that he didn't want to see her go, either. A lump was forming in his throat, making it difficult to say what he needed to. The longer he waited, the harder it would be. He finally spit it out, despite the protests from his heart.

"Wildflower, I'm going to get you back to your daddy. I promise. I never meant to take you." She looked up at him with a tear-stained face. "I was, ah, just borrowing you." He smiled a lop-sided smile that made her heart sing just a little more.

They sat in companionable silence for a few more minutes before Charlie stood. "You need to finish washing. I'll watch the hill, and you move it along. We've been gone for a while now, and I don't want anyone else getting the idea that they need to be down here, too." He turned his back and could hear her in the water, finishing her bathing. Gritting his teeth, he pictured her water-caressed body—Annabelle, rinsing her hair clean by leaning her head back into the water, her breasts raised to the sky like an offering. When she finished that, she'd run her soapy hand down her limbs and across those very breasts, then lower. The pressure he felt below the belt increased after she got out of the water and dressed. He could hear the rustling of clothing, and her soft footstep as she came up behind him and stopped. He casually turned around but lost his smile, bellowing when he got a good look at her, throwing his arms wide.

"What the hell, Annabelle!"

"What?"

"Your clothes—my clothes."

"I'm sorry I didn't think you'd—"

"What if someone *sees* you like that? You're welcome to my things, but you can't run around looking like that."

"Like what, Charlie?" Now her ire was raised. His name came out in a growl.

"All—like—like…a bedtime angel." His hand waved in front of her person. "It looks like you're wearing nightclothes and all." He blushed to the roots of his hair.

"I—" For a moment, she was flummoxed, but then her practical side kicked in. She stamped her foot. "Charlie Stapleton. What *am* I supposed to wear?" She leaned forward and began jabbing her finger at him. "I don't *have* any other clothes to wear. You can be darn sure that after bathing I am *not* putting on filthy clothes." She straightened her back and sniffed, turning her head to the side. "I was beginning to smell like Elwood."

Anger dropped from his face, his laughter breaking the tension. "Wildflower." He extended his arm. "I'll walk you to the table and then get you some water. You better get a move on. No one's going to hold back with you looking like that."

It was her turn for blushing to her roots, and Charlie found it delightful.

❧ **26** ❧

nnabelle was back working with Jimmy the following day. Even though she was wanting to keep a little cleaner after bathing, she relished talking to all the horses. They were so peaceful, unaffected by their riders who did bad things. Jimmy took good care of them, and they had each other. They seemed fairly satisfied. Most of the men treated their horses well, which made her feel better.

She had a brush in her hand, grooming a horse she had started calling Buttercup because of the mare's buttercream hue as well as her sweet nature. Buttercup liked it when Annabelle brushed her and would push her with her muzzle whenever she took a break or even paused in her brushing. It would make Annabelle giggle, and Buttercup would respond with a nicker and a horsey grin of her own. The sun was brightening the day while the other horses were gently milling around their makeshift pen—one that Jimmy and Charlie had made larger to accommodate for the gang's growing herd. Jimmy was watching her from the awkward little stool he sat on.

"What?"

"You seem a little different today." He continued to take a long look at her. "Lighter. Happier?" He cocked his head in question.

She looked thoughtful for a moment. "I suppose I do. I feel like Charlie understands me better than I thought he did."

"How so?"

"He seems to know I feel bad and guilty about Papa—he's also concerned about getting me back to him."

"Hmm."

Annabelle stopped brushing Buttercup, who immediately nudged her arm. Annabelle gently pushed her muzzle away but stroked her absentmindedly anyway. "What do you mean, *hmm*?" She put one fist on her hip.

Jimmy sighed, straightening himself out. "That's what Charlie does for people, especially those he cares for. Even when they don't want it."

"I don't understand—I miss Papa. I—"

"Not you, me."

Annabelle grabbed the other stool, dragging it closer to Jimmy. "I think you better share your story with me."

Jimmy let out a belabored sigh, knowing that he'd opened the can and now he had to finish what he started. They had a stare-down of sorts, but Jimmy starting speaking anyway.

"If Charlie is planning to get you back to your papa, then he's also planning for both of us to escape with you."

"What's wrong with that? You don't like being here, right?" Annabelle's brows knotted, and her lips pursed.

"Remember how I told you that we were kidnapped?" She nodded her head. "There's that and watching Charlie begging to save me and being taunted by Wrighty and a couple of the others—it all built up in me. All this pressure, then something broke inside. I'm not the same. Charlie wants to get justice—actually escape, and go out and get it. I want revenge. Revenge for all they stole from us and so many others. For the abuse they've made us suffer. For repeatedly humiliating me and Charlie until we were too big and strong for that. And especially for making Charlie an outlaw. He didn't deserve that—

he's too good and kind for that. You know that's why he took you, right?" He looked long and hard at her. When she didn't answer, he asked her another question. "He didn't go in with a gun, did he?"

Annabelle pursed her lips for a moment, her eyes going wide when she remembered that he didn't have a gun. She slowly shook her head.

"I figured. They gave him one, but I was sure he wouldn't use it. On the rare occasions they give him one, he always keeps it holstered. I'm not sure it's even loaded."

"Ahhh. That makes more sense."

Jimmy cocked his head at her.

"He said he kidnapped me so no one got hurt. He was kind of using me as a barrier because he knew Papa wouldn't shoot around me."

"Mm-hmm."

They looked at each other for a long time. Annabelle had dropped her head, feeling a little guilty about some of the judgment she'd thrown at Charlie—especially since he'd been nothing but good to her, when she really thought about it.

"So, what do we do now?"

"We? We don't do anything. Charlie has some sort of plan, and he'll expect us to follow it. I, however, can no longer think about escaping."

"What?" Annabelle's face fell in horror.

"No escaping."

Annabelle swallowed hard. She had to be very careful with the words she used. She didn't want to offend Jimmy, and neither did she want him to stop talking now that he'd finally opened up to her.

"Why not, Jimmy?" She let that hang for a moment. "Do you want to continue living with these men?"

"Hell, no. I'm getting revenge. The good, old-fashioned way. From the inside out—keep your friends close and your enemies closer."

"How?"

"Charlie's probably still planning a way for the three of us to escape, except I'm not going."

"Jimmy, you—"

He held up a hand. "Hear me out, Annabelle. I cannot go. Charlie needs to get you out of here safely. I don't know how negotiations will go, but he needs a backup plan, just in case. He can try to get all the help he wants from the outside, but I'm not banking on it working. The only way we can bring them down is from the inside. I need time to figure that out."

"Charlie'll be heartbroken. He loves you, Jimmy."

"And I love him, but as the preachers always say, I have my own path to walk. You need to help him understand that for me. Will you do that for me? Help him understand?"

"I—"

Jimmy had a hopeful look on his face, the first one she'd really seen since she'd been here. She couldn't disappoint him. She nodded. Her lips pulled in on each other to keep her from crying for him. She knew he wouldn't want her tears for that—instead, he needed something to hold on to.

"You're a good woman, Annabelle. You're good for Charlie. I'm sorry you had to meet him this way. This life isn't who we are."

"Oh, Jimmy. I know that. You stand out like sore thumbs, but I didn't know why, or even try to know, until you said something. I was too scared and angry, at first. Then, I thought maybe you somehow belonged to someone here, even by accident, maybe."

Jimmy didn't say anything. He handed her the brush and went back to Buttercup's hoof. He started picking away at it, and Annabelle knew that was all she was getting out of him for the day.

It didn't surprise Annabelle that Charlie had been cooking up a plan for them, probably even before her personal washing day. She blushed thinking about that day. She felt things she hadn't felt before and was still feeling warm all over when she thought about it. She especially felt it lower down, wondering at it. No one had talked to her about *relations*. She pursed her lips, recalling the horses she'd seen mating—it wasn't particularly pretty, but this didn't feel like *that*. What she was feeling, though, was so much nicer than what she thought she knew, and she knew that she didn't know much. What she definitely knew was that she liked the way he made her feel, and she wanted more of those feelings. She *needed* something more. What that was, exactly, she wasn't sure. She was so confused. She slouched at the thought of it all.

Her forbidden thoughts were interrupted by Charlie calling out to someone. She stopped sweeping to watch him stalk toward her. His shoulders were broad and strong—his entire body was muscular and hard. There was nothing little or weak about the man. It was her resolve and heart that were weakening. When he grabbed her in the river, she could feel all that strength in a different way, in spite of all those restless nights sleeping next to him—sometimes wrapped up with him. She loved the feel of his calloused hands on her skin when he held her hand or cupped her face, as well as when his long arms were wrapped around her.

Closing in on her, a big smile lit up his face, and he had a glimmer in his eye. He was up to something. After talking to

Jimmy, she was pretty sure it was his escape plan. Nodding to him, she couldn't help but return his with a bright smile of her own as she leaned against the broom, waiting for him to stop in front of her.

When he did, he tilted his head to the side, admiring her. As he bent down to give her a sweet kiss on her cheek, she looked up at him, eyes wide and a little star-struck, hoping for more. His eyes sparkled as their faces paused, close. He kissed the side of her head, cupping her chin and tilting her face before planting a soft kiss on her lips. Annabelle's heart beat like hummingbirds' wings in her chest. His lips lingered and she thought she'd die of happiness—this was *some of the more* she was looking for. Releasing the broom, her hands went over his shoulders to pull him closer to her. She stood on tiptoes to meet him halfway and sighed against his lips.

Charlie tilted his head further to allow his mouth to gain better access to her, growling as he grasped her shoulder blades, holding her in place. The polite and reserved broke in him. He wanted Annabelle, and she clearly wanted him. Their lips moved across each other's, pressing, tasting, and seeking, as their hands echoed their lips in exploration. One hand slid behind up her head and the other moved to the middle of her back, eliminating any space between them. Their kisses became more insistent and needy as Annabelle's hands moved up Charlie's neck to his hair, running through it and mussing it up. They couldn't seem to get enough of each other, or even close enough, until a throat cleared behind them.

Annabelle thought she may have heard something but chose to ignore it. Then she heard it again—a distinct throat clearing coming from behind. Charlie must've heard it at the same time because they jumped apart simultaneously, trying to act casual. Laughter flustered the pair even more.

"I knew you two were bound to be a pair when I saw you riding into camp the day of the robbery." More chuckling. "I want to introduce you to somebody. This here's Travis."

Charlie had pulled Annabelle behind him but not before the men saw her embarrassment. Her skin was already infused with a pink tinge of arousal. Now she was flushing to her roots at being caught in such a compromising position—out in the open during daylight, no less.

The man called Travis had the decency to lower his eyes and take off his hat. Orrin just hooted at the poor pair. They were innocents, really, despite all of Charlie's earlier claims. Some seemed to sense it, but there were a few who knew it. Orrin was one of the newly confirmed on that count. Ironically, at this point no one really cared, except for Wrighty. The rest of the men figured Charlie deserved a break, and however he wanted to handle her was up to him. Besides, they couldn't help but joke about his awkward innocence behind his back. Occasionally to his face, for that matter.

Charlie stuck his hand out to Travis, who took Charlie's in a firm and steady grip. They locked eyes and leaned toward each other as they pumped their arms in a handshake. Everyone could feel the tension as they sized each other up. It built until they finally released their handshake. Travis seemed convinced of whatever it was that he was looking for, nodding for good measure. He was a man of few words but keen observation. He'd been watching the two of them together before Orrin even noticed.

Travis wasn't the only one who was being covert. Moris was in the shade, watching intently. He finally had found Annabelle, but he had also found Travis. Wrighty needed to know.

27

Van Der Kamp had been watching and not interacting the past few days. He was trying to figure out whose side Gabe and Lafayette were on. Gabe was benign enough, but Van Der Kamp needed hard numbers, and that man was easily swayed. He was wanting to make a move against Mack, but he wouldn't do that until he decided who he could truly count on. He knew that Wrighty had been itching to take over the gang—his actions with Charlie and Annabelle confirmed it. He'd been blatant in his disregard of Van Der Kamp's orders, and they were especially important this time, given who they were dealing with—Mack Pennington meant business and didn't suffer fools. The sheriff had to be dealt with, and not just because of Annabelle. Having Annabelle made it easier, in Van Der Kamp's mind, because there didn't have to be unnecessary killing.

To satisfy this man who seemed to think he was their boss, they had to get the sheriff to somehow quit being the sheriff, or get him ousted. There was no way that would happen successfully with Annabelle here and part of the gang wanting to splinter off. Sheriff O'Donnell was a man of his word and of the people. He wouldn't let the town down, and he wouldn't be bullied into something he didn't want, either. Van Der Kamp hadn't let Wrighty in on the entire story of Sheriff O'Donnell. What little Wrighty knew he was distorting and making O'Donnell the bad guy; Van Der Kamp knew otherwise. Somehow, Wrighty had managed to convince some of the others that the sheriff was their problem, aside from being the law. Wrighty was writing checks that couldn't be cashed. So Van Der Kamp was giving Wrighty plenty of rope to hang himself. He just wished that Wrighty would get on with it. He was a patient man and could wait out the enemy longer than most. Mack wasn't. He was rude, opinionated, and rash. He'd also been breathing down Van Der Kamp's neck the past few days by telegraph.

Stretching, he walked into the common area and checked the rations. Sweet Annabelle was fixin' to get dinner ready, and Goat had wandered off to bring back more firewood. He lifted pot lids and looked at the ingredients she'd spread out on the worktable. Annabelle was humming a little tune and wasn't paying attention to her surroundings. Good thing Charlie assigned himself as her protector. She'd have been done in long ago if he hadn't. He straightened up from the pot he was looking into and cleared his throat so that she'd notice him.

"Argh!" Her hand flew to her chest. "Mr. Van Der Kamp, you scared me! Perhaps you shouldn't kill the cook with fright." Her face scrunched up at that thought.

His laughter was deep and genuine, surprising her. "Annabelle, your mind is always somewhere else. You ought to learn to pay better attention to your surroundings."

"Papa always told me that, too." The corners of her mouth turned down.

He patted her shoulder as one would a child, very out of character for a man who spoke little and rarely showed emotion. "It's true. No better place to do that than here. Although, you're pretty lucky to have Charlie looking after you."

She blushed brightly because she was thinking the same thing. She couldn't always rely on him, however. She had been forced to rely too much on Papa, and look where that got her. Breaking from her thoughts, she realized that Van Der Kamp was watching her carefully.

"Ah, yes. He's been very good to me, sir."

That made him laugh even more.

"Annabelle, you keep telling yourself that. That boy is as smitten with you as you are with him. There's no need to pretend with me. I see *everything*."

Even though his eyes were warm at the moment, the way he emphasized *everything* made a chill run down her spine. She wasn't sure what he was getting at, so she quickly nodded and looked down at the ground for a moment before hustling back to filling the pots with more ingredients, then stirring them.

Truth be told, he made her nervous. He was a nice-looking older man, even respectable-looking. He kept himself tidy and walked tall with pride, even with the slight limp. He never raised his voice and didn't waste words. He didn't speak meanly or crassly, but there was an edge to him that made her feel that letting down one's guard around him was a bad idea. He felt dangerous, for lack of a better word. She'd seen men brawling over minor things, and they'd go at each other as if they wanted to kill. Van Der Kamp, however, didn't operate that way. He was calm like the surface of a still pond—it was what was underneath it that was so frightening. She was pretty sure that he could kill a man with his bare hands and not break a sweat. That he'd kill before the victim knew what was coming—it was that kind of lethality that had her on edge. He didn't need to flex his muscles to prove that he had them—just having them was enough for him. The rest of the gang were amateurs compared to him.

Turning back to the table, she realized that he was still watching her. It took everything in her not to start shaking like a leaf. Wiping her hands on Goat's apron, she chopped some more vegetables. Unable to pretend she was ignoring him any longer, she put her knife on the table and turned to Van Der Kamp.

"I think you weren't done talking yet."

"Yup."

"I'm ready to listen."

"Mmm-hmm." Biting into a carrot, he watched her squirm a little. "How close are you two?"

"What do you mean, *close?*" Her eyes narrowed at him as she put her hands on her hips.

"I'm not trying to get your dander up, woman." Annabelle gasped at him, her hands slipping off her hips. "I need to know how—intimate—you two are."

"What!" Annabelle practically screeched at him.

"Hold on, now. I have my reasons for asking, and it's important. I, personally, don't care either way. I think you're suited for each other, but that's your choice. There are other things at play here—bigger than you and Charlie or this gang, for that matter."

Annabelle looked surprised at that and was thoughtful for a moment. Initially, she wondered if he'd heard about their passionate kiss from Orrin, the blabbermouth. Beyond that, she really didn't know how to answer that question. She was really wanting there to be more but didn't want to be strapped into something. She liked Charlie—it felt good to be around him. He made her feel good. But she wanted to be free from all this.

Fortunately for her, she didn't have to answer. Just as she was opening her mouth to respond, Charlie came down the hill. He didn't see them tucked away in the cooking area, and he called out for her.

"Wildflower. Wildflower, you around?"

Van Der Kamp quirked his brow at Annabelle, and she blushed, hard. Stretching out his legs and crossing his arms, he waited for Charlie to catch up to them. They were both looking toward Charlie when he landed at the bottom of the hill, twisting his head in either direction. When he caught sight of them, his eyes opened wide and his pace quickened.

"Annabelle. Van Der Kamp. Everything all right?" His long strides brought him there before he finished asking his question.

"Yes. I was just talking to your *Wildflower* about the nature of your relationship with her." Half of his mouth quirked as he shifted so he was looking directly at Charlie. "Care to elaborate?"

The air hung heavy with lies and unfulfilled desires. Charlie wasn't sure how to answer that, and they hadn't had much of a chance to discuss their feelings, either. Aside from this morning's lengthy public display, Charlie showed his care and concern by keeping her safe and promising to return her to her father, which felt contrary to what he really wanted to do. There were things he wanted to do, too, that her father wouldn't approve of. The longer he took to respond, the deeper shade of red he turned.

Finally, Van Der Kamp straightened up and let out a long breath of air. "I see how it is between you two. You're going to have to decide where you stand with each other and how you want things to pan out." He looked back and forth between the two of them. "Charlie, you're in charge of negotiating a deal with her father. Between the messenger we sent and the time it takes to get responses back and forth, it'll be upwards to three days, max, that you'll have together. You need to make plans."

"Why?"

"This'll all be over soon. You'll need to decide your own fates after that."

An uneasy stillness hung in the air. Annabelle and Charlie passed glances at each other before looking back at Van Der Kamp.

"But why are you telling us all this? You don't usually share information unless it's necessary."

Van Der Kamp pulled a frown while breathing in deeply. "You're a good kid, Charlie. You and Jimmy both. Like I told Annabelle, here, there are things at play here that are bigger than all of us. I've seen the way the two of you look at each other, too. It's a good thing. The other things aren't. You have to make some decisions between the two of you before I tell you anything more."

With that, Van Der Kamp slowly limped away, leaving a stunned Charlie and Annabelle in his wake.

Travis had been trailing Charlie since their initial meeting. He wasn't sure what to make of the kid. He was certainly a hard worker and didn't cause trouble. He was also smitten with O'Donnell's daughter. As far as he could tell, he was treating her well. Aside from that passionate kiss he witnessed, they were pretty green in the sexual arena. He'd been watching camp for a couple of days before he made himself known. He liked to know what he was up against when he arrived. He didn't necessarily trust Van Der Kamp to tell him the whole truth, or any of the others, for that matter. He especially didn't trust that snake Wrighty to be up front. He was always out for himself. Van Der Kamp seemed to be up to something as well. He was talking to Charlie and Annabelle longer than he'd normally talk to someone that he wasn't giving commands or orders to. Their voices weren't carrying to him so he either had to give up his location or find something closer. By the time he shifted to move, Van Der Kamp had left. As good a time as any to make himself known. Stepping out into the path, he meandered toward the clearing.

Van Der Kamp didn't let on that he was watching; he just assumed Travis was aware. "Travis. Good to see you." He held out his hand. Travis took his and shook it with earnestness.

"You, too, Van Der Kamp. I have some letters from Pennington for you and some other information that I can report when you're ready."

Van Der Kamp seemed to be considering what Travis said, but he was studying his face closely. He had done interrogation during the war. It was something he was good at because he so seldom showed emotion. These days, his emotions were practically nonexistent—hazard of the job. Travis didn't flinch under his scrutiny, which was something Van Der Kamp respected. He respected it a lot. It was also one of many things he admired in Charlie, along with his extreme loyalty to those he loved. He was sure that kid was going to make a great husband if he saw what was right in front of him and found his way. He hoped for Annabelle's sake that the kid did.

He'd sure as hell hated that kid's father. He didn't feel bad putting a bullet in the man. He didn't feel too bad when he let Wrighty and his men loose on him, either. Bastard deserved what he got. He didn't cotton to killing the wife, but that was what Mack wanted. This job was becoming more complicated and demanding than was initially presented to him. He had Mack and his enormous ego to thank for that. He'd underestimated the size of that man's pride. Wrighty and his dealings with the deputy also complicated matters. Wrighty thought he was being sly with that one, but he was too full of himself, overstepping boundaries and forgetting—*that I see everything*.

Besides, Van Der Kamp didn't hold with dealing with corrupt law, either—he was ready to put all of this to bed. Robbing these entitled rich folk and fighting the government was coming to an end for him. He was tired of his reign of terror. Hell, he was becoming soft if he was rooting for the likes of Charlie. The thing is—Charlie and Annabelle were the very type of people, like himself, that he was fighting for—even Sheriff O'Donnell. It was the Mr. Stapletons and Mack Penningtons that he was fighting against. The greedy bastards who clawed their way to the top, regardless of who they had to tear down to get there. Even if those poor, hapless fools were family, like the sheriff, Annabelle, Charlie, and Jimmy.

He shook these thoughts from his mind, jerking his head to indicate that Travis should walk with him. They went up the path together toward Van Der Kamp's cabin. Travis had a lot of things he needed to share, but he also had some questions of his own.

"So, what's going on with that giant kid and the girl?" Travis had been in and out of communication with the gang over the past four years; it made it easy to pretend ignorance. He never stayed long enough to meet Charlie and Jimmy, anyway, although he'd briefly seen them when they were younger and much smaller. Now, they had grown into big, strong men.

"Ah, Charlie. He's Stapleton's kid. You remember the teens we captured, after that stagecoach robbery about five years ago? He's the older brother."

"His girl?"

Now Van Der Kamp looked interested. Curious. "Whadya mean, girl?"

"I caught him in a lip lock with a pretty brunette. Little gal with lots of hair."

"Ah, sweet Annabelle."

Travis's head cocked. His turn for interest. "I suppose that's what he called her. Annabelle, that is."

"Sheriff O'Donnell's daughter. Casualty of Charlie's first robbery. He did pretty well for himself."

"Because he got a girl?"

"No, he hit pay dirt. Girl was a bonus. She's like a wildcat but is a good worker and excellent cook. They seem to be sweet on each other."

"Seem to be? He was practically mauling her out in daylight. She could've been a lady of line for all I knew. Didn't think you'd get into that kind of business."

Van Der Kamp made a noise that was a cross between a grunt and a snort. "You know I don't cotton to that. Who do you take me for, anyway?"

Travis gave him a long, sideways look. "Why's he got a girl?"

"She needed protection."

"Can't you control your beasts?"

"It's not them." He ran his tongue behind his teeth, making a sucking sound.

"Wrighty."

"Yup. He'd been warned. Didn't listen."

"What're you gonna do?"

"He's done."

Travis knew not to ask anymore or he'd be "done" as well. Since he didn't say anything else, Van Der Kamp moved forward. "What do you have for me?"

"Here's something interesting I found out when I was back east. Apparently, Stapleton tried to back out of the contract that he'd signed with Pennington. The bank had loaned him the money for mining, but there was a side deal they had put together—that's what he was trying to squirrel out of."

"How so?"

"Well, Pennington had added a clause about the foreman of the mine. He wanted the same one present for two consecutive years. They were having troubles keeping one."

"Why didn't Pennington have his son do that?"

"That's why O'Donnell initially came out here, to run the mine. I can guess what stopped him—he figured out what Pennington was up to. What I do know for sure is that everyone in that town loves him and elected him the sheriff. It's clear that there's bad blood between the sheriff and his father, which is why he's the sheriff and not running the operation. It's also why he has a different last name. Took on his mother's maiden name when he came here, wanting to distance himself from his old man."

"What does that have to do with Stapleton?"

"Stapleton wanted his older son, Joseph, to be the foreman, but he wanted him to have a big East Coast kind of salary and a home built. Joseph didn't really want to get his hands soiled with Mack's dirty business and all. He wanted to be more of a figurehead. Pennington said that wouldn't fly until the operation got off the ground. Then, he'd consider it. So Stapleton insisted it be added to the contract—"

"What, a house and salary?"

Travis nodded. "But there had to be someone watching the mines consistently, otherwise the deal was off."

"You mean running off the remaining prospectors."

Travis's face was grim, confirming violence beyond what the gang had already done for Pennington. "Stapleton thought that someone else would just take over the dirty work until his son could manage to come back from California. As you know, the dirty work was getting done, but no one was really handling the mine itself. Foremen, yes, but beyond that, no one. He said his son was technically managing the mine from afar *in name*. Stapleton didn't agree to ridding the land of the prospectors or any violence. The time period had come and gone and Stapleton insisted that Joseph had upheld his end of the bargain, that Pennington should start building some mansion-like home out here."

They guffawed at the thought of a mansion out in the middle of nowhere in the Arizona Territory. The rich had fancy homes but not to the extent of the eastern spreads Stapleton had in mind. Homes were being built and wives and families were moving out—slowly. It was still no real place for fancy ladies, however. Those ladies usually returned east; they didn't last long. The women who lived out here had to be made of sterner stuff. Stapleton didn't have what it took. His youngest sons were a different story, however. Perhaps that was just the circumstances they found themselves in, but Travis didn't think so.

"That makes no sense, Travis. You're telling me that Stapleton signed a contract that said the mine had to be staffed for two years before Pennington would build a fancy home for his eldest, Joseph, and pay an exorbitant salary for him? That he didn't bother looking at this mine before he agreed to this and didn't have anyone out here to fill the position?"

"Yup. He thought he could outsmart Pennington, but Pennington's pretty sly himself. He's conned quite a few people out of their hard-earned coin, but not in ways that he could be legally held accountable. He has someone who's capable of running the operation. Brute of a man, but things are going well enough—he no longer needs the Stapletons. Stapleton was the dumb one—the damn mine had to be producing, and if no one steady is watching over them, the miners are going to rob the mine blind."

Van Der Kamp threw himself back into his chair with a heavy sigh. "There's got to be more to that than this. That's the stupidest contract I ever heard of. He didn't need the money; he owned a bank that had plenty. Right? Bank did well?"

"Bank checked out. It's on the up and up. It was the slight dealings behind closed doors that had me concerned. Stapleton'd blackmailed these people, somehow."

Van Der Kamp threw him a look. Travis shrugged. "Hear me out. You get legitimate businessmen into your bank needing money to expand their businesses or float them until their next big pay dirt. Things check out, and they sign the papers for the loans. However, he sends Pinkerton agents after these men and comes up with other dirt. He calls them back to share his "findings" or tells them at the signing—either way, they're men caught in a hard spot—they need the money or have already signed. And to keep Stapleton quiet they sign another, different contract. These wouldn't show up on the bank records because they're private contracts."

"Mmm." Van Der Kamp snorted air in through his right nostril, indicating that he was intrigued and thinking. He pointed a finger at Travis. "Now that I could see. Man was a weasel of the biggest sort." Travis looked like he was going to say something but Van Der Kamp quickly added, "Pennington's no better, though."

"Agreed. That's what I have on that front. I have some contacts out, figuring out the sheriff. He left so long ago that people have stopped talking about him. We'll get something. We're also looking into the missing wife."

"Missing?"

"Apparently, she walked out on Sheriff O'Donnell and their little girl when Annabelle was about three. Went to run an errand and never came back. Some say she was abducted, others say she ran away."

"That's why the sheriff never remarried, even with a little girl to care for?"

"He's very protective of her—there's something else I'm missing. Here's what we do know about her." Travis shared a few details before adding, "The wife has to be connected to Mack somehow. I just haven't figured out exactly how."

"Must be money. Everything with those two comes up money—money and lies."

The two men, hardened members of an outlaw gang, whose profession was robbing, sometimes killing, and generally causing disruption for the rich and wreaking havoc for the government, rolled that thought around individually, reflecting for several long moments.

Money and lies. Together they sat in silence with that truth.

Moris found Wrighty leaning against a tree, his hat tilted forward, shading his face. He wanted to walk up to him and kick his boots but knew that wouldn't go over well. Especially since Wrighty looked like he might actually be sleeping and not just resting. Wrighty had always had an odd feeling about Travis. Maybe telling him about Travis would get him off the hook with Annabelle. He wanted no hand in helping Wrighty with those dirty deeds. *What the hell, let's just get this over with.*

"Wrighty." Wrighty made a grunting sound but didn't bother looking up. "Wrighty, I need to talk to you. Travis is back."

That got Wrighty shooting straight up, pushing his hat off his face. "What? When? What're you talking about?" He shook his head slightly to clear it before looking up at Moris.

"You heard me. He's back. I saw him shaking hands with Charlie, sizing him up."

"And?"

"He seemed to pass muster."

"Shit."

"That's right. And I won't be able to get near Annabelle, alone, for some time. Charlie's going to be on high alert with Travis around, even if they agree to disagree, so to speak."

"I'm going to have to welcome Travis back personally, it sounds like."

Moris didn't want to respond to that. He was tired of Wrighty and didn't have a good feeling about any of it. There was something else going on that Wrighty wasn't catching and wasn't supposed to catch—he was sure of it. He'd leave that to Wrighty and his need for revenge.

"Well, I'm out of here. Thought you'd want to know about Travis and all."

"I'm not done with you. You get on Annabelle, anyway. You hear?"

Moris had already turned around and was walking away. He flipped his hand back and managed to shout out, "You betcha." Whatever that meant.

28

Travis left Van Der Kamp with his big news and some miscellaneous items and went in search of Jimmy. He wasn't sure what he looked like, but he knew he would most likely find him with the horses. He trudged up the hill and rounded the bend toward the sound of nickering and blowing. He stopped behind the extended stable to watch how Jimmy handled the animals. It said a lot about a person's character, as well as how the animals responded. Leaning against the wall, he waited.

Jimmy was working a beautiful black, running it through its paces. They were like one, dodging the barrels and other obstacles that Jimmy had set up in the ring. He held the reins loosely, communicating through the slight pressure of his legs and a mental connection that astute riders have with their animals. They anticipated each others' moves, each working in tandem. It was clear that what they were doing was more for exercise and entertainment, but it served a solid training purpose, too. Good sign. He waited until they were finished with that round and Jimmy was riding him out for water. Another good sign. So far, these boys were proving to be far better than their sire, that's for damn sure. He stepped out to make his presence known.

Jimmy saw the movement out of the corner of his eye as they headed toward the trough. He decided to ignore it as he slid off Cole. Allowing the horse to drink his fill, he went to grab a brush to rub him down. When he returned, a trim man with a larger build was stroking Cole's beautiful black coat, admiring the horse. Jimmy stopped and gave the man a once-over. He had dark hair and tanned skin from being out in the elements. By the way he held himself, Jimmy could tell that he was strong and used to labor. His feet braced the ground, and he stood tall like a poplar. He had a cat-like quality to him as well—his movement was sleek and efficient. Dark, unreadable eyes were watching his perusal.

Jimmy nodded to the man. "Morning. Well, what's left of it."

"Morning. You Jimmy?"

"Yup."

"Pretty good with the horses."

"I like it."

"Mind if I watch you work?"

"Already were, weren't you?"

"I always watch before I enter, keeps things safe for me."

"Suit yourself." With that, Jimmy walked around Travis and brushed down Cole. He didn't bother to ask Travis his name or what he wanted. He didn't care.

That night Wrighty came sauntering in toward the end of dinner. Annabelle and Goat had already served everyone and were just settling down to eat, themselves. Wrighty went up to Annabelle and stood so close that his boots touched her skirts. It was one of his many favorite tactics to use on Annabelle— he liked being in her space, and it usually bought him time to mess with her.

"Darling, don't get comfortable yet. I just got here."

She rolled her eyes and started to move back toward the cooking area. Travis, however, reached out and put his hand on her arm, stalling her.

"Annabelle, dear, you've already worked real hard. You go on and sit down here with Goat and Charlie, and enjoy yourself some dinner. Wrighty can come on time if he'd like your lovely meal service."

Wrighty scowled at Travis. "The prodigal son has returned. When'd you get back?"

"I've been back. I already checked in with Van Der Camp." He tilted his head to indicate Van Der Kamp, who was watching them. "I didn't know I needed to check in with you, too." Their eyes locked, each waiting for the other to make the next move.

Annabelle looked at Charlie. He barely dipped his head at her before she walked off to get Wrighty his food. The two men were still having their standoff when Annabelle pressed the plate into Wrighty's hand before sitting down. She did, however, turn to Travis.

"Thank you for your kind words. I do appreciate them."

While Annabelle always felt safe around Charlie, and she was pretty sure the others wouldn't bother her, Wrighty left her nerves frayed. She still hadn't told Charlie what Wrighty had done or *how* he threatened her, but neither did she discount the fact that he would try to make good on his promise. It was always in the back of her mind. Everyone sat down and started eating, but Wrighty wasn't content to let it go. He kept leering at Annabelle, signaling what she had feared earlier.

"Annabelle, darlin', would you fetch me something to drink? I'm feeling a little parched today." He displayed his biggest, and what the gang called women-getting, smile for show.

Annabelle's mouth dropped open in shock, but before she could say anything, Charlie and Travis were out of their seats. Travis had vaulted the table and pulled Wrighty up by his collar. She could hear his fist making contact with Wrighty's face. There was a terrible cracking sound when he broke Wrighty's nose. Blood splattered around them as the men jumped from their seats, and Annabelle screamed. Charlie pulled her away from the fight, but not before she saw Travis throw two consecutive punches to Wrighty's gut. Wrighty thrust his leg out, catching Travis's foot and knocking him over. Before Wrighty could get on top of him, Van Der Kamp had him by the shoulder, pulling him back.

"I wouldn't do that if I were you." Everyone halted in their tracks. There was something about Van Der Kamp's smooth voice that forced others to take note. They all looked at him as they waited to see what Wrighty's fate was. "I told you to leave Annabelle alone." He thrust Wrighty away from him like a fishwife throwing away fish heads. He didn't wait for Wrighty to respond but walked away. His departure signaled the fight was over, and everyone went slowly back to what they were doing. Wrighty still hadn't learned his lesson, however. He shouted after Travis, pointing at him. All the while holding his nose to keep it from bleeding all over.

"I ain't done with you!"

"Let it rest, Wrighty. And start treating Annabelle with some respect, will ya?"

Wrighty growled in response but didn't do anything.

"Go fix your nose, Wrighty, so the rest of us can finish dinner." Van Der Kamp sat down, picked up his fork, and continued eating.

The remainder of dinner was a tense affair, but at least Annabelle knew she had two more people on her side, two people who really counted—Travis and Van Der Kamp.

That night, Charlie pulled Annabelle close to him on the cot. They had shared a very intimate moment in public, and he was curious how much further this should go. He didn't like that Travis got a jump on him with Wrighty, either. He had promised to protect her, and then Travis jumped his claim. At any rate, she was going back to her father—he had promised.

Van Der Kamp's words hung over him as well—they had three days together, at best. But he was falling in love with her, and everybody seemed to realize it but him. That is, until now. He knew that he admired her and wanted to protect her—but love? He didn't know what that was. He had no experience with women, even though the men tried to get him and Jimmy to visit the painted ladies at the various stops they'd made. They both refused. It was too embarrassing, and he wanted to be with someone he could love and court. Ironic, really. He didn't have the chance to court Annabelle, but here she was, sharing a bed with him. And he really liked having her there. It was the first time in a long time he didn't feel so alone. He had Jimmy, but Jimmy had become withdrawn over the years. The beatings and teasing had been especially hard on Jimmy, no matter how hard Charlie tried to protect him from them. Sometimes, he worried he'd made it worse for Jimmy, but he couldn't stop protecting him if he tried. It'd feel wrong. It'd feel like he'd given up, and that wasn't something he was willing to do.

He wrapped his arm around Annabelle a little tighter, and she gave a soft hum in return. Scooting closer to her, he placed a soft kiss to the side of her hair and nuzzled his face into it.

"Your hair's so soft now that you've washed it."

Annabelle's laughter rang out in the tent. "Charlie, you're such a romantic." She continued laughing, her back to him.

Instead of answering, he kissed down her neck, eliciting a gasp from her. "Annabelle," he whispered into her neck, like a plea.

Simultaneously and unbidden, she rolled toward him as he rolled her over. Facing each other, they suddenly became shy. Their eyes locked with longing before they inched their faces closer, pressing their lips into a soft, tentative kiss.

The kiss was different in the dark. Their bodies were nestled intimately, and they didn't have an audience. Initially, it was a kiss of exploration and question. Exploration soon turned hungry and greedy as their breathing increased, and their hands roamed. Their bodies moved against and with each other. Fortunately for them, Jimmy had chosen to stay by the campfire a little longer. He had been watching Travis, who asked too many questions and was a little too kind and sophisticated for being one of the gang.

Charlie was becoming painfully aroused, but he didn't want to do anything that would make Annabelle feel uncomfortable or ashamed. Still, he couldn't help pressing his hard length against her, and when she made gasping and sighing noises, it urged him on even more. Finally, he had to break himself free when she threw her leg over his—the contact of the junction of her thighs connecting with his hard length was overwhelming. They both gasped at it.

"Wildflower." She had her arm tangled around his neck, and he was trying to nudge her loose.

"Mmm." She pulled him closer and continued kissing and nuzzling him.

"Wildflower."

"Charlie." She pressed another kiss to his neck.

"We have to stop."

"Hm? What, no." Although she did stop what she was doing.

"Yes. I don't want to compromise you."

With that, Annabelle sat up looking him in the eye with fire shooting out of hers. "You can't be serious, Charlie."

Charlie looked stricken. "Of course I am."

"Charlie, you *claimed me*. Everyone already thinks we're doing this." She gestured wildly between the two of them.

He blushed, realizing that not only was she right, but the whole situation was even more awkward now. He ran his hand through his hair and wasn't sure how to respond to that, although his body had some rather specific ideas. Annabelle sat up and looked down at him.

"Charlie—you make me feel things I've never felt before. I—I don't know what to do with these feelings, these sensations. Whatever I'm feeling feels right with you."

"Wildflower." Charlie swallowed hard. "I put you in a bad, bad position. I'm so sorry."

"Don't you be sorry, Charlie Stapleton. What we have is good. So good, it scares me."

"It's not that, it's—you're too good. You're a good girl. You deserve to be courted and have sweet gifts given to you—not to be kidnapped and forced to work for a gang." He put his head in his hands.

Annabelle moved to kneel and rubbed his shoulder in soothing circles as she leaned toward him. "Charlie, what you did you couldn't avoid. You did what you had to do. I wouldn't have met you if you hadn't taken me." Her lips tucked inward, pulling her nose down and her eyes wider to keep from laughing. Charlie looked at her and started to laugh. He put his hand behind her head and pulled her to his chest.

"Sweet Annabelle, you're too kind. I know I didn't do a good job of defending you tonight, but we'll get out of here, don't you worry. I'll get you home safe."

"I know you will."

Resuming their cocoon of love, they snuggled closer together and finally, eventually, into a contented sleep.

❦ 29 ❦

Jimmy finally cornered Travis the next day when he was grooming his horse. Very few of the men took much time with their horses, taking it for granted that Jimmy would handle everything. Travis, however, was different from the others—one of the many reasons Jimmy kept an eye on him. Take, for example, his curiosity about him the day before and then his swift defense of Annabelle. Jimmy couldn't figure him out.

Travis was exercising his horse in the ring before breakfast. He was already there by the time Jimmy got to the stables to muck and feed, which was generally early. Jimmy watched him from a distance, much like Travis had watched him earlier. He slid out of the saddle and walked his horse to water. Jimmy stood with his arms crossed by the trough, waiting for them.

They eyed each other before nodding. Travis said, "I'm sure you have questions."

That threw Jimmy off guard, which caused him to slip out of his protective stance. He shifted and uncrossed his arms. Travis smiled at him, clapping him on the shoulder. "It's okay, go ahead."

Jimmy swallowed. He didn't expect it to be that easy. Eyeing him warily, he finally asked some of his burning questions.

"How come you know who we are?"

"Easy. I've been coming and going for the past four years, shortly after you and Charlie showed up. You've grown a lot, that's all. I had to make sure it was you and not someone new."

"Why'd you have to ask? What's it to you?"

"I always know who I'm surrounded by—be deadly if I didn't."

Jimmy nodded at that. It seemed reasonable. "Why didn't you just ask someone who I was?"

"I had to see for myself—and to see what kind of person you are. I don't need someone else's opinion of you. I want to form my own."

"And?"

"And, what?"

"What did you decide?"

"Does it matter?"

Jimmy thought about it. Shaking his head, he said, "No, I don't suppose it does."

They continued to look at each other.

"Are they treating you all right?"

Once again, Jimmy's eyes went momentarily wide before they shuttered. He narrowed his eyes at Travis. "Why'd you ask?"

"I'm not sure I like the circumstances that landed you here, that's all."

"I can't say I've enjoyed it here." He shrugged after rolling the words around in his head. "It's been getting better."

"You mean, you've grown so they've finally left you alone." Travis gave it a moment. "You and Charlie are quite a bit bigger than the rest of them, in case you haven't noticed."

Jimmy gave a half-smile. "Best day ever when Charlie was noticeably bigger than them all." They both smiled at that.

"Why are you asking all these questions? It's more than knowing who you're with." He dipped his head toward Travis.

"I'm thinking I have to talk to you and Charlie about something important—real soon. I have to do it before Charlie negotiates with the sheriff to get Annabelle back."

"What's it have to do with her?"

"It's not so much her but the window of time involving the trade that's important. Although I'm thinking that Annabelle's more important to Charlie than he'd like to let on. Am I right?" He cocked his head at Jimmy.

Jimmy was weighing how sincere Travis was. He finally nodded. "He likes her, a lot. I'm not sure if he realizes how much. At least, he didn't before. I'm thinking Annabelle's pretty sweet on him, too."

"Guessing by what I saw yesterday, I'm pretty sure they feel something toward each other." He chuckled at that, causing Jimmy's hackles to rise, his shoulders to bunch up, and his hands to curl into fists. "No need to get your dander up." Travis put his hand on Jimmy's shoulder, straightening his arm. "I caught them kissing, that's all."

Jimmy shoulders relaxed, and his face took on a slight tinge. "I suppose it's about time. They've been making moon eyes at each other since he brought her here."

"I don't doubt it, Jimmy. They're a handsome couple, and they're of age."

Jimmy just shrugged at that. While he was forced to grow up early, he was still young in the ways of women.

"How about we find Charlie and Annabelle and have a little talk with them?"

Annabelle's scheduled washing day was today. Charlie went down to the river with her and helped carry a load of laundry wrapped in a sheet. Annabelle had the soap in her hand, and a brush. The washboard was already there. When they got to the bottom of the hill, however, Jimmy and Travis were waiting for them. Charlie pushed Annabelle behind him and called out to Jimmy.

"Jimmy, what's going on?"

"Travis here needs to tell us some things. I think we should at least listen to what he has to say."

"What could he possibly have to say to us?"

"Damn it Charlie, ask the man. He's standing right here."

Travis chuckled at that and pushed off the tree he was leaning against.

"We need to talk about the trade and what you're planning to do about it." Charlie eyed him, unwilling to talk about it with anyone. Seeing that Charlie was a harder sell than Jimmy, Travis tried a different tack. "I have information about your parents."

Charlie and Jimmy exchanged looks.

Jimmy interjected. "They're dead."

"I know."

"What could you possibility tell us that'd make any difference?" This time Charlie responded.

"Your father had a hit put out on him."

The brothers looked at each other, stunned. Charlie was the one who spoke up. "Dad was a banker. Did someone want his money? We have older brothers who would inherit—that doesn't make sense."

"Your dad was blackmailing some powerful men." He waited for that to sink in before continuing. "It was a kind of side business, if you like."

"I don't like. Our dad wasn't a criminal!" Jimmy was starting to close up again.

"Jimmy, I'm only sharing this with you because I can't tell you everything I know about what's going on. Not right at this moment. Soon, I promise you. I'm telling you because you need to leave this gang, and that has to happen when Annabelle is traded or before."

"I'm not leaving."

Everyone went silent at Jimmy's admission. Charlie's mouth dropped open, and Annabelle looked at the ground. That's when Travis realized that Annabelle knew more than she was willing to share.

"What's going on?" Travis looked around at the three of them.

"I'm done here." Jimmy stalked away while giving Annabelle a pointed look that left her mighty uncomfortable. Charlie turned to her.

"What's that all about?"

Annabelle went a little wide-eyed, not wanting to answer. "I—you should probably talk to Jimmy about it."

"No, I'm asking you. You know something. What's Jimmy said to you? What did you say to Jimmy?"

Annabelle's hand flew to her chest. "Charlie, I didn't say anything to him. I listened to him. You should try that on for size."

"What's that supposed to mean?"

"It means, he clearly doesn't want to leave for reasons of his own. Why don't you ask him yourself if you want to know so badly?" Her mouth quirked up on one side, eyes widening in an *I dare you* look.

"He's told you something, and I think you should tell me, Annabelle."

She remembered Jimmy begging her to persuade Charlie to leave him behind, but she couldn't help pushing at Charlie and his self-righteous attitude. Sometimes, he was no better than her father, or that deputy. "Really? Would you listen to me if I told you?"

"Annabelle!"

"Fine. You'd best listen, Charlie."

Travis watched this exchange with great interest. They were like an old couple, the way they bantered. He didn't think she'd been with the gang for that long. Shrugging, he continued to watch them, fascinated.

"He thinks that the best way to bring down the gang is from the *inside*. He knows that you've been doing everything you can to try to protect him and that you are probably planning another escape. He doesn't want to be a part of it."

"Why?"

"Charlie, listen! He thinks he can do better on the *inside*. He said that you'll just go to the authorities when you break free, and they won't be able to do anything."

Charlie digested that, but then he said, "If we leave, then they'll harm Jimmy. It's what they've always done and threatened to do."

Travis interrupted. "No, I think they'll see that Jimmy has decided to throw in with them. They're overconfident that way. Besides, Jimmy's still young in many ways, and maybe they'll think he's afraid of what's out there. Better the devil you know, kind of thing. He's grown to be a man here, and they'll be arrogant enough to think they've shaped him, especially since he's so quiet and hasn't been proven otherwise. Lazy bastards will want to keep him for the horses' sake, anyway."

They looked at Travis, then each other. Finally, Annabelle spoke.

Placing her hand on Charlie's arm, she said, "Charlie, Jimmy feels bad about all the things you've been through for his sake." She held up her other hand to stop his interruption. "He really needs to do this for himself. It's his rite of passage, so to speak. I think he's felt very cut down by the gang and is tired of feeling helpless. He loves you, but he has to do this for himself." She waited for that to sink in. "You can't do everything for him all the time."

The air went out of Charlie, and his shoulders sagged. Annabelle wrapped her arms around him, holding him with a slight swaying motion. "He loves you dearly, but all the guilt and pain he's carrying…"

"Why didn't he say anything to me?"

"Would you have listened before?"

Charlie didn't respond. Annabelle continued to hold him.

Travis interrupted after a minute. He put a hand on each of their shoulders. "We need to talk strategy. Soon, the messenger'll be back from the sheriff and Van Der Kamp will have Charlie making arrangements. You don't have much time."

Charlie's hold on Annabelle tightened when he looked at Travis. "Why're you doing all this, anyway? I'm not sure why Jimmy went along with you to begin with. What'd you say to him to make him cooperate?"

"I didn't say anything. I'm sure he has a feeling that I'm on your side." He paused before adding, "He'll make a good lawman someday."

Charlie and Annabelle just stared at him as if he'd sprouted horns.

"Jimmy is still waters run deep. He has a knowing from all the watching he does. It'll work in his favor—it already has."

"Then humor *me* and tell me why? What's going on?"

Travis looked around and leaned in. "I'm a federal agent. I've infiltrated for a variety of reasons, but Van Der Kamp is one of them. I'm here to handle both of your cases, as well. But this all extends further than I can safely explain. It's better that you just trust me, and wait for better timing to hear it all. You didn't handle your father's news very well." He cocked a brow at them.

"Coming from a supposed bandit and criminal, no, I didn't. Why should I?"

"Fair enough. Trust me with this, however. You don't want to risk Annabelle, do you?"

Charlie pulled back to look down at Annabelle, and his whole demeanor changed. His face softened, and his body relaxed. He put a hand out and cupped her face. His thumb caressed her cheek. "No, I don't. I promised to get her home safely to her daddy." He turned back to Travis. "What do you have in mind?"

"Jimmy just mentioned you're planning an escape?"

"Yes, I've been planning it for a while. I don't have the details worked out, and now it'll be harder because Jimmy won't be around to help."

Annabelle chimed in. "I'm sure he'll help you with whatever you need. He just wants to finish business here, on his own terms."

"And I can help him with whatever he needs—from the inside. Don't worry about that. Focus on Annabelle."

Charlie looked between Annabelle and Travis—between concern and earnestness—and gave a curt nod. They breathed a collective sigh of relief. Charlie went into great detail about a back trail that he'd found, running from one of the abandoned mines that never produced. It was on the steep side of the protective hill they were ensconced in, and no one from below could easily get to it, especially since they couldn't see it. No one from the camp paid attention to it because the area around the mine had caved in. It was too dangerous to be bothered with, which was perfect for them. Charlie had scoped it out when he was supposed to be helping Jimmy with the horses, before Annabelle even came. He started investigating with more vigor after she arrived.

They decided when and how Charlie would smuggle Annabelle out while Jimmy and Goat would keep Wrighty occupied. Goat wouldn't know what was going on, and if he asked, they'd have Jimmy tell him that Charlie and Annabelle needed some privacy. He wouldn't ask any more questions after that. He'd been pretty delicate about the pair since he got an eyeful of Annabelle bathing. While Charlie didn't like the fact that another man saw her in a state of undress, he did think it was funny that it discombobulated Goat so much. Especially since he'd been pushing for Charlie to "lay claim" to Annabelle.

Van Der Kamp called Charlie to his cabin a day later, shortly before dinner. Charlie figured it was about the negotiations but wasn't sure. Jaems had come down to the river, telling him he was summoned, and that was it. He walked a brisk pace up the hill to Van Der Kamp's cabin and knocked firmly on the door.

"Come in."

Van Der Kamp was situated like usual—legs up on the table, leaning back in his chair. He seemed to position himself in this casual pose to disarm his visitors. Charlie wasn't fooled by it; he knew Van Der Kamp better than that. Additionally, he had a certain amount of respect for the man. He didn't abuse his power like Wrighty did. Van Der Kamp had always been fair to them, as fair as a gang leader could be, he supposed.

"Jaems said you wanted to see me, sir."

"Take a seat." He untwined his long legs and pulled them off the table, leaning on his forearms instead. He looked at Charlie intently.

"The messenger's come back. The sheriff will meet you at the edge of town two days from now, at noon." He watched Charlie for a reaction. He didn't give one, so he continued. "He can have Annabelle back, but you'll need to find out what he's willing to give for her. I'm not sure he has much. These are the amounts and forms I'd accept as an exchange." He slipped Charlie a piece of paper that Charlie picked up and read. He looked at it for a long while, astonishment clear on his face, before he looked back up and nodded. "If he can't do any of those—you can press him first—then we'll take a two-day head start. We hand her over, and we get two days where they don't follow us. They can track us on the third."

"What if he doesn't agree?"

"Oh, he will. He's attached to his sweet Annabelle. She's all he has." He looked hard at Charlie. "He'll do anything to protect her, always has." He leaned back again, but didn't put his feet on the table. He watched Charlie with hawk-like eyes.

"Do I ride by myself?"

"Yup. Straight there and straight back. Leave after breakfast, and you'll get there a little before noon. Don't want to keep the sheriff waiting and all. That'd be rude." With that he got up and went to the kitchen to pour himself some coffee. Charlie stood and waited to see if he'd say anything else.

Van Der Kamp didn't say anything else; neither did he turn around. Charlie finally said, "Thank you. I won't let you down."

"I know you won't, son. I'm counting on it."

With that, Charlie left the cabin feeling a little more unsettled. He hurried to find Annabelle, not only to settle his discomfort, but to make sure everything was okay with her. Something about this felt wrong, and he couldn't place why.

Annabelle was making supper with Goat when Charlie rushed into the main meeting area. Their heads whipped back at him and then swiveled, looking around to see what he was running from.

"Is everything okay, Charlie?" and "What set your pants on fire?" Annabelle and Goat asked at the same time, casting worried looks at Charlie and then at each other, surprised.

Charlie was breathing hard from exertion and anxiety. He couldn't explain the pressure in his chest or the uneasiness he was feeling. The palm of his hand actually went to his chest because he was sure that his heart was going to jump out of it. He dropped onto the bench and slumped over his legs, elbows on knees. Annabelle rushed to his side, wrapped one arm around him as far as she could reach and placed her other hand on his forearm. She squeezed his shoulder and rubbed his arm while he caught his breath.

"Charlie." Annabelle said sternly, trying to shake him out of his fog. She shook his shoulder as best she could for good measure. "What is going on?" His normally even-keeled nature was shaken, and his anxiety was palpable.

Goat stood there watching them. He'd never seen Charlie so out of sorts before. The only other time was when he threw Annabelle over his shoulder—and that he could understand.

The wolves were closing in on his desert hen. This was something altogether different.

Charlie faced Annabelle, looking as if he was seeing her for the first time. He put his hand on the side of her cheek, and his eyes roamed over her face. Grabbing his hand, she said, "Charlie, talk. You're starting to scare me—even more than Wrighty does."

Mention of Wrighty snapped him out of his panic and confusion. "What do you mean about Wrighty scaring you?" He barked at her.

Annabelle jerked away from him. His demeanor changed so quickly even Goat moved protectively closer toward Annabelle, ready to guard her.

"We're talking about you, not Wrighty. What's got you so bothered?"

"Not now, Wildflower. Wrighty first."

"Charlie, it's not important." Her voice held a tinge of desperation to it, but they all knew how important it was because she started to shake ever so slightly, and a sheen broke out around her hairline as well as between her nose and lip.

Charlie grabbed her before she realized what was happening, making her squeak. He drew out his words long and low. "What did he do to you?"

"Why—I—nothing. Nothing, Charlie. You're making something out of nothing." Annabelle didn't realize it, but she was wildly looking around herself for an escape path. It didn't pass unnoticed by Charlie and Goat.

"Wildflower." He said her nickname low and soft, gentling her like he would a skittish colt. Meanwhile, Goat moved in on her from the other side. Charlie bent forward and continued coaxing her. "Talk to me, darling. I know something happened. You can tell me. You're safe with me and Goat here. We won't let anything happen to you. Neither will Van Der Kamp or Jimmy."

"I…he…he just scares me a little, that's all." She tried brushing them off but still had a wild look in her eyes.

Charlie looked over at Goat, who shook his head, anger flashing in his eyes. They were already guessing what Wrighty did to her.

"Honey, you changed after your days in the tent. You stayed there for a few days because you were supposedly under the weather, but you didn't act the same after that, either. What did he do to you?"

"It's nothing like that! Nothing happened. Nothing happened." Annabelle started to thrash, but both Charlie and Goat had a good grip on her.

"Take a deep breath, darling. Breathe—in through your nose and out your mouth. Breathe." Goat was rubbing her back, and Charlie held her gaze and her hands. "Talk to me, Wildflower. You can't tell me anything that'll make me mad at you. I'll protect you. I love you, darling."

Goat's eyebrows rose with Charlie's confession, but he didn't seem to realize that he'd made it. Annabelle did, and she burst into tears. He pulled her into his arms as she sobbed, rocking her. Goat sat behind her on the bench, looking back at Charlie with wide eyes. They waited for her tears to subside before trying, again. This time Goat spoke up.

"Annabelle, girl, you have to tell us what he did. Van Der Kamp said you weren't to be touched or bothered—that means if Wrighty did something, he broke Van's law. *Never a good idea.* Van Der Kamp won't be pleased to hear this." She looked about to protest again, but he talked over her, pointing a finger in the air. "If he finds out you've been hiding something, you'll be in a heap of trouble, too."

The hysterical look on her face returned, and she tried to bolt, but Charlie held her firm. "You have to tell us now. Wrighty's been getting worse and even more unpredictable."

"Charlie's right. He even challenged Travis, which is not good."

Annabelle's chest was heaving, and she was sniffling, but she nodded, coming down from her hysterical crying. When she finally caught her breath, she whispered, "He said he'd get me if I told. I was too scared to tell, and I wasn't sure if anyone would do anything, anyway."

Charlie's face fell, and he looked crushed. Annabelle quickly added, "That was just in the beginning. I know better now. I do. Then he tried to poison you—there was too much to worry about." Her eyes pleaded for Charlie to believe her. He leaned in and kissed her softly on the forehead, smoothing wispy curls away from her face. His hand remained on the back of her head, steadying her.

"Go on." Goat urged her.

"I—he—he tried to force himself on me—" Charlie tensed up and jerked as if he was going to fly out of there to find Wrighty, but Annabelle grabbed his arm, hard. "Moris stopped him. He came running in and said that Van Der Kamp was coming, but he never did." She hung her head, and Charlie stroked her hair. "He took off his belt, and he whipped my exposed leg with it. He…" she blushed so hard she looked ready to combust "…he was trying to lift my skirts, and I was trying to scoot away from him. My leg was exposed, and the belt came down on it—a couple of times." She started crying again, heaving sobs that wrenched at Charlie's heart. Sobs that made his gut churn with anger and upset, both at Wrighty for what he did and at himself for leaving her unprotected.

Charlie clenched his teeth, trying to be patient, but it was hard. He wanted to pummel Wrighty more than anything. She continued, the words coming in between her stuttered breaths. "He said if I told anyone he'd do worse to me. Then he told me he'd be back to finish what he started." Her hands flew to her face, covering them from shame and embarrassment. The sobs wracked her entire body as Charlie pulled her into his lap, cradling her.

Goat looked right at Charlie and said, "I know, I feel the same way. But don't do it. Not now."

"I'll get him. He won't get away with this." He leaned his body protectively over hers and let her cry it out. When she finally had let loose the tears that had been hiding all these weeks, she sat up and finished her story.

"That's why I stayed in the tent. Not because of, well, you know…he cut open my leg and bruised the bone. I couldn't walk. Moris had to take care of me, otherwise I'd have to explain what happened and then…"

"He won't get you. I've got you. We're all looking out for you. I'm sorry you had to suffer through this alone, Wildflower. Never again. Never."

He gently stood up with her still cradled in his arms. He looked down at Goat, who was still seated. "I'm taking Annabelle back to the tent. She needs a little rest. Can you handle the rest of supper?"

Goat waved his hand at them. "Go on, git. I'll be fine. Whaddya think I did before y'all came?"

Annabelle gave him a watery smile before burrowing her head into Charlie's chest and wrapping her arms around his neck. Goat watched Charlie carry her away. "This is gonna git interesting, real interesting," he said aloud to no one in particular. He hobbled off to finish preparing for supper. There really wasn't much left to do.

He made a mental note to ask Charlie later what he was in such a lather about.

Annabelle was exhausted from crying and the release of emotions she'd been holding close to her vest for so long. She was still afraid of Wrighty, but both Charlie and Goat took what she said to heart, all things considered. At least she didn't get blamed for doing something wrong. She was usually the culprit. Once the panic subsided, she snuggled closer to Charlie, thinking about how angry Charlie was for her, the way he held and soothed her, and what he said. *He loved her.* Smiling, she felt warm all over, and it smoothed away some of fear's sharp edge. She knew that, no matter what happened, she could count on Charlie. Whether she should or not was the question. Loving how she always felt safe around him and that he birthed new and wonderful feelings within her chased the thought away—things were always better with Charlie. They made a good team. With her mind made up and her exhausted body relaxing, she fell into a deep sleep.

Charlie laid her gently on the cot and slid in beside her. He held her until she fell asleep, which was pretty quick. He stroked her hair while he watched the rhythmic rise and fall of her chest. Occasionally, she'd suck in a stuttered breath. How could someone beat a woman like that? He'd seen some of the gang be overly rough with a few of the painted ladies, but to beat them—as far as he knew, none of them did. None of them were that low. Van Der Kamp didn't go for that kind of violence, either. All he knew was that Annabelle needed to leave, the sooner the better. He was glad they were in agreement about the escape plan. However, he still needed to talk to

Travis about how he was going to help Jimmy and make sure Jimmy was on board with this. He didn't want to leave him behind—maybe he could return for him. They'd have to work that out, and quick. While Van Der Kamp had always been fair to him and Jimmy, he didn't trust his tone this afternoon. Something was up his sleeve, and he didn't have a good feeling about it. Maybe he should tell Van Der Kamp that he wanted to keep Annabelle, and he wouldn't negotiate for her return. Maybe he'd tell him that she didn't want to go back. He'd have to talk to Travis and Jimmy about what happened. It'd have to wait until he could find a safe place to put Annabelle, because there was no way in Hell he was leaving her alone for a minute.

✑~31~✑

Annabelle woke up feeling heavy-headed and disoriented. It took her a minute to remember what happened. When she did, it threw her into a momentary panic before she realized that it was all going to be over soon. Charlie was going to help her escape, and she'd get to go home. But then what? Papa wasn't going to welcome Charlie with open arms, especially when he'd practically begged her to take Jake into consideration. *Hi, Papa. This here's Charlie—you know, the man who snatched me from the mercantile? Yes, we love each other.* That'd go over like a rock in the grist—difficult and potentially harmful to the mill. If it made it past the mill, it'd be like bits of that rock remaining in the flour while trying to bake—gritty and distasteful. *Even if Papa does welcome him, what would we do? Charlie's been in a gang for the past five or so years. We aren't promised to each other, and he isn't exactly courting me, either. How could he be?* She mentally smacked herself on the forehead. *Charlie made things feel normal when they were anything but normal. We've been playing house, just like Wrighty accused us of doing. Although he did tell me he loved me.* Her face broke into a smile that shot warmth and happiness into her entire body. *Was that just panic and stress making him talk, or does he really love me?* Before she got carried away, she tapped her finger to her mouth and mulled that one over.

The idea of his love made her warm all over, but she thought about her papa, again. Love had made him weak. Something died in him the day her mama disappeared. She was too young to remember much, but that's what everyone seemed to say. Maybe she was just being selfish because she had Papa all to herself. She did catch him looking sad on occasion when he thought she wasn't paying attention, and she thought he was probably lonely with just her and a deputy for any real company. The Johanssons were friends of his, but they were more like kindly relations than friends.

Then there was the issue of being forced to marry—she'd have to give up her freedom and independence. That wasn't something she was really willing to do. Depending on another man would just make her weak, even if it was someone strong and handsome like Charlie. Someone who was willing to drop everything to help her out and protect her from even herself. Would she just be trading one man for another when she married? That's what it felt like when Papa talked to her about it. She wasn't so sure she wanted that. She had her papa, if that's the way it had to be.

Darn it, now she was confused. All she wanted was to go back home and see Papa, but now she had Charlie. She loved being with him and looked forward to spending time with him. She didn't really want to stay here, although she had things she was responsible for and the men mostly respected her—excluding Wrighty, that is.

Then there was handsome, brave Charlie who made her feel things that she wanted to feel more of. He made her feel safe, protected, and loved in ways that Papa couldn't. Perhaps that was what Papa was trying to tell her when he talked about marriage. Maybe that made her weak. She craved those feelings. Tapping her upper lip again, she *hmm*'d to herself. She hadn't considered that yet. She rebelled against Papa because he was doing many of the same things Charlie was doing here—why was it so different?

Before she could delve into that, the tent flap opened, and she heard Jimmy and Charlie talking.

"Oh, you're up. I'm glad. Jimmy brought you food."

Annabelle sat up. "Thank you. How long have I been asleep?"

"Couple of hours."

"What?"

"You were exhausted. You had a long afternoon. Goat took care of everything. Even sent Jimmy with food for both of us." Her eyes opened wide at that. "I told you I wasn't going to leave you alone, and I meant it."

Jimmy looked between the two of them but didn't say anything. They sat side by side on the cot, eating peacefully. Jimmy went out to get them water and returned with two filled tin cans. He handed them over before sitting back down on his own cot. Looking at Charlie, he raised his brows. Charlie wiped his mouth before speaking.

"Annabelle, we need to move the escape up a day. I've already explained things to Jimmy, and he agrees. If we need it, he'll be ready to cause a diversion so we can get down the backside of the old mining hill without any notice. We'll walk one mount out, mine. It'll be quicker that way."

She looked between them but couldn't get a good read. "What about you, Jimmy? You still good with this?"

He nodded, but Annabelle held his eyes until he answered with words. "I told you before, this is just something I have to do on my own. Travis is going to help me from the inside."

"How do you know he's who he says he is? I mean, he seems like a lawman all right, but why did Van Der Kamp just let a man like that into his gang? He had to know."

"Van Der Kamp has a lot of things up his sleeve. He doesn't let anybody know everything. Keeps us all on our toes and following *his* law. It also keeps us safe, in a strange sort of way."

"Wildflower, like Jimmy said, Van Der Kamp has something up his sleeve—I could feel it today."

"Is that why you were so panicked?"

"Yes." Charlie ran his hand through his hair. "He knows things we don't know, and I need to get you out of here before something really bad happens." He smoothed her hair. "You've suffered enough."

"Don't worry, I have a good feeling about Travis. Besides, anyone who comes back from the trail and kicks Wrighty's ass for looking crossways at you is my kind of guy." Jimmy blushed, looking down at his lap after saying that.

Annabelle reached out and put a hand over his. "You're a good man, Jimmy. Don't you ever forget that." He nodded his head without meeting her eyes.

Charlie knew that Jimmy felt uncomfortable with displays of affection, so he interrupted them. "Jimmy's going to stay with you right now. After we finish eating, I'll take the plates back down and go talk to Van Der Kamp. I'm not sure what I'll tell him, but maybe I'll get him to let me keep you or something. Then, we can sneak off during the night tomorrow. If it's money he wants, I've earned him more in that robbery than he's asking for—maybe I can convince him I'll rob again."

Neither Annabelle or Jimmy looked comfortable with that idea, but they didn't say anything. Once Charlie made up his mind, there was no changing it. They exchanged looks when he got up to leave.

Once he left, Annabelle said, "I don't like the sound of that. He might give an accidental hint to Van Der Kamp, he's canny that way. It could be dangerous for him."

"I know. I'm not sure what to do with that."

Annabelle thought about it for a moment and decided. "I do. I'm going to tell him to negotiate. That I won't run away with him."

Jimmy's face dropped at that. "You're going to trust a bunch of bandits to bargain your way home? Are you serious? Charlie's escape plan sounds more solid than that!"

"No, it doesn't. The only person we really have to worry about is Wrighty. He's the one no one trusts, not even his cronies."

"I don't like it, Annabelle. Not at all. Charlie's going to have a fit."

"So you get to say what you're doing and stand up to Charlie, but I don't?"

"Charlie's looking out for your best interests."

"And he isn't with you?"

"You got me there, but our stories are different. You have people to go home to. I don't."

"You don't have *any* family?"

Jimmy shook his head. "We were going to see an older brother, Joseph, but Charlie and I don't know anything about him. They never said anything. Something to do with business. His mother was our father's first wife, who died. He remarried our mom and had three boys—Charlie, me, and Chester. Chester drowned when he was five."

"Oh, Jimmy!"

"Yeah, Charlie holds that against himself, too."

"Poor Charlie."

They sat in silence for a while, thinking about their sad situation, when Annabelle finally perked up. "Do you think that Travis knows anything about your older half brother?"

Jimmy's eyes lit up. "I don't know. I hadn't thought about him for a long time. I'd been cursing him like a prayer for bringing us out this way."

"You'll have to ask. You might learn something important."

Even though their conversation took a turn away from why their stories were different where Charlie was concerned, Annabelle didn't forget. It made her all the more determined not to leave with Charlie and to insist on the barter. Why men got away with things that women didn't was beyond her. But if Jimmy was able to get his way, then she would, too.

Charlie knocked on Van Der Kamp's door and was surprised when he called out, "Come in, Charlie."

When Charlie walked in, Van Der Kamp was seated in a chair away from the table, smoking. He motioned for Charlie to join him. Walking over, he sat in the chair Van Der Kamp pointed at. Leaning back, he watched Charlie's hands clenching and unclenching and the nervous jiggle of his leg.

"What's on your mind? Is your sweet Annabelle feeling better? Goat said she was a little under the weather." He took a long drag on his cigarillo, waiting for Charlie to respond.

"She's feeling better, thanks. She was a little overworked this afternoon." They continued to stare at each other. Van Der Kamp's face held a small glimmer of humor as he watched Charlie sweat it out. "About Annabelle—"

"Yes, we didn't get much of an opportunity to discuss her, did we."

"No, sir. I was hoping that I could keep her, not do a trade. She's very helpful around here, and I did bring in a lot from my haul…"

Van Der Kamp straightened out and leaned forward. He made pointing motions with his fingers holding the cigarillo. "You see, Charlie, Annabelle is part of something bigger that she has no idea about. She has to go back."

In general, Charlie was adept at keeping a neutral expression, but since Annabelle's arrival, his emotions had been too plain to see. Charlie was the only one who couldn't see that he was wearing his heart on his sleeve. His face fell at Van Der Kamp's words.

"I—"

"Son, listen to me. Listen real good. I know you've fallen for her. She's your first, and they're always special. But she has to go back. We didn't end up here by happenstance. No. We were hired to come here and get the sheriff to cooperate with the man who hired us—his daddy."

It took a moment for Charlie to process what Van Der Kamp was saying. "Annabelle's grandfather hired you?"

Van Der Kamp nodded. Now that he had Charlie's rapt attention, he leaned back and took a long drag and leisurely blew out the smoke from his upturned face. "Neither of them know and, for now, we need to keep it that way. Mack Pennington has plans for his son, and he thinks he's hired us to help see them through—that's debatable in my mind, and it's a long story you don't need to hear. But know, we can't keep her— Mack will want to use her against the sheriff, and I won't have that." He looked lost in thought for a moment before adding, "It was an interesting turn of events that put the two of you together." He chuckled, flicking the ashes to the floor.

Charlie's mind was galloping—he'd had no idea, but neither did Annabelle. He loved her, but now he had to let her go—and he wasn't ready to do that. Despite his promises, he didn't think he'd ever be ready to let her go. He thought he'd forgotten how to truly laugh and smile until she came, even with her exasperating ways and her mulish persistence. His face hurt thinking about all the times she made him laugh and smile, even when he was trying hard not to. He was smiling right now, despite himself.

Van Der Kamp shook his head, looking ruefully at Charlie. "I can hear you thinking—you have to let her go. It's for the best. Mack's a dangerous man, and he doesn't suffer fools or plans going awry, if you catch my meaning." He quirked a brow at Charlie. Charlie could only nod in response. "Annabelle's a special girl, I'll give you that. I like you, Charlie, and I wish it were different, but it's not. In any other situation, I'd give you my blessing, but here and now? You have to do the right thing by her. Mack has no problems killing either of you. He's still mad because his son became sheriff and didn't continue running the mine. And that was nearly a score ago."

Charlie was about to ask a question, but Van Der Kamp raised his hand. "I don't know the details, and I don't care. The sheriff is a good man, for all intents and purposes—despite what the rest of the gang thinks. Those lies are on Wrighty. I have no beef with the sheriff. He'll do what he says he will. Negotiate with him, and Annabelle will be safe. If you love her like I think you do, then negotiate well—make sure she gets home to her daddy and don't piss anyone off while doing it."

Charlie swallowed hard. He swallowed his pride, his fear, and his love before giving Van Der Kamp the affirmative.

"Well, you best go on and say your goodbyes. You don't have much time."

With that, Charlie was dismissed, and his hopes and dreams dashed. Walking down the path, he realized that it was the first time in a long time that he'd allowed himself to hope, to feel light, and to feel like he was basking in something good. All for nothing now.

~ **32** ~

Charlie walked slowly back to the tent, dreading every step of the way. He wanted to hold Annabelle in his arms, but he didn't want to make the immediate decision that needed to be made. Either way, he broke with everything he held true—protection, promises, and keeping his word. Even if it were to a criminal, that criminal seemed to be looking out for him and Annabelle. He could beg Annabelle to leave with him, but that'd make matters worse for everyone if they were caught, Jimmy included, despite what Travis said. He also ran the risk of raising Mack Pennington's ire, even though they were unknown to each other. He didn't doubt Van Der Kamp on that account. No matter what, Annabelle's safety came first. He let out a huge sigh, throwing his head back, looking skyward, as if the stars could tell him what to do. His arms hung as limp as his hope.

When he reached the tent, Annabelle seemed to be sitting in the same spot he'd left her. He looked between Jimmy and Annabelle, both looking about as glum as he felt. Since they didn't say anything, he got right to the point.

"Van Der Kamp said no. I have to negotiate with your daddy, Annabelle. I've been thinking—" he ran his hand through his hair, looking between the two people he loved the most in the world, "we should just run, tonight. Van Der Kamp is saying the same things Travis is saying about everything being bigger than we know. No one's sharing any information, and I'll be damned if they put you in any danger."

His statement was met with silence. Annabelle's lips were pressed together, and Jimmy wouldn't make eye contact.

"What's going on?" When Annabelle wouldn't say anything, he looked at Jimmy. "Talk to me—we don't have much time." Jimmy had the same pain in his eyes the night he said he didn't want to run when they were kids.

Annabelle cleared her throat. "Charlie." She reached for his hand, holding it between hers. "I'm not running with you. It won't work. You need to negotiate with Papa. He'll be fair."

Charlie's face fell, and his mouth wouldn't cooperate. He stared at her in disbelief. Shaking his head, he said, "That's what Van Der Kamp said—the sheriff'd be fair. This whole situation isn't fair, damn it. Wildflower, honey—"

"Charlie, no. We know nothing about nothing." Her sniffling started up as she dabbed her eyes with the handkerchief he'd loaned her the first day in camp. "You've done so much for me. I don't want you to get hurt." Her crying was really kicking in, now. "Besides—what's out there for us when you return me to my father? What are we going to do? I want freedom."

"I don't want to control you, I want to protect—" Charlie cleared his throat. He changed his wording, "I want to provide you with protection—I thought you understood."

"Charlie, I don't think you understand—I don't want to go from one gilded cage to another."

"Annabelle, you can't roam free here, 'cuz it's dangerous. I can't rightly say how I'd operate out there," he made a broad sweep of his arm. "I don't know what's out there. But I *promise* I'll always protect you and keep you safe. That's important to me—I care for you. Hell, Wildflower, I love you."

Annabelle's weeping grew until it became sobs. Covering her face with her hands and bending over her lap, her body shook with her weeping. Charlie sat down next to her, rubbing her back to soothe her. Slowly, she started to quiet down. When she could finally talk without choking, she took Charlie's face in her hands.

"Charlie, I love you, too. But after watching my father pine for my missing mother, I don't know that love is enough. I refuse to be tied down with that lie. You're a good man, and you always do the right thing." She swallowed hard, cocking her head to the side. "Do you know why I was at the mercantile, alone, that day?"

Charlie looked a little confused by that question but shook his head.

"I was there getting supplies. I was going to store up things, bit by bit, and then run off to my aunt's. I wanted to get away from Papa telling me what to do, and the deputy pushing himself on me."

Mention of anyone pushing themselves on her got Charlie's dander up, but she put her hand on his. "He wanted to court me, and I don't like him. There's something—off, yes, off about him. Something's not right. I don't want to get married. I want *freedom*. Most men don't understand that—freedom. Charlie, I know you want it, too." She was leaning toward him in her excitement, grasping his hand and nodding her head.

"Shoot, Annabelle. What'm I supposed to say?"

"That you'll negotiate. It's the right thing to do."

He held her gaze, hoping she'd change her mind, but she didn't. Hanging his head, he continued holding her hand. When he looked up, Jimmy was watching him from the depths of his being.

Jimmy inhaled deeply through his nose and pursed his lips. "I tried to talk her out of it. She's not having it."

Charlie could only nod at his brother, who also wouldn't escape with him. All he wanted to do was provide and protect, but no one was willing to go along with him. He couldn't very well leave these two, but he didn't feel as if he had a place here, either. He was as stuck as he was before he talked to anyone. It didn't make any sense to him, but he supposed he didn't have much of a choice. No one was willing to budge or hear him out. Tomorrow, he was riding out for the edge of town and negotiating with the sheriff.

"Well, we better get some shut-eye. I've got to ride out in the morning and figure out what I'm going to say to your daddy."

"Charlie—"

"It's all right, Wildflower." Charlie cleared his throat and brushed his hand over his mouth, covering for the emotion that was itching to bust out. "I'll get you some water to wash up. I'll be back."

In a rush to escape, Charlie walked fast toward the long path to the cistern but returned as slowly as he could. He couldn't face either of them right now. Somehow, he felt like he'd let them down even though he was trying his damnedest to help them in every way possible.

❧ **33** ☙

Charlie didn't sleep a wink that night. He spent it watching Annabelle toss and turn, knowing that soon, they'd be apart. He wanted to memorize her so he had something to tuck away and keep. She didn't look very rested come sunrise, either. After taking care of their morning necessities, he walked her down to the cooking area and left her with Goat.

"I have some things to take care of before I leave. I'm leaving before everyone comes for breakfast. I don't want to make your daddy wait. I'm sure he's anxious to hear how you're doing." His voice was flat, and he wouldn't look directly at her.

Annabelle's lips were turned down, and her eyes had a mournful look to them. She nodded but didn't say anything. Goat looked between them but snorted in disgust, returning to the bacon he had spread out on the griddle. Charlie and Annabelle stared at each other, but neither was willing to say how they really felt. Annabelle wasn't willing to compromise, and Charlie felt like he'd given all that he could—leaving them with what they thought was nothing to say. Charlie pivoted, taking extra long strides away from a scene that used to bring him comfort. Annabelle slowly turned away from his retreating back.

Goat was adding eggs to the already sizzling bacon. He didn't bother turning around. "Don't bother explaining yerself. I'm pretty sure I can guess what's going on."

Annabelle sullenly brought over tin plates and stacked them on the table, then plopped herself on the bench. Her head sunk into her hands, propped up by her elbows. It was a pathetic sight. Goat could feel it happening behind him, so he turned around and pointed his spatula at her.

"Girl, I don't know what you've done and gone, but you've gone and done it this time." He whirled back to his skillet, flipping eggs and checking the bacon.

"You don't understand the situation, Goat. I—"

"*You* don't understand the situation, girl. Now, I like you, and I like Charlie. He's a stand-up fella. He dotes on you. Say no more. He'd make it work because that's just the way Charlie is."

"Goat—"

"You just hush. Make yourself useful and git some coffee brewing. Them others will be here soon, surly as all git-out if you don't have some o' that brew a-goin'."

Dejected and shamed, she trudged over to the cistern for water and back to the potbelly to make coffee. This was going to be a long, long day.

Jimmy had beat Charlie to the stables and was saddling up his horse. Charlie quirked his brow at him.

"Can't wait to rid yourself of me?"

"Nothing like that and you know it, too."

"Do I? I'm not so sure, anymore. You and Annabelle sure seem to be sharing a lot of opinions these days."

"What's that supposed to mean?"

"It means you and Annabelle have secrets. I could tell when I walked in something was going on. You're shutting me out."

Jimmy's arms dropped to his sides. "Charlie, for once, just listen."

"What the hell, Jimmy."

Jimmy widened his eyes with a look of *you're proving my point*. He looked at Charlie until he conceded.

"Fine. Go ahead. I'm *listening*."

"She's just scared, Charlie." He stopped and gave him a stern look. "Don't go giving me that protection spiel, either. Your protection can border on bossy. Annabelle says that men get away with everything, and women aren't allowed to do anything. She seems to think you'll do the same thing to her even though deep down she knows you're different. She's running away because she's never been allowed to do much of anything else. It's what she does best. You can understand that, can't you?"

Charlie was tight-lipped while he thought about it. "Yes, I suppose I can give you that."

They both turned at the sound of footfall. Wrighty came in and leaned against the doorframe.

"Van Der Kamp wants to see you before breakfast. Better go on, then." He lips curled up in a sneer. "Don't know why he's sending a whelp like you to do a man's job."

Charlie straightened to his full six foot four, giving Wrighty a moment of pause. He stepped away from the doorframe as if he were allowing Charlie to pass. Charlie didn't bother with a response and shouldered past him.

Taking another cheap shot, Wrighty called out after him. "Don't you worry about your little Wildflower. I'll make sure she is taken care of."

Charlie stiffened, deliberately choosing how to respond. "Don't worry yourself, Wrighty. Jimmy and Van Der Kamp have everything under control."

Wrighty gritted his teeth but didn't have a good comeback. Besides, Charlie was gone, his long legs eating up the path.

$$\textit{34}$$

After talking to Van Der Kamp and reconfirming the details, Charlie left camp without having breakfast. Jimmy managed to pass him a parcel for his saddlebags, but other than that, he didn't talk to anyone on his way out. Some felt bad for him, knowing what was happening, and others wondered what he'd do after Annabelle was sent away. Charlie was still a hard-working member of the gang, but he'd been so much happier and more purposeful with Annabelle around. They'd hate to see him crushed like Jimmy. Despite the brothers' initial prisoner status, most of the gang had come to see them as one of their own.

Charlie's true concern for others, as well as his strong work ethic, made him a favorite among the men. He was a problem solver and he didn't complain. The rest of the gang cut loose every chance they got, but Charlie and Jimmy didn't. They figured he deserved a little fun, and who wouldn't want a little fun with little spitfire Annabelle? Some of them also knew that being pretty to look at wasn't her only advantage. She worked just as hard as the brothers, but she had a mouth on her and, they were guessing, was probably good in bed, too. Shaking their heads as they watched him go, there wasn't much they could say to him. Everyone was fairly morose watching Charlie ride out.

It took a few hours to wind down the hills to the edge of town. The morning was growing hot and dusty, adding to his general irritability. Despite Charlie's being early, the sheriff was already waiting for him in the shade, arms crossed. Charlie rode closer and held his arms out, slowly moving only one open hand to the pommel so he could slide off of his horse. He held his hands up, moving his arms to indicate that he was unarmed. They watched each other the entire time, Charlie with curiosity and the sheriff with suspicion.

While the sheriff had thick, curly hair like his daughter and intelligent, bright eyes like hers, clearly his build was much broader and stronger. The facial features held a strong similarity. While on Annabelle they were sweet and delicate, on the sheriff, it was if they were set in granite.

The sheriff's sharp eyes took in everything about Charlie. The massive frame and height of the rider was a dead giveaway. He was sure the man in front of him was the same man who'd taken Annabelle, although they couldn't find any wanted posters matching his description.

"Hold there." Daniel held up his hand. "Don't mind if I pat you down, do you?"

Charlie kept his hands raised. "No, sir. I'd expect you to." He patiently stood spread-eagled while Daniel made sure he wasn't armed. When he was satisfied, he stepped back and looked Charlie right in the eye. Tipping his hat back and putting his fists on his waist, he inclined his head to him.

"What's your name?"

"Charlie."

"Charlie what?"

"Stapleton."

"You the one who stole Annabelle?"

"Yessir."

"Why?"

"I didn't want anyone to get hurt."

Daniel's jaw ticked while his fists clenched. "Why you—" He was about to cock his arm back and let loose, but good sense and Charlie's words interrupted him.

"Sheriff, I was unarmed. Would you have believed me if I told you?"

Daniel took a hard look at the man in front of him. While he may have been a giant, there was still a boyishness to his expression. "No, I don't believe I would've."

"I knew you wouldn't start shooting if I had Annabelle. There were other people in the mercantile who could've caught a bullet or something in the crossfire. I didn't plan on you being there, and I certainly didn't plan on taking her."

Daniel drew in a long breath. "Is she all right?"

"She's well. I've taken good care of her—made sure she was safe."

Daniel visibly relaxed. His shoulders fell from his ears and some of the tension in his face melted. For whatever reason, he seemed to believe Charlie, but he still couldn't forgive him for all of the days he missed with Annabelle and all the potential dangers she was exposed to. He wanted to pummel the man in front of him, but he needed to get Annabelle back safely. His calmer self prevailed.

"Was she in any imminent danger?"

"A lone woman is always in danger surrounded by a bunch of lawless men who've been without."

Daniel's lips pulled tight, icy eyes narrowing to crescents, but Charlie went on. "I felt very responsible for the predicament she was in. She did nothing and no woman deserves any harm to come to them. My brother and I watched over her and made sure no one bothered her. Van Der Kamp decreed that she be left alone, as well."

That caused Daniel's eyes to widen, but he didn't comment on Van Der Kamp. Instead, he focused on Charlie—he was curious about him. "Why'd they send you?"

"I'm not a criminal, at least I wasn't until that robbery and accidental kidnapping. It's not something I wanted to do."

"All right, then. Let's get on with it. What does Van Der Kamp want, and how do I know she's still alive?"

"Van Der Kamp sent me with a list of monetary demands that I'm to negotiate, and Annabelle is very much alive. I tried to get her to escape with me, but she wouldn't go. She's the one who wanted to barter."

Again, Daniel was surprised by the turn of events. He usually was the one who was one step ahead of the others.

His voice went low, and his brows knitted together. "You didn't do anything to make her not want to go with you, did you?"

"No, sir." He responded with firmness and heat. Charlie cleared his throat but resisted the urge to look down and run the tip of his boot through the dirt. Admitting the next part was more difficult. "She said that she wanted her freedom and that going from one gilded cage to another wasn't her idea of that—or something to that effect." Pausing, he cleared his throat again, blushing. "She seems to think that I'm overbearing in my protection." It was still a sore subject for Charlie, but he had to be as honest as he could with this man. There was the fact that he stole his daughter. On top of robbing a mercantile. And was associated with a known gang. Things added up against him in a pretty big way, considering the man was a by-the-book sheriff.

Daniel's hard look dropped as he threw his head back in laughter. He clapped his hand on Charlie's shoulder, much to Charlie's surprise.

"Now, that sounds like my Annabelle. She must be okay if she's bossing you like that." He chuckled some more before locking eyes with Charlie.

"Yes, she's just fine, sir. Some of the men call her a spitfire on account of her ability to hold her own—"

"And her sharp tongue." Daniel was unsuccessful at suppressing a grin.

Charlie made a choking sound but answered with a straight face. "Yes, she has a way with words." Charlie blushed, thinking about all the times Annabelle put him in his place, or someone else, for that matter. She didn't mince words.

Daniel watched Charlie blush and noticed his polite nature—there was something terribly off about him being associated with Van Der Kamp. Jake aside, his instincts were usually correct.

"Son, I like you. You seem real honest, despite the fact that you've robbed and kidnapped. I'm not sure what's going on with you and why you and your brother are with Van Der Kamp, but I have a good feeling that you've done what you said you did." He nodded his thanks, and they proceeded to discuss Van Der Kamp's financial terms.

It didn't take much time at all for them to be at an impasse when Charlie finally laid out his cards. "The final thing Van Der Kamp is willing to agree to is a head start." Daniel cocked his head. "You all give us a two-day head start, and we'll give you Annabelle, unharmed." Saying *unharmed* made him wince. "You know what I mean, don't you?"

Daniel nodded but looked grim. "Technically, I'm not supposed to do that, seeing's how you all could get away. Your gang is very much wanted and every one of you has a poster, except you and probably your brother."

"We don't have posters. Mine was our first offense. Jimmy's done nothing wrong. *Nothing.*"

Daniel was getting ready to ask about Jimmy and Charlie's situation and why they were with the gang in the first place but decided against it, since he was already breaking two of his hard and fast rules—don't let criminals get away, and don't negotiate. For Annabelle's sake, he had to be at least a little flexible.

He let out a big sigh; his shoulders sagged. Hanging his head, he looked at his boots before responding. It was taboo for him to break the law. Charlie beat him to the punch.

"Van Der Kamp says that you're a man who's good on his word. He said that I could trust you."

Daniel looked up at Charlie, who had hope in his eyes. He wasn't sure what was going on, but he took it as a good sign. He certainly wouldn't and couldn't give the gang money. That would be the beginning of the end if anyone found out. He'd never retain control over these lawless lands if he did that— Annabelle would never be safe, either.

"You promise to keep Annabelle safe and return her yourself?"

"Yes, sir. As long as Van Der Kamp allows it, I will. I don't stand much of a chance against his law, but I made a promise to Annabelle to get her back to you and that's what I'm aiming to do."

"Yet here you are. There must be another reason he sent you. Did Van Der Kamp say why you and not Jimmy or someone else?"

Daniel was hitting too close to home. Charlie didn't want the sheriff to know that he had taken a shine to his daughter and that he thought she liked him, too. He didn't really want to discuss how he was feeling about letting her go, either. Worse than that—under no circumstances did he want to clue the sheriff in to the thoughts he had about Annabelle. His mouth went dry, and his face burned thinking about her, which didn't go unnoticed by Daniel.

"I see. You're close to Annabelle?"

"I was in charge of keeping her safe, especially since I—ah—*borrowed* her for a bit." He cleared his throat, giving the sheriff a lopsided smile that made him look much younger.

"How old are you?" Daniel's eyes narrowed at him.

"Twenty-one, sir."

"Your brother?"

"Nineteen."

"Hmm." Something was niggling the back of his mind, but he couldn't figure out why. He decided he'd work that out later but would finish this now. "Well, Charlie, let's make an exchange tomorrow, then. Same time? Bring Annabelle here at noon, and I'll take her home. Van Der Kamp's gang gets a two-day head start from the moment I leave with her. Are we agreed?"

Charlie swallowed hard, because this was it. He'd make good on his promise, but he'd also lose the one thing that had brought him joy the past few weeks—Annabelle. He nodded quickly before sticking his hand out for a handshake. Daniel's face opened for a moment, registering surprise, before he shuttered it, sticking out his own hand. They grasped each other firmly but not in an aggressive manner. Their handshake demonstrated the strength of each man and his willing agreement—not the posturing or one-upsmanship that might've come from Wrighty or the likes of him. Nodding, they walked off in opposite directions. One looking forward to tomorrow and the other dreading it.

35

Daniel rode off, still perplexed by the young man representing the gang. Not much of this made sense to him. As soon as he got Annabelle back he'd do more investigating. He headed toward town to talk to Jake about tomorrow's plan.

He hitched his horse out back and, after giving it a quick brush down, hurried in to give his update. Jake was leaning back at the desk with his feet on it. He didn't bother putting his feet down when Daniel walked in, which was odd—he usually showed the sheriff more deference than that. Frowning, Daniel hung up his hat and got a cup of coffee.

He was waiting for a barrage of questions, especially since Jake was so interested in Annabelle, but none came his way. That was also odd. He waited for a few extra minutes with his back to Jake, but still, nothing. Slowly turning around, he lifted the cup to his mouth and took a long sip. He watched Jake over the rim of the tin, but Jake was behaving as if it were an ordinary afternoon.

He sat down and decided to ignore what Jake was pretending. "I'll need you to go with me to pick up Annabelle at noon tomorrow."

"Edge of town?" He asked without looking up.

"No." That finally made Jake look up. "How'd you know it was the edge of town?"

Jake's feet slid off the desk. "I didn't know. It was a logical guess."

"Logical, how?"

"Where else would you meet him?"

Daniel kept watching Jake for any tell he might give, but so far he wasn't letting on. Daniel just nodded to him. "Yup. Edge of town. Noon."

"I'll be there, you know that."

No, I really don't know that. Daniel didn't say anything. Shuffling through some papers, he decided to test Jake some more. "Say, you familiar with anyone by the last name of Stapleton?"

Daniel thought Jake went slightly pale at the mention of it, but if he did, he recovered pretty quickly—he responded a little too quickly, as well. "Nope, can't rightly say I do. Why?"

"Just curious." Daniel could feel Jake watching him intently at this point but decided to wait before saying anything else. He wanted to see how long Jake could hold out before asking any more questions or giving himself away. He was pretty sure Jake knew something but wasn't letting on. It was a gut feeling more than anything. He reached into his desk, pulled out a ledger and began leafing through it. He was pretending to look for the place he left off but was paying attention to Jake with everything but his eyes.

It took less than five minutes for Jake to break. "Who met with you? Did Van Der Kamp meet with you?"

Daniel quirked a brow at him. "You honestly think Van Der Kamp would crawl out of his safe hole to come meet with me? Don't you think this is a task better suited for one of his minions?" The bait was set. He leaned back and waited.

"Well, I—"

"You, *what*, Jake? What is it you're getting at?"

"Sheesh, Daniel. You're sure up in arms. Didn't things go well enough for you?"

"What do you mean by *well enough*?" His eyes went narrow as he leaned forward.

"Well, you got Annabelle back, didn't you? That is, you're going to get her back. What more do you want?"

"I want some justice, that's what I want. I don't want anyone just coming here and taking people and things from us. We're honest and hard-working people, Jake. Haven't you noticed that by now? Even Mr. Dooley is all right, although he spends too much time drunk, and we have to lock him up from time to time."

"What's that got to do with getting Annabelle back?"

Daniel huffed out a breath, exasperated by the turn of events. "Because, Jake, I have to let Van Der Kamp have a two-day head start to get Annabelle back."

"I thought you'd just give him some money and be done with it."

Daniel's lips tightened like a vise. He had to wait a moment before responding or else he'd knock Jake on his ass. "I am not going to give criminals money, especially money I don't have."

"You sure you don't have any money?"

Daniel was near shouting at this point. "What the hell is that supposed to mean? What're you getting at?"

"It means, I'm sure you have some money somewhere. Don't you?"

Daniel stood up so fast his chair collided with the wall behind him. The action took Jake off guard and he was too slow to get up. Daniel stalked over to him and lifted him by the front of his shirt. Jake was roughly the same height as Daniel, so he didn't have to lift him very high to look him eye to eye. When their eyes were level, he leaned in close and, in a near whisper, said, "Don't you ever talk about something you know nothing about—especially if it has anything to do with me or Annabelle. You hear?"

He held him for a moment longer before giving him a hard shake and dropping him back into his chair. Jake rolled his neck and pulled his shirt back down before giving Daniel an annoyed look.

"What'dchya do that for, Daniel? I didn't mean anything by it. Most everyone in this town has some money. God damn it." He was fussing with his shirt and straightening himself. "Town's doing real well—everyone's got more money than they did when they got here."

"Quit your griping. I don't want to hear it." He caught himself from kicking the chair Jake was sitting in—he wanted to lash out at something, anything. The room suddenly became too small for him, so he grabbed his hat, stalking out the front door.

He walked down the street until he found himself in front of the bakery. He seemed to find himself in front of the Johansson's storefront a lot, lately. This time he decided to just walk on in instead of waiting for an invite or for Mrs. Johansson to come out and drag him in. He needed to figure some things out, and she was good about that in her own sort of way.

He gently pushed open the front door, and the little bell chimed. Mrs. Johansson came scurrying out, wiping her hands with a towel as she did. When she looked up, her face broke out into a smile.

"Sheriff! So good to see you. Have you come with good news about our dear Annabelle?" Placing the towel on the back counter, she grabbed a mug and filled it with coffee. "Sorry, this has been sitting around warming for a while. Might be a little chewy, but better than none. I'll brew us up a fresh pot—you drink that while you wait."

"No, no. Please sit, Mrs. Johansson. I didn't come to make you work. I came to talk."

"Oh? Everything okay?"

Daniel pulled in a deep breath and let it out, loudly. Scratching his head, he leaned across the table. "There's something off about Jake."

"Pfft." She made a flapping motion with her hand. "I could've saved you the trouble and told you that. That boy isn't right."

Daniel's face scrunched up and he leaned back. "What do you mean by that—*not right?*"

"Annabelle's been telling you all along that he does things that aren't appropriate—he's not on the up and up. I'm surprised you didn't notice before. He's like one of your father's men." Her lips went into a seam, and her eyes narrowed. She crossed her arms and waited for either yelling or questions to start. Instead, what she got was a look of confusion.

Daniel put his elbow on the table, and his fist covered his mouth. He sat like that for a few moments before pulling a half face with his deep nostril breath.

"How long have you noticed this?"

"Not right away, mind you. He's always been polite and friendly. Says the right things. It's not until Annabelle started getting older that he changed. He seemed more territorial around her. He always seemed to be looking for things, for something." She shook her head. "What, I don't know, exactly. It's like those men your father hired to 'take care' of business for him. That kind of looking." She tilted her head to look up at Daniel. "Does that make sense?"

"Mmm-hmm. It does, sadly. Wish I caught that earlier. It didn't occur to me until, well, now, I suppose." He stretched his legs out and leaned back in his chair.

Mrs. Johansson went into mother mode. She placed a hand over his. "Daniel, honey, what happened to bring all this up?"

Mrs. Johansson's touch felt like home. His mind temporarily drifted back to the big kitchen in the Pennington mansion where the Johanssons were both cooks. He could still smell the pastries she made for Mack and the warmth of the kitchen. He covered her hand with his, squeezing. The Johanssons were more like parents than his own were. They had practically raised him in their kitchen. When Daniel and his wife had moved out West, the Johanssons went with them, much to Mack's displeasure.

Daniel always went to them when he needed something, even if it were only to feel love or safety. That was exactly what she was giving him now—it's why he kept ending up unwittingly at the bakery. Remembering Mack's anger—the bribes, the rages, the threats—at their leaving with him, he dragged himself out of his reverie.

Daniel looked up at her and shook his head. "I came back from negotiating Annabelle's return, and Jake didn't say a word. He's been all hot to trot about courting her and all that, but when something this important happens to the woman he says he wants to marry? He keeps quiet and acts as if nothing's happening. I had an odd feeling when I walked into the jail, anyway."

"You know to stick to your gut—it's saved you so many times before—"

"It's okay, we don't have to go there." It was Daniel's turn to pat Mrs. Johansson's hand and comfort her. They sat in silence until it was broken by Mr. Johansson's bellowing in the back.

"Honey? I need your help. Something's stuck back here, and I can't get it to budge."

Daniel rose before she could respond. "Stay, I'll go help."

When they returned, Mr. Johansson had his hand on Daniel's shoulder, which seemed to ease some of his tension. It made Mrs. Johansson smile. Daniel had always been the son they couldn't have.

"Say, does the name Stapleton ring any bells with you?"

"No, I can't say it does." Mr. Johansson said, pondering. After a minute, he raised his index finger in the air. "You know, it does. Your father had a business associate by that name, if I'm recalling correctly."

The Johanssons discussed who this person could possibly be until Daniel interrupted them.

"Was he married? Had children?"

Mrs. Johansson said, "I think he might have had a couple of boys, but they were older. They didn't live with him—they lived out west somewhere. One might've been newly married, if I'm recalling correctly." She looked at her husband as they nodded to one another. Looking back at Daniel, she asked, "Why do you ask?"

"The man they sent to negotiate with me said he's Charlie Stapleton—he's actually the one who took Annabelle. There's something off about his being there and being the one Van Der Kamp sent, but I can't get a good read on him. He's young, for one. Not really a criminal, either."

Mrs. Johansson tensed, and Mr. Johansson patted her hand. There seemed to be a lot of patting of hands that afternoon.

"He's nice and polite—"

"Like that deputy of yours?" She gave Daniel her stern mother voice.

"Mrs. Johansson—"

"Fine," she sniffed. "I'm listening."

He waited for another outburst that, thankfully, didn't come. "I wanted to pummel the man for taking Annabelle, but I knew that wouldn't get us anywhere. He didn't struggle with me or posture—he was cooperative and polite. Then he was so contrite—he really feels sorry for taking her, and not because he got caught, either. It's strange."

"Well, maybe the young man likes Annabelle. She's a pretty young lady." She gasped. "You don't think—"

Daniel's face fell at the possibility but quickly recovered. "No." He shook his head. "His posture and words indicate protectiveness, and he's contrite. He's been raised right. He has manners and knows his place. He kept calling me sir, without any sarcasm or subtext to it. None of the other men would do that. It's not in keeping with the men Van Der Kamp keeps around him. They're more of a surly lot with a bone to pick. They're also loyal as hell."

"Hrumph." Mrs. Johansson threw him a reproving look, crossing her arms.

"Sorry, ma'am. Like I was saying, Charlie is more concerned about Annabelle than his loyalty to Van Der Kamp, although he seems to respect Van Der Kamp's law, so to speak. He even worded it that way. Said that he promised Annabelle that he'd get her back to me."

"He could be lying," Mr. Johansson chimed in.

"Could be, but I doubt it."

"Why's that?"

"When I asked him to prove Annabelle was alive and well, he told me about her going on about wanting her independence and that whole thing. I knew that she was doing all right if she was running on about that." Mrs. Johansson looked askance at Daniel. "A man can't make up that kind of nonsense." He shrugged his shoulders as Mr. Johansson laughed, earning a dirty look from his wife.

"Well, what do we do about your deputy, then? I'm guessing that's what brought you out this way."

Daniel was looking above the Johanssons at nothing in particular. "Yup."

"Were you going to take the deputy with you to fetch Annabelle?"

"Mary, you're acting like she's been out on a social call."

"Pshaw—you know what I mean, George. Is he taking the deputy as some sort of backup, or does he trust this Charlie person?" She turned back to Daniel, "So, are you taking him or not? Do you trust him enough at this point? I don't want you getting into any extra danger." She shook her finger at him, scolding him.

"Mary, he's been sheriff for long enough now. I suspect he knows how to do his job."

"I suppose I'll take him with the posse, but I'm not giving him my back, just yet. His behavior was somewhat unsettling when we were tracking Annabelle to the abandoned mining camp. We'll see how he behaves when he sees Annabelle. That'll be the true test—he's been hankering for her for a while, according to what he's been saying."

"Do you think that'll put Annabelle in more danger with him around?" Mrs. Johansson's hand went to her chest.

"No, I wouldn't test things out with her. He won't harm her, but I'm not sure what his game is, either. He clearly wants her but there's something going on in the background with him. When I came back, I was going to ask him to do some research on Stapleton, but he was acting off. That's when I headed down here to see what you knew. *You* I can trust." He winked at Mrs. Johansson, who blushed, slapping playfully at his arm.

"Don't go getting fresh with me, young man." Everyone laughed at that as Mrs. Johansson got up to serve the coffee she'd made while they were in the storage area.

Daniel decided to test Jake, anyway, despite the conflicting misgivings he had about him. If they didn't get information right away, he'd know that Jake had something to hide. He'd also follow up later. Jake wouldn't be deputy for long if that was the way he rolled. Come to think about it, things had been off with him for a while. He just let it go because there was always something else more pressing, and the offenses seemed minor.

Unfortunately, he did the same thing with Annabelle— shoved her concerns and desires to the bottom of his list. The town and the law always came first, and that had to change, even if just a little. Annabelle wouldn't always be his little Annabelle. In fact, she no longer was "little," according to Mrs. Johansson. She didn't have much time left with him before she'd find herself a man to take care of her. He wanted their last bits of time together to be good.

Unlike her mother. Lissa had never given him the chance to say goodbye or to make their last bit of time together good. *That's because she was always in it for herself. I wonder if she ever thought about or missed Annabelle, or me. Probably not. Always was a very selfish, vain woman. She was in it for the money. I wonder if Mack ever gave it to her. We didn't really fulfill our end of the bargain. Although I never agreed to that bargain, either.*

Daniel let the door slam behind him because Jake looked like he was about to fall asleep. Fortunately, no one was in the jail, but that was still ridiculous. The odds were against Jake,

Daniel was afraid. It made him sad, because he really liked Jake and had high hopes for him.

Jake jumped like a skittish colt. "What the hell?"

"Should be more aware of your surroundings, deputy. Sleeping on the job could be deadly."

Jake snorted. "Only you, Mr. Perfect."

Daniel just quirked a brow at him and sat on the side of his desk. "I want you to do some research on a Charlie Stapleton and any information you can find on any Stapletons. Start with the East coast and work your way across the map if you have to."

"What's this all about?"

"I'm just curious, that's all. Problem with that?"

Jake looked like he was going to protest but decided against it.

"Good, I'm glad we're in agreement."

36

The warning bells were going off in Jake's head when Daniel came back from the meet. He knew that Daniel was beginning to put the pieces together. He was a smart man—Jake was just surprised that it took this long for him to figure things out. Annabelle had really been giving Daniel grief about her "independence," trying to get him to loosen the reins, so he wasn't on top of things like he usually was. To top it off, it really messed with Daniel when he'd started asking about courting. They both knew that Annabelle wasn't amenable to it, but he pushed anyway. It didn't matter none to him. He had ways of making women cooperate. Daniel never need know. He liked the man, but he could be a self-righteous son of a gun at times.

Annabelle was too outspoken and needed to be put in her place. "Independence," he snorted. He figured he'd saddle her with a bunch of babies and that'd take care of her for a while. He'd have fun making them, too. Jake refused to let his thoughts go too far down that path because he had a lot of riding to do tonight, and he didn't want to ride with all the blood going to his groin. He was ready for this to be over with so he could have a go at her. He'd been waiting patiently—a little too patiently for his liking.

He had to find out what Wrighty knew about Charlie and what Daniel was so hot to figure out about him. Daniel couldn't possibility know about his personal connection to Wrighty. They'd been very careful. He also wanted to cover his own tracks in case he had to leave in a hurry—with Annabelle, of course. Since Daniel was keeping watch tonight, he was free to "go home." He would set off as soon as he could to meet up with Wrighty.

The message he sent was to meet just outside the mines closer to town so he wouldn't be missed. They'd meet where there wasn't active mining so no one would accidentally stumble upon them. Wrighty was already waiting when he arrived.

"Where's the fire? You know we shouldn't be contacting each other—especially this close to the deal." He spit out the toothpick he had in his mouth. He would've lit a cigarette, but he didn't want anyone to see the light or smell smoke. He pushed off the wall and walked toward Jake.

"O'Donnell's on to us. He keeps asking questions—he's asking a lot of questions about that Stapleton pup. Why would he be doing that?"

"How the hell should I know? You're the one who's worked with him for a bunch of years."

"Yeah, well, it has something to do with what's going on with the gang—and that isn't something *I'd* know about."

"You're law and not part of the gang—need-to-know basis, you know." He smirked at Jake.

Jake moved into Wrighty's space, jabbing his finger at him. "You keep everything too close to the vest. I need to know more because what I don't know might get one of us put in jail or killed."

Jake's finger-jabbing didn't faze Wrighty. His response was calm. "If anyone's going to jail, it's going to be you. *You* ought to know better, deputy." He chuckled at that, making Jake angrier.

"What do you know about Charlie?"

"Charlie? What's this with Charlie? He's a nobody, just like his pansy-ass little brother. They were little runts when we killed their parents and now they're over-sized servants. They do what we tell them to do and they generally don't talk back." He made a sound of disgust.

"*Why* did y'all keep 'em? Why go to the trouble to murder their parents and keep the witnesses alive? That ain't smart, and Van Der Kamp is, if anything, smart. What aren't you telling me?"

"Pfft. Goat—Goat's going soft and wanted slaves to help him do work, that's all. He was feeling bad for those boys and begged Van Der Kamp not to kill them. We really ought to put Goat out of his misery. If it weren't for him, we wouldn't be dealing with any of this." He spit on the ground, wiping his mouth with the back of his hand.

Jake watched Wrighty for a long time, not moving. He was trying to decide if Wrighty was on the up-and-up. More often than not, he wasn't.

"Why would Van Der Kamp listen to Goat? Especially if he's going soft on two young boys?"

"Somehow they're related. Goat looked after Van Der Kamp's sister when she was ill, and he was at war. He's indebted. You know how loyal he can be about certain things. It doesn't matter what Goat says or does, he has an out. Although Goat's smart enough not to push him too far."

"So we're back to my original question—why is Daniel so concerned about Charlie? What's the deal between the two of them? What did Charlie do to make him so suspicious?"

"For Christ's sake, man. Let it go. He's a sheriff, he's suspicious by nature. You sneeze around that man and he's asking you all sorts of questions. Charlie's young—why wouldn't he be suspicious that Van Der Kamp sent him? He's a little too green for that kind of task. I wanted to go, but Van Der Kamp wouldn't let me. He said it was Charlie's job to do it. God only knows why, but he has a soft spot for that kid, too."

"Doesn't that strike you as odd?" Wrighty didn't look like he understood. "Why would those two be soft on those boys? To what end? They have to mean something to them or be valuable in some way. What would they get out of being nice to them otherwise?"

"You're overthinking this. Let it go. Van Der Kamp's letting Charlie do this because he feels so responsible—overly responsible—for Annabelle. He wants her, and Van Der Kamp feels sorry for the kid because he has to let his new toy go."

Jake grabbed Wrighty by the collar and pulled him up to his face. "He didn't mess with her, did he?" He growled. "I'm going to rearrange that pretty-boy face of his, if he did. She's mine!" He shoved Wrighty away from him, shaking out his hands.

"Look at you, deputy. You think you have some sort of claim over the little girl because you work for her daddy?" He looked at Jake from head to toe and back again. "Mmm, mmm, mmm. Look at you, getting all defensive over something that ain't yours to begin with."

"I asked her daddy permission to court her—that was before your buffoon botched the robbery and took her."

"Ain't you all proper—courting and all. I have a mind to go back to camp and sample some of that before she goes back home. I'd been staying away because I felt bad for Charlie and all. He never gets none. You? You get plenty and ruin it all." He spit on the ground at Jake's feet.

"You're still sore that Josie chose me and not you, that's all."

"No, I'm sore that you beat the woman before I could have her. You had no right to do that, you somabitch."

Jake straight-armed Wrighty before he could get one up on him. "Not here. Not now. We have a problem with Daniel, and you need to be aware of it. Besides, Josie's old history." He shoved his fist into Wrighty's face. "You better not touch Annabelle."

"Don't worry about me. It's Charlie that you have to worry about. She has moon eyes for him, and he returns the favor." It was Jake's turn to shove at Wrighty, but he was ready for it, being that he purposely provoked Jake. He hated the bastard, but he was still useful, being on the other side of the law, with questionable ethics. Wrighty blocked Jake and continued talking.

"I'll ask Van Der Kamp some 'round-the-bush questions so he doesn't suspect I'm talking to you and see what comes up. Just let the sheriff go on with his plan for tomorrow, and if anything changes, I'll send Moris with a message."

Jake nodded, going back to his horse. He could see why Daniel was in such a state of questioning with Charlie Stapleton. None of this made sense. Someone knew what was going on, but no one was telling. As much as he hated to admit it, he didn't think Wrighty knew. That could only spell trouble for Wrighty, because Van Der Kamp was accustomed to keeping him informed. That probably meant Wrighty was on the outs, for whatever reason. He didn't care, but he didn't want to be taken down by that fool, either. He had to figure out how to get out of there with his head still intact. If Wrighty went down, he was taking everyone he could with him.

Turning his horse back toward town, he took a slower pace so he could work out a plan. Wrighty was no longer useful to him.

❧ **37** ❧

The next day, Charlie and Annabelle were waiting for the sheriff. They had arrived extra early because Charlie didn't want a prolonged goodbye, and Annabelle was harboring guilt for hurting Charlie's feelings. It was easier to ride and wait, ignoring what was in their hearts and minds. They weren't speaking when Daniel rode up to them. He stopped right in front of the pair, assessing Annabelle with his eyes then nodding to Charlie. Charlie slid off his horse and held his arms out to his side.

"Thanks, son, for making this easier." Daniel patted Charlie down. Finding no weapons, he turned to Annabelle, who was still atop the horse, looking down at them.

"Annabelle, honey. You okay?" He felt like he was going to crumble for the first time since his mother died. Outwardly, he looked as solid as a mountain. Inward, he was a giant mass of rumbling and quaking. He wanted to grab Annabelle off of the horse and hold her tight. He resisted because he wasn't sure how she'd take the display, and he didn't want to look weak in front of Charlie or Annabelle.

"Yes, Papa. Charlie took real good care of me and kept me safe. I'm fine. No need to worry." She looked sad while she spoke, speaking softer and with less enthusiasm than she normally did. She looked directly at Daniel, acting as if Charlie wasn't there, which was interesting. Charlie looked a little stricken himself.

"I'm so glad to see you, honey. Let's get this straightened out, and we'll talk, later."

Annabelle nodded and looked down at her saddle horn, fiddling with the reins. He turned back toward Charlie.

"I'm going to take Annabelle and put her on my horse before I saddle up. As soon as I do that, the timer starts. Two days." He thrust out two fingers out. "That's all I'll give Van Der Kamp. At—" glancing at his timepiece—"11:45 a.m., two days from now, my posse and I are riding out to find you. We will arrest you when we find you—a head start is all you get, remember? Got any questions?"

"No, sir."

"All right." He turned back toward Annabelle, raising his arms to her. "Let's go, I've got you."

She slid down the horse into her father's arms. Pivoting, he quickly lifted her up onto his horse and followed her. He nodded to Charlie as he turned the horse back toward town. He stopped when he heard Charlie speak.

"Sheriff?" Daniel looked back, but Annabelle refused, tensing when she heard Charlie speak. "I'm real sorry for all the trouble I caused. I was trying to do the right thing, so no more harm would be done. Annabelle, I tried to take good care of you, and I really enjoyed your company. You made things brighter for me and Jimmy, and we appreciate all you've done. I'm sorry for all the trouble you've been through."

Daniel could feel Annabelle shaking. He quickly nodded and hurried his horse off so they could put as much distance between that ordeal and themselves as they could. It didn't stop the flood of tears from Annabelle, however. By the time they were home she had soaked Daniel's vest.

Jake was waiting on the steps of the jailhouse when they returned. He reached for Annabelle, but she remained on the horse facing forward until her father handed her down. She wouldn't look at him, either. When her feet hit the ground, she broke away from them, running into the house. The men watched her retreat, dumbfounded.

Jake took off his hat, brushed his hair back, and returned his hat to his head.

"Well, I'll be. Where's the fire with that one?" He squinted toward the house.

Daniel was ready to beat some sense into Jake, or at least some sensitivity. "Are you that big of a fool? She's a kidnapping victim who's been stuck with Van Der Kamp's gang for almost a month. She has every right to be emotional. It took us a damn long time to breach their defenses and get cooperative communication going. She might've even given up hope of being saved. Who knows what she's thinking."

"She didn't talk to you?"

"Not a word."

"Hmm." They stood watching the house before Daniel made a move to go.

"I'll give her a few minutes to collect herself before I start asking questions. You get a posse together. We ride out in two days."

"Two days?"

"Yep. That was the deal I finally struck. I wasn't going to give them money, especially money I didn't have. They know they're fair game after their head start. Weren't you even listening?"

Jake's eyes narrowed at Daniel, but he didn't say anything. Daniel didn't care, because he was going to make sure that Jake wasn't long for this town.

Daniel looked away from the house and straight at Jake. "You better go on then. At least give these men some time to gather supplies and say goodbye to their people. I want everyone ready to ride at 11:45 a.m. I was precise about the time and I need you to be, too."

Jake's lips twisted as if he were keeping words in his mouth, but he nodded anyway. Turning away from the house, he went down the street to round up some men. Daniel watched until he walked into the smithy. He wanted to make sure Jake wasn't going to sabotage his search efforts. Daniel wasn't sure of much right this moment, but the blacksmith had always been a fair man. That, he could trust. Shaking his head, he headed into the house to face Annabelle.

Gently rapping on her door, Daniel called out to her, "Annabelle, darling. Annabelle, you doing all right in there?"

He didn't get an immediate response. He leaned his head closer to the door, trying to make out any noises. Before he could try the doorknob, she answered him. "Papa, I just need a minute or two. I'd like to lie down for a bit. Okay?"

He hung his head and leaned it against the door. "It's all right, darling. You have a good rest while I make you something to eat." He slowly walked down the hall, dreading the next few hours.

◈ **38** ◈

Charlie made it back to camp in record time. Fueled by agitation, irritation, and a profound emptiness within, he needed to work something out of his system—he just didn't know exactly what that was. All he knew was that it just needed to go—he didn't feel right. Everything went well with the handoff, and the sheriff was courteous, all things considered. Annabelle, however, didn't talk to him the whole way down and wouldn't look at him. He didn't know what he did wrong. He did what she asked and what he had initially promised her, and now she was mad at him. Sad thing was, he was willing to break his stringent rules for her—he didn't want to let her go. He shook his head as he spurred his horse faster on the straightaway. Instead of checking in with Van Der Kamp, he went to the corral and found Jimmy. He leaned against the fencing as he watched him work with Wrighty's horse. It'd come back from an outing with a strange gait. Jimmy was great with the horses. He didn't have formal training, but he learned from careful observation and experience. With his gentle nature, the horses trusted him.

Jimmy cantered the horse back to the gate and Charlie opened it for him, following them back to the stable.

"Figure out what's wrong with her?"

"I think Wrighty just rode her too hard. She might've stepped wrong in a pit or on a rock, but it's hard to tell. He'll have to stay off of her for a few days."

"Not possible. We have to clear out—they're coming in two days."

Jimmy raised his eyebrows, but he didn't speak.

"Yup. That's what I got for Annabelle."

"Seems to me she's worth more than two days." When Charlie didn't answer, Jimmy looked up at him. His face was tight and his lips stretched across it, as if they were holding him together. "You know she loves you, right?"

"No, I don't." Charlie turned on his heel and walked away. All Jimmy could do was shake his head and go back to working on the horse.

Charlie didn't have to knock on Van Der Kamp's door. He was standing outside of it, leaning against the wall with a coffee in hand. He watched Charlie slowly trudge up the trail before Charlie realized he was there.

"Charlie." He took a sip of coffee, watching him over the rim.

"Sir." Charlie gave a curt nod. "Trade went without a hitch—the sheriff has Annabelle, and we have a two-day head start. Posse sets out at 11:45 a.m. The sheriff was real specific about that." He was lackluster, and his words fell out of his mouth more than they were spoken.

Van Der Kamp stared at him a little longer than usual. He took another sip of coffee. None of his tactics fazed Charlie. He remained, waiting to be given an order. Waiting to be told what to do.

"How was the sheriff?"

"Good. He said that he'd keep his bargain but that it didn't include not arresting us when he caught us. He's sure of it."

"I'm sure he will."

Charlie stood straighter, and his eyes became clearer. "You're not worried about that?"

"Nope." Charlie just stood there looking at him. "Aren't you going to ask why?"

"I'm not so sure it's my place. You have your reasoning."

"Let's just say I have some things I need to tell the sheriff, and we need to be on neutral ground before I do. Sometime tomorrow, spread the word and start getting camp torn down. There's no need to hurry, we have plenty of time—don't want to make the sheriff work too hard, but a couple of the men are lazy. They need an extra kick in the ass to get moving. That or they can stay behind. Don't rightly care either way." He didn't wait for Charlie to respond. He went back into his cabin, shutting the door behind him.

Annabelle could hear them talking. They weren't trying to be quiet, but they didn't want her to hear, either. Initially, she tried to ignore them, but when she heard Charlie's name mentioned a couple of times, as well as "Stapleton," in general, her ears tuned in. She could make out bits and pieces but not enough. She already knew the posse was leaving tomorrow morning. They'd meet outside of town and wait until 11:45 a.m., then whoever was there would head out. Any stragglers were free to catch up. Papa was impatient, and the terse responses he gave indicated as such. Her curiosity was getting the best of her, so much so that she accidentally bumped into the door, making a loud sound.

"Annabelle! I know you're listening. Come on out if you really want to hear. Eavesdropping isn't polite." Daniel's boots hit the floor hard as he headed toward her door. He yanked it open before she could straighten herself up off the floor. She was lying there in an undignified heap, looking up at him.

"Hi, Papa. I thought I might come out, maybe make some coffee for you all. I just hit the door's all." She gave him a lopsided smirk, but it failed to crack a smile on his face. Her usual tactics didn't work. They backfired—if anything, he looked sterner.

He jerked his arm down and offered her a hand up. She took it, dusting off her skirts. "Go on and make coffee, but no interrupting. Talking happens between me and you before I set out."

She nodded, skirting around him as she looked down at the floor. Daniel shook his head in frustration on his way after her.

Jake and a couple of other men were in the living room, but Daniel followed Annabelle into the kitchen. The house wasn't big enough to afford them much privacy, but he was broad enough to block their conversation from the others' hearing.

"What's going on with you?" She tried to keep busy, but her hands were shaking. She decided to be up front with him. Setting the coffee down, she turned around.

"I heard you keep mentioning Charlie, that's all. I wondered what he had to do with all this."

"You tell me." He crossed his arms over his broad chest, his legs braced apart in a ready stance. While Daniel wasn't as big or tall as Charlie, his size was still impressive. His body told the story of a man who put in a hard day's work.

Annabelle sighed. "Charlie and his brother are innocent." Daniel cocked his head forward. "Yes, innocent. Charlie always tries to do what's right."

"And robbery and kidnapping are the right things to do?" He rocked back and forth on his feet.

"No. Look, I don't want to talk about it with"—she tried peering around him before lowering her voice—"them here." She lifted her chin in the general direction of the sitting room.

"You mean, Jake."

"Yes, him. I need to tell you some things—alone." She gave him her best wide-eyed *please* look. "Can you at least allow me that?"

Daniel's lips tightened, but he nodded anyway. "Bring out the coffee when you're done. You can stay and listen or leave, it's up to you. We'll talk after everyone's left." The discussion grew louder, but Jake had managed to come up behind Daniel.

"Is there anything I can help you with, Annabelle? How're you feeling? We didn't get a chance to talk."

Annabelle looked ready to take a swing at Jake, and Daniel was ready to pull him out of the house by the back of his shirt.

Daniel gave Jake a shove. "What she needs is some space. She'll be bringing us coffee in a minute. Let's go back to the meeting." He didn't bother looking back at Annabelle but concentrated on getting Jake away from her. The more he had to deal with Jake these past few days, the more he wondered how he'd missed all the warning signs. *Was I so desperate for help that I took someone else's word about Jake? No, Jake has changed, but I didn't see the change happening because I let him get too close. That's the problem—never let 'em get too close. That's when things go south.* Nodding to himself, he dropped into a chair and listened to the men. He continued to watch Jake out of the corner of his eye while Jake kept craning his head toward the kitchen.

Before the door fully shut, Daniel turned to Annabelle. "You've had your time, now spit it out. No more fooling around."

"Papa, I couldn't talk about it before. Remember when I tried to tell you about Jake? You wouldn't hear it. I don't want this to be the same. This is even more important, the more I think about it."

"What do you mean, more important?" Daniel leaned forward, his jaw clenched.

Without stopping for a breath, Annabelle blurted out, "Charlie and Jimmy were kidnapped by the gang. They aren't really members of it. Goat, an older man, he felt bad for them and told Van Der Kamp to keep them for the hard work. He said when they got bigger, they could help with robbing and such."

"Now slow down, honey." He held out his hands as if he had to physically impede her as her words rapidly tumbled out. "What do you mean, kidnapped?"

"Van Der Kamp's gang ambushed the Stapletons' stage-coach—the gang killed their parents and the driver. Wrighty—he's the meanest of them all—he was getting ready to kill Charlie when this older man, Goat, pleaded for him. Wrighty has it out for Charlie and now me. He thinks Van Der Kamp should've just killed the brothers, and he holds everything against Charlie."

"Why does Wrighty have it out for you?" The muscle in Daniel's jaw began flexing.

Annabelle blushed to her roots.

"Did he touch you?" She didn't respond, so Daniel reached out and touched her arm. "Annabelle, I know it's embarrassing, but you have to tell me. I'll find him if it's the last thing I do."

She put a hand on his. "Papa, it's okay. He didn't—didn't touch me, not in that way."

"In what way did he touch you?"

She cleared her throat, eyes welling. "He whipped me with his belt." Her words came out in a strangled whisper.

"What?" Daniel jumped out of his seat. "Show me."

"No, Papa. It's on my leg. I don't want to show you. It's better now. It just bruised me badly so I couldn't walk without help for a couple of days."

"How'd you get around? Who helped you?" He gripped both of her arms with his as his voice raised slightly.

"Moris did. I think he's kind of Wrighty's main lackey, but he was getting irritated with Wrighty. He was kind to me, despite everything." Taking in a deep breath, she added, "Please, just let it go."

"I'm getting the posters—you point them out to me. I'll get them." His fists were clenching, and his eyes were hard.

"Please, just sit down." She tried leading him back to the chair. "I have more to tell you. You can't arrest Charlie or Jimmy—whatever they've done, they were forced to do. Wrighty kept threatening to beat up or kill Jimmy, depending on the day and his mood. Charlie was trying to protect his brother. Remember—he told you that he didn't have a gun. He didn't want to rob. Elroy was just so afraid of Charlie—he's as big as a bear," she said, nodding in earnestness "—that he took out the money before Charlie was even to the counter. I watched the whole thing happen. I was standing right there."

Daniel looked at his daughter with disbelief. Here she was defending a gang member. She couldn't stand Jake and was averse to the whole marriage thing. But here she was defending someone who's pretty much a stranger to her and did her wrong.

"Tell me exactly what happened that day."

"I snuck out to get supplies. I was thinking about going to your sister's house—"

"You don't even know where she lives."

"Well, I was going to work on that. I was just collecting some necessities for the trip."

"What trip?"

"Ah, yeah, well—"

"Annabelle."

Annabelle released a heavy sigh. "I was going to run away. You pushed me to it. You were going to force me to be with Jake, and I can't stand him. I've been around a lot of other men now. I've seen them interact with each other and how they treat me. Even though they were bandits, most of them treated me with more respect than Jake did. He's not right. There's something going on with him. He's a lot like Wrighty, except that Jake hasn't had the opportunity to beat and threaten me like Wrighty did." She burst into tears and sobbed into her hands.

Daniel's face crumpled and his eyes misted over. He folded a weeping, shaking Annabelle into his arms and held her until she'd cried it out. He stroked her hair and rocked her, doing his best to comfort her. Growing up with Mack, he didn't have a lot of affection. His mother was a little distant before she died, as well. Mrs. Johansson was the only one who gave him affection, but he had to be careful and not hang around the kitchen too much or he'd get in trouble with his father. That was a *woman's place—no son of mine is going to hide behind a woman's skirts,* Mack's voice suddenly thundered in his head. He thought he'd distanced himself from that nightmare years ago.

"It's okay, honey. I was never, ever going to force you to do something you didn't want to do. I'm only doing the things I do to protect you. After we talked that day, I took a long, hard look at Jake. I'm sorry I didn't see the things you were telling me. I didn't want to believe he could be like that—I couldn't believe that I'd missed something that important. Please forgive me, Annabelle. I've only ever tried to protect you, and I failed. Not only with Jake but with Van Der Kamp. I let you walk right into that trap."

Annabelle's shoulders shook even harder. She was having a big, ugly cry. It was the culmination of the past year's frustrations. She was so sheltered that she couldn't fully articulate what she found so offensive about Jake. Being around Wrighty and the gang had given her a better idea of what Jake was about. She liked him even less, once she figured it out. Her sobbing slowed and she heaved a jagged breath in. Blowing her nose and calming her breath, she finally was able to talk.

"Papa—that was *my* fault. I didn't listen. I didn't think that kind of danger would come here." Her lower lip trembled. "The thing is—Charlie was always good to me. He was kind and always took care of me." Fat tears were rolling down her cheeks as she sniffled again. "I—I," more sniffles, "I love him, Papa. I realized that these past few days that I love Charlie. I know what you're talking about when you said I needed someone to protect me and show me things. Charlie's it for me. He didn't have to take care of me, but he felt so responsible for me that he kept me safe and comfortable. He never got angry with me when I yelled at him or was mean to him." She began crying so hard Daniel couldn't understand her words.

"Annabelle, breathe. I can't understand you. You're going to make yourself sick with all this crying. We'll figure this out. Breathe, honey."

"Papa, I was so mean to him because I was scared."

"You had every right to be scared. You—"

"No, I was scared because I liked being in his company. I really liked him, and I missed him when he wasn't around. He made me happy. I didn't know what to do. I told him he was stifling me—that I didn't want to lose my independence and not have any freedom. He wanted to help me escape, and I forced him to barter. I told him we didn't have a future because you wouldn't accept him because he was just a bandit and a kidnapper—that's the furthest thing from the truth. All the things he's done with the gang he's done reluctantly. Why, he's no bandit at all!" She heaved out another sob before whispering, "Papa, he's a reluctant bandit."

She threw her head down on his shoulder and starting weeping anew. Daniel just held her until she was sniffling, then carried her to bed. He laid her down and promised to talk more about it after she rested. He went to the living room and drank some more coffee. How was he going to handle this? At least his instincts were spot on about Charlie—he didn't belong and now he knew why. He'd have to look into the stagecoach ambush and see what he could find. There had to be more to this story than either of them knew. He was going to find out.

❧ 40 ❧

Charlie went around camp after breakfast to let everyone know that they were moving out and to pack up their necessities. He answered the same questions over and over. *No, I don't know where we're going. Yes, Annabelle is gone.* He moved quickly enough so everyone had enough time, but his heart wasn't in it. The last person he found was Travis. He stopped in front of him, shoving his hands in his pockets.

"She gone?"

"Yup."

"How're you doing there?"

"Not good. She wouldn't talk to me the whole way down—she's the one who wanted to negotiate, too."

"Hmm. You better come with me to find Jimmy. Time to talk, seriously."

They had found Jimmy still with the horses. He was brushing them down and checking hooves again. Not that they needed it, but there were a couple of men who kept taking mysterious night rides that, between them, they pretended didn't happen, like Wrighty and Moris. He wanted to make sure no one else threw a shoe or had any minor injuries needing looking after. Jimmy stopped brushing to look up at Charlie and Travis.

"What now?" Jimmy was squinting up at them, the sun blinding him. He didn't bother shading his eyes; his attention was already back on the horse he was brushing.

"We need to have a game plan—let's go inside where we can't be seen talking."

"Better make it quick because everyone's going to be hollering to have their horses 'tended to,' as if I'm up here twiddling my thumbs."

Travis chuckled at that. "They just like to pretend that they're important. Makes 'em feel good. Never mind them. Look—" he nodded between the brothers, "We have a situation here. Van Der Kamp seems to want to have a confrontation with the sheriff, I can sense it. He's not at all in hurry to leave. He hasn't even packed. He might even wait until sundown to get moving, which is very unlike him."

Charlie bobbed his head. "I agree. He was pretty casual when I told him the sheriff was certain he was going to catch up to us. He said the sheriff and him had things to discuss in neutral territory. I don't know what that means and if it has anything to do with Annabelle or not."

"No, more likely Mack—the sheriff's father. He's the one who hired the gang to put out a hit on your father." Charlie and Jimmy looked at each other, mouths open. "They had some sort of side agreement—outside normal banking business. It had something to do with your older brother."

"Annabelle told me to ask you about him. What do you know?" Jimmy sounded hopeful, and Travis cringed at the thought of crushing his hopes.

"Nothing good, I'm sorry, Jimmy. He was supposed to run the mine for Mack. He's the one who owns these mines."

"But the band of prospectors lived here. We ran them off."

"By Mack's orders. He owns the rest of the land and has been driving off the other miners. He hasn't paid for much of the land but 'owns' the whole parcel. He's taking it over."

"Is the sheriff crooked? He seemed on the up and up."

"No, that's the problem. Mack wanted Daniel, the sheriff, to run the mines. For whatever reason, Daniel looked into it but didn't stay there long. I'm not sure what happened, but he went into law enforcement almost immediately after he arrived. Him and Mack haven't talked since. Talk in the town is that he cares more about the townspeople than he does the mine, although he's good to the miners themselves."

"What do you want us to do?"

"Wrighty wants to take over the gang. He's been doing things here and there to undermine Van Der Kamp for a long while. Van Der Kamp's aware of this. He's been giving Wrighty enough rope to hang himself. Wrighty's collecting men to go into town and take Annabelle for himself." He grabbed Charlie's arm just as Charlie jerked, then continued. "You and I are going to town and settle this with Wrighty, once and for all. Together—got it?" Travis tilted his head toward Charlie and quirked his brow. "He might not openly defy Van Der Kamp, but he's still enough of a skunk to sneak off. And when he does, we'll trail him."

Charlie blew out a breath but gave a curt nod. "Got it."

"Jimmy, I know you want to stay with Van Der Kamp and get justice from within—is that still the case with Wrighty breaking off into his own gang of sorts?"

Locking eyes with Travis, Jimmy gave a slow nod but didn't say anything.

"Fine. This is what's going to happen. Jimmy, you just keep working the horses and getting men ready to leave. If anyone asks where we're going, say that we saw Wrighty and some others leave, and we went after them. That'll be the truth, so you won't be lying. I'll be coming back, but Charlie won't. He's going to stay with the sheriff and Annabelle. I'll let the sheriff know about you and what's going on and together we'll get you help. I'll keep you updated, but until you hear from me, it's business as usual. Understand?"

Charlie just stood there with slack shoulders, his features pulled downward. "She's not going to have me, Travis. Sheriff won't, either. Not after what I've done. I have to come back with you."

Travis grabbed Charlie by his shoulders and looked him right in the eye. "Charlie, I bet you dollars that by now, Annabelle has spilled the beans about how she feels about you. The sheriff would be glad to have you for his daughter. You kept her safe, healthy, and happy—despite everything. You did what you had to do. I promise you, he'll understand. He's that kind of guy."

"But Jimmy—"

"As soon as Jimmy's done doing what he needs to do, I'll get him back to you and prove he's better than all right. You two can go from there. It may be a long while, but we'll know where to find you." He winked at Jimmy, who smiled his first broad, genuine smile in a long time. It made him look younger and lightened up his face. "Jimmy's going to be a great lawman if that's what he decides to do with himself. He's got plenty of time to decide, don't you Jimmy?"

Jimmy nodded enthusiastically, which made Charlie smile. They drew close, slapping each other on the back.

"Don't worry, Charlie. I told you, Annabelle loves you. She was just scared. It'll all work out. Remember? That's what you've always told me, and I always believed you." Jimmy clapped him on the shoulder.

"Thanks for everything, Jimmy." Charlie started to turn away but thought better of it. He had to say his piece to Jimmy now. "Look, Jimmy—I don't know when we'll have to be leaving, or when we'll see each other next. But I love you and I'll always help you if you want it or need it. You know where to find me." He looked at Travis, who nodded.

"We've got to get moving, men. No telling when Van Der Kamp is going to want to pull out—he's hard to read right now." Travis clapped Jimmy on the shoulder. "Hang tight. I'll be back as soon as I can. I have to report back to Van Der Kamp after we take care of this business."

Charlie and Travis went off to get ready to leave at the drop of a hat, whenever Van Der Kamp made his move. No one seemed to take the threat of Sheriff O'Donnell too seriously, given that they assumed Mack was in charge of this operation. Travis shook his head, thinking about the gang's general pridefulness. *Sheriff O'Donnell won't be a threat, but not for the reasons they expected.*

~41~

The posse rode out at exactly 11:45 a.m., two days after the handoff. Daniel thought the time would never come. He was eager to meet up with this Wrighty
character. He'd done some more checking on him, and the
more he found out, the less inclined he was to be gentle with
him. He hoped that he found Wrighty before finding Van Der
Kamp, oddly enough. He wondered how much Wrighty was
behind all of the violence attributed to the gang, after what
Annabelle had told him. She was safely with the Johanssons,
and he knew that she wouldn't stray this time. She'd learned
a lesson the hard way. He also suspected she harbored secret
hopes of Charlie finding her.

They'd been on the trail for a couple of hours when two
riders approached them. Everyone tensed, hands to firearms.
Daniel squinted and saw that one of them was very tall and
broad—Charlie. He couldn't make out the other man with
him, but he looked like he could hold his own. He held up his
hand to halt the posse's progression and waited for the strangers to approach. Firearms were at the ready.

Just like he did the first time he met the sheriff, Charlie
held his arms out wide to his sides, dropping the reins. They
slowed their approach as Travis called out to them.

"Travis Hendersen—federal marshal." He held up his
badge. "This here is Charlie Stapleton—he's a former cap-

tive of the Van Der Kamp gang. We're looking for Sheriff O'Donnell." They stopped about twenty yards away from the posse, waiting for a response.

Daniel sized Travis up. "Charlie, this man telling true?"

"Yes, sir. He knows about my parents' deaths, although he wasn't there when it happened. He knows things about you. I recommend we talk—Annabelle's in danger again."

The sheriff rode his horse closer to the pair, staying the posse.

"Better talk quick. Annabelle told me about Wrighty, and he's the first one on my list."

Charlie's face went dark, confirming what he knew about the man.

Travis stuck out his hand. "Good to meet you, Sheriff. I was assigned to infiltrate Van Der Kamp's gang and relay whatever information I could back to the government. He'd been hitting some high-profile people and doing some damage to government operations. I go in and out of contact with them—Van Der Kamp sometimes sends me out for reconnaissance but mostly for personal information. He knows I have contacts. Last time I went out, it was to gather information about you."

The sheriff's usually neutral demeanor fell. "What the hell for?"

"Mack."

Daniel's face went red, and his jaw twitched. "What the hell has he done now?"

"I'm glad to see I was correct in my assessments and intel. He put a hit out on Frank Stapleton; that's why Van Der Kamp's here. He was hired for the job. That was further south, when they were traveling to see the mines. The mines Mack still wants you to run."

Daniel's jaw clamped down, and his knuckles went white clutching the reins. He nodded for Travis to continue.

"Stapleton was trying to blackmail Mack; that's when Mack had the hit put out on him. I don't know the complete plans, but Van Der Kamp was supposed to secure the area around the mines he already owns. He did that by scaring off some of the last prospectors—they killed old Davy and then spread the ghost story about him so they'd have that area undisturbed for a base camp. That's where you found the gang hiding. They're heading due east from there but weren't in a hurry to leave. In fact, you should catch up to them fairly soon, if you ride hard. Charlie came back and Van Der Kamp didn't sound the alarm. Took their time gathering up and heading out. Didn't head out until this morning—he waited until the last minute to leave. We departed from the gang, with Van Der Kamp's blessing." Travis cocked his head for Charlie to continue.

"Van Der Kamp told me that he had some unfinished business with you and some things to tell you on neutral ground," Charlie added. "He was vague, and I didn't press him."

"For obvious reasons."

"Where're you heading out now?"

"We're going to town to find Annabelle. Wrighty may be after her. He doesn't let things go—he considers Annabelle his for some odd reason." Travis shifted in the saddle. "It's just a hunch—a good one based on Wrighty's previous behavior."

"He took off in a different direction than the rest of the gang, and some of his cronies went with him. We really have to find her, sir. Where is she?"

Daniel looked between the two men, assessing their faces and body language. The horses shifted nervously from the energy of the hunt. Finally, he said, "She's with the Johanssons; they own the bakery. She's to stay put." The three of them looked at each other and shared a chuckle. "She will this time. She's been contrite and remorseful about the way things have panned out." This time Daniel looked directly at Charlie. "Son, I think you should really talk to her, you know?"

Charlie nodded, hope springing anew in him. He was getting a second chance—a second chance at so many things. He smiled brightly and nodded, looking younger than his twenty-one years. Before Travis knew what he was about, Charlie touched his horse's flanks with his boots and was off like lightning toward town. Travis and Daniel had a moment of being dumbfounded before Travis sprinted after him, throwing a wave back at Daniel. Daniel watched for only a moment, shaking his head and smiling, before turning back to the posse.

"They're heading east and not moving fast according to the fed. Subdue as many men as you can, but don't be afraid to shoot. If anyone sees Van Der Kamp, he's mine. Apparently, he has some things to say to me, and I want to get to the bottom of all this. Willard Wright—the one they call Wrighty— is mine, as well. Don't kill Van Der Kamp, though. I'm tired of this nonsense. All clear?"

Everyone nodded. They heard the conversation and they were fully aware of how dangerous Wrighty was. They also had an inkling of what he'd done to Annabelle, which made them furious.

Daniel raised his arm and, as he kicked his horse's flanks, shouted, "Let's ride!"

They left in a cloud of dust, riding in the opposite direction of Travis and Charlie, but with no less emotion or purpose.

✦ **42** ✦

The posse could see the cloud of dust ahead of them. Just like Travis indicated, they weren't that far out. Daniel spurred his horse on, signaling for the others to come around the flanks of the gang. There were fewer of them than they anticipated, which was a good sign. Oddly enough, as they neared, the entire gang slowed down, allowing themselves to be surrounded. They had their hands on their firearms but didn't draw. The posse had their firearms trained on the bandits. Van Der Kamp was casual, as if he were waiting for his comrades to catch up. His hand was on his pommel, face and shoulders were relaxed. He looked ready to smile—odd, coming from a taciturn man.

Daniel rode through the middle of the group and stopped in front of Van Der Kamp. They took measure of each other before simultaneously nodding. Daniel tipped his hat back as he leaned forward.

"Heard you wanted to have a little chat with me, Mr. Van Der Kamp."

Van Der Kamp ran his tongue over his teeth, making a sucking sound before answering. "Yup. How about we ride aways from them, and I'll tell you."

Daniel eyed him warily, wondering if this was just a ploy. Everything had been too easy so far. It was as if Van Der Kamp had invited the posse to tea. He was hardly behaving like a criminal who had a two-day head start—which he didn't even use.

Nodding, he said, "You don't mind if you I ask you to throw down your firearms, do you?"

Van Der Kamp shook his head. Holding one arm out and reaching for his pistol nice and slow with the other, he pulled it out of the holster and handed it to the sheriff by the barrel. He did the same thing for the gun in his left holster and the shotgun holstered on the saddle. He also handed him a large knife for good measure. Daniel took each item, one by one, and put them in his saddlebag. He'd return them—he just wasn't sure when that would be.

"Keep an eye on the men. Nothing is going to happen to Van Der Kamp as long as everyone keeps a cool head. Understand?"

All the men nodded in a variety of ways, albeit some begrudgingly. After giving everyone the once-over, Daniel nodded to Van Der Kamp. "Lead the way."

They rode off quite a few paces from everyone, despite being downwind of them. When Van Der Kamp stopped, he turned around and gave Daniel a steady perusal. Daniel was curious about this, as they didn't know each other personally, and Daniel had never had any business with him before the robbery, which seemed, at best, to be a standard-issue robbery. He submitted to it because he was curious, but he was also accustomed to it because of all his years of enduring Mack. When Van Der Kamp seemed satisfied, he leaned forward.

"Your daddy is Mack Pennington, and he hired my gang to do a series of jobs for him." When Daniel didn't say anything, he continued. "It was fine, at first, because we were running low on funds, and I only do jobs that send a message to the government."

"What do you mean, send messages?"

"The war did us all in, and it's the stubbornness of the men in the government and those with money who put us there. We didn't have to spend that many years killing our own kin, not even a day—over what? Nothing. Nothing to the common man. Money to those who already have it. Freedom to the slaves who'll never really be completely free—all because of the man who has money and power. We're a bunch of vets who no longer have a place in society. We did what we were told, but we no longer fit in—in some cases, we're patently rejected. Well, I don't cotton with that, and I decided to send a few messages of my own."

"How's Mack fit into that?"

"He just came at the right time. I'm tiring of all this." He waved his hand around. "Been ready to leave it but still needed some money to settle down. This was supposed to be a one-off thing, and he's turned it into a logistical nightmare."

Daniel barked a bitter laugh. "I could've told you that. He's the devil himself. Why him?"

"He came to us because of Stapleton—he double-crossed Mack."

"How am I involved?"

"You wouldn't cooperate. He's still trying to get you to run that damn mine of his and not be sheriff. That's unless you decided to go crooked and look the other way."

"Absolutely not. He knows that."

Van Der Kamp nodded, turning his head away from Daniel to spit tobacco. "I know."

"So, why're you here, then?"

"Unfinished business."

Daniel quirked a brow at him and waited him out.

"Mack's done and crossed a hard line with me. He asked me to take out Stapleton—fine by me, he's as crooked as the day is long. No problem there. But he knew the whole family was on that coach and *neglected to tell me*. Intel is important to a soldier and a hired hand like me, you know?" He raised his brows at Daniel who gave him a slow nod. He knew where this story was going. "Wrighty got his hands all over this one. Slaughtered the driver and Stapleton. Made the boys watch while he taunted them first. I had Jaems shoot the wife, put her out of her misery—bad enough her and the boys had to watch. I wasn't going to let anything else happen to her. He was going for the boys when Goat intervened, convincing me to spare them." He waved his hand. "I didn't need convincing—Goat just threw me a bone on that one. I'll spare you the details, but you can guess who one of them is. That's why I sent him—he didn't make sense to you, did he, Sheriff?"

"No, he was a puzzling piece to me. Very polite and caring toward Annabelle, too."

"I'm not officially betraying any confidences—as far as it goes, you caught me and I escaped. But I wanted you up here to tell you what you needed to know. Charlie, he's about as different from his pa as night is from day." He pulled in a long breath through one nostril, looking out at nothing.

"It was fortuitous that Charlie kidnapped your sweet Annabelle there—made what I'd been thinking all right."

"And what was that?"

"That I was no longer doing what Mack asked. I did the first job and hated it. No women or children—he knew that and set me up to be the butcher everyone thinks I am. It was too late by the time we pulled the coach over—ironically, it set the wheels in motion, so to speak. They saw us and knew who we were. Besides, Wrighty and his cronies were on it like stink on shit. That's why he's so pissed at Charlie—he got saved. Besides, that boy stands up for what's right. Helps his brother no matter what. Helped Annabelle." He pulled in another single nostril breath then spit again. He turned to look at Daniel.

"When I met Annabelle I knew that she could never get into the hands of the likes of Mack. That you must've done something right by defying him and raising that little girl all on your own out here." Van Der Kamp went thoughtful for moment. "That whore of a wife is back with Mack, you know." This time he cleared his throat and spit with venom. "You deserve better than that."

Daniel went pale at the thought of Lissa. He had a love-hate relationship with that woman. More hate than anything, especially these days.

"There's got to be more than that. The Stapleton job was small vittles for you—what'd Mack do to you, personally? He gets under people's skin easily, but he usually has something on everyone, whether they know it or not."

"That's between me and Mack." His lips twitched. "What you need to know is that he probably knows about Annabelle and will come for her. He's not beyond using her against you. Why he's so set on you running this mine is beyond me. No offense."

"None taken. He just doesn't like being denied, that's all." They were quiet for a moment. "I've been keeping my eyes open for him, wondering when he'd come."

"Here's what I have on you—your ex-wife or whatever you want to call her—she's spreading rumors that you're doing dirty business out here. We all know who is, but she's fingering you for it. That's supposedly why she's run to Mack for *support*. Load of bullshit if you ask me. Why anyone would believe that poor excuse of a woman, I do not know. Pardon me for saying so. Annabelle is all your doing and none of hers."

The sheriff blinked, then frowned. "What am I supposed to do about that? They're back east, and I'm here."

Nodding, he deeply exhaled. "They're going to try to pin you for the murder of the prospector."

"The ghost of Davy? That prospector?" Daniel snorted until he realized that Van Der Kamp was dead serious. "You've got to be kidding me."

"Nope."

"Well, what can I do about that?"

"You can let me go."

"What?"

"It was another hit our gang did, per Mack. He wanted all this land and didn't want to pay for it. We killed him and scared off the others, spreading ghost rumors. I have damning evidence that can lay the blame at Wrighty's door for that one, I'll mail it after I reach my next destination. You let me and the gang go—you go back and help Travis and Charlie get Wrighty and his followers, and you'll still have a win."

Daniel couldn't believe his ears. Here he had one of the most notorious bandits and Wanted men in the territory within his reach, and he was supposed to just let him walk away. He was shaking his head in disbelief. It went against everything he believed in and worked for.

It was as if Van Der Kamp could hear his thoughts. "You're stuck either way with Mack. You either bend the rules a bit and let me and my men go, or you get pinned with a crime you didn't commit. Lissa is the one who's trying to pin you with it. She's planning on telling how you were abusive and threatened her when she heard you planning the murder—that's supposedly why she escaped."

Air expelled from the back of Daniel's throat. "You've got to be kidding." He slapped his thigh with his palm. He would've thrown his tin cup if he had it in hand. "That damned bitch. I stood up for her and she just played me. Played me *and* Annabelle."

"Should've known better with that one. I'm sure the warning signs were there." Daniel glared at him, and Van Der Kamp held up his hands. "I'm not here to judge. I'm just saying you have a choice, and I think I'm the one to bet on, not them. You also need to hurry and make your decision because Charlie and that fed are going to be needing your help, real soon." Van Der Kamp leaned back in his saddle and let Daniel work that out for himself. He'd already led that horse to water; he was just waiting for it to drink.

"Damn. Damn, damn, damn it!" His horse started shifting and snorting beneath him, bobbing his head in agitation. "Fine." He shook his head. "Wait—how'd you know?"

"I've known—needed better intel and he provided it. Don't worry, it's for the greater good—anything to bring Mack down." Tilting his head toward Daniel's saddlebags, he said, "I'll just take my weapons back, if you please? Me and my men will ride out nice and slow, and you won't be seeing us around here, again. I'll mail you the evidence against Wrighty."

"Why are you turning on him, now?"

"Not now, been a while. I've been watching him—he's been chomping at the bit to run this gang, and he's making promises he can't deliver. I've been giving him enough rope to hang himself. Looks like a woman rejecting him was all that was needed to send him over the edge. Mmm-hmm. Can't take a blow like that to his ego."

Daniel's face went red with rage, and he nodded to Van Der Kamp. He handed over the shotgun, then proceeded to dig out the guns and knife and hand them over. "I'll follow you back to the men, and you tell them how it's going to play out. I'll let my men know."

Before they reached the group of men, Van Der Kamp gave his orders in his usual low, slow voice. "We're leaving here nice and slow. Plans are still the same, but the sheriff's posse won't be taking us or following us. They're going after Wrighty, y'all hear?" There were murmurs, and grumbling, but their hands relaxed from their ready postures, and they turned their horses in Van Der Kamp's direction.

The sheriff raised his voice to his men. "We're heading back to help Travis and Charlie get Wrighty. He's got a small gang of men with him and they're after Annabelle. There are greater forces at play here. The fed knows all about them." Daniel looked around him, wondering where Jake went. "Where's Jake?" Apparently, the blacksmith noticed and called out to him.

"Sheriff, the deputy said he had something he had to take care of a ways back. Told me not to question him."

Daniel shot a look back at Van Der Kamp who shook his head, lips turned downward. They were thinking the same thing—Wrighty. Daniel kicked his horse's flanks, and they flew off toward the path, the posse hot on his heels.

Annabelle promised Mrs. Johansson she wouldn't go far. She was quickly collecting more eggs from the chicken coop and coming directly back to the kitchen. They'd decided to bake some more pies to keep themselves busy. Mrs. Johansson also wanted to spend some woman time alone with Annabelle to hear about what happened and how she was doing. She figured there was more to the story than the sheriff was telling her, but she didn't want to upset him by asking. He already looked fit to be tied about multiple things—she'd seen that look on him before and knew she wouldn't get far when he was in such a state.

She was laying out the rolling pins and getting the flour measured out when Annabelle came back into the kitchen.

"I actually found quite a few eggs out there. Your helper must've missed 'em. There were a few in the bushes as well." Annabelle held up the basket to show Mrs. Johansson.

"Wonderful! Then I won't have to go out first thing collecting because we'll have some left over, plus what little Nellie brought in for me this morning." Nodding, she took the basket and set it on the counter behind them.

Divvying up the sugar, salt, and flour, she had Annabelle begin sifting while she went for the spices. Over her shoulder, she called out, "Annabelle, honey? Are you ready to talk about what happened and how you kept yourself out there? If you aren't, I understand." She scurried over to the worktable with the spices. She put her hand on Annabelle's arm, looking at her with a sweet, kind expression. "I just thought it might be nice to talk to a woman about what happened, as well as someone who isn't your father." Winking, she went about her business, letting Annabelle decide whether or not she wanted to talk.

Annabelle sifted the flour, moving it from one bowl to another. Pushing a strand of hair out of her face, she said, "You're right. I've been surrounded by men; it'd be nice to have a woman's opinion for a change. I don't get one very often, after all."

"MaryAnne doesn't come around very often, does she?"

"Not since she got married. She has better things to do." Annabelle gave Mrs. Johansson a wry grin.

"Cheeky girl! Well, go on. Tell me what you want to share. I'm all ears—and heart, honey." She gave Annabelle a loving look. "Your daddy means a lot to us."

Annabelle smiled back at the kindly woman. "You know, he speaks very fondly of you and Mr. Johansson, too."

Mrs. Johansson clasped her hands at her breast, and her eyes got misty. "Go on, girl."

"Well, I don't rightly know where to start. I guess I have to say that my ways have caused some people a lot of trouble—I didn't mean for that to happen. You know?"

"I do. You're a good girl, you really are." She cupped Annabelle's face with the palm of her hand. "What did you learn?"

Swallowing, Annabelle went on. "I always thought that Papa was heartbroken because Mama wasn't here with us anymore…" Mrs. Johansson wasn't able to keep from making a sour face. Annabelle tilted her head in question but didn't ask. "When I met Charlie—he's the one who took me from the mercantile—I was scared and hoppin' mad. I was readying to run away and find some space for myself, be my own person, when I found myself being tossed from one set of men to another. I was tired of being unable to do anything without an escort, and Papa suggested it was time I thought about marrying and that's when the deputy said he wanted to court me. I don't like him; he looks at me funny, and he touches me inappropriately and too often." She drew in a big breath, releasing it loudly. Her words came out in whirl of one breath, but Mrs. Johansson was able to catch the last part. Her eyes narrowed and her lips thinned.

"Tell me about the deputy, Annabelle." Her voice went low exactly like Papa's when he was angry but wasn't quite ready to lay it on the line.

"Well, he'd offer to escort me to the mercantile and different places—he checked in on me a lot, too. Just stopping by the house when he knew Papa wasn't home." She stopped what she was doing and looked up at the ceiling to think. "You know—he seemed to show up when I was doing laundry or if I was pumping water for a bath. But he always showed up after I drew and carried all the water in…odd."

Mrs. Johansson's face went three shades darker as she clutched the spoon in her hand. She finally gave vent to her anger, smacking the spoon the counter, startling Annabelle out of her thoughts.

"Why that no-good, dirty scoundrel! Your daddy was wanting you to think about marrying *him*?" She quirked her brow at a wide-eyed, open-mouthed Annabelle, who lamely nodded back at her. "When the sheriff gets back, I'm having a word with him." She was muttering to herself, sorting out the spices. "Men! I need something to chop. Let's get the apples." They went to the pantry and brought out a large basket of apples. By the time they got it on the worktable, it was too late to notice that they weren't alone. Their mouths dropped open at the sight of a handsome blonde man leaning against the doorframe, arms and legs crossed, looking smug. He watched them stare at him with perverse satisfaction. Pushing off the doorframe, he stalked toward Annabelle. He stopped too close with his boots touching the hem of her skirt and brushed hair from her face. She was still too shocked to get angry at or step away from this intimacy. Mrs. Johansson, however, was not.

"Sir—you get your hands off Miss O'Donnell right this instant." She stamped her foot on the floor, her blood pumping through her veins like a racehorse. She was still fired up from their earlier conversation.

Wrighty had the nerve to tip his hat to her. "Why madam, lovely to see that you're taking good care of our Annabelle here." He tilted his head in Annabelle's direction. "I'll be taking over now." He went to reach for her when she stepped back, holding up her hand.

"Wait a minute—is the gang here? You were supposed to leave—my father's out hunting you." There weren't any windows for her to look out of, but she tried looking around Wrighty anyway, hoping to see someone else with him.

"Nope. They have things handled. Your pa was nearing Van Der Kamp when I left."

"Why'd you leave? I thought you were Van Der Kamp's right-hand man." Her voice pitched higher.

"Van Der Kamp has everything under control, darling. You're to come with me." This time he grabbed her elbow, pulling her closer to him.

Annabelle yanked her elbow back, her eyes burning into him. "I will not, Wrighty. Papa told me to wait for him and that's what I intend to do." She crossed her arms over her chest, giving him a firm nod. Her time with Charlie had emboldened her. Boring her eyes into him, she dared him to say otherwise.

Wrighty laughed in response. "Oh, Annabelle," he shook his head, mirth spread across his face. "You had no problem disobeying before and now you're suddenly a model daughter? Why the sudden change? You aren't actually hoping someone's going to come save you, are you?" He leaned into her space with curiosity written all over his face.

"Sir!" Mrs. Johansson shrieked.

Annabelle had started to shuffle her feet and look away when he asked his question. Wrighty's face lit up at the opportunity to take another jab at her. He laughed, throwing his head back. "You think Charlie's coming!" The smile fell from his face as it went dark. "He ain't gonna come. You made it clear you didn't want any part of him."

Annabelle cut him off. "Why are you here? Why haven't you rode out? If you get caught, you're going to jail—or worse." She spoke the last part on a low breath.

"I don't like repeating myself, woman. Once we leave, there won't be any more sass from you—do you hear? If you're good, I might even marry you. You seem like the marrying type."

"Marry? I told my father—no marriage. Especially not to you."

"Why I'm gonna—"

"You're gonna what, Wrighty?"

The women audibly sucked in air, looking up at another man filling the doorframe.

"Deputy Collins!"

"Jake—" Annabelle gasped. Her eyes went wide and wild at the sight of him. "How'd you know? What's going on?"

The deputy grinned at her. "Glad to see you missed me, too." His eyes moved to Wrighty. "I'll be taking Annabelle now."

"No, you won't. She's going with me. Van Der Kamp owes me—she's as good as promised to me."

"I don't think so. She's mine."

"I don't belong to any of you. Get out of here." Annabelle pointed, directing them to the door. The men looked at her, then at each other. They both started laughing.

"Not likely, darlin'." Jake shook his head, crossing his arms.

"Like I said before, we have unfinished business." Wrighty winked at her.

Mrs. Johansson had moved herself in front of Annabelle, urging her with small arm motions to run out the back way, but Jake was quicker. His arm flew out, grabbing her hard. She shrieked in pain as he yanked her from Mrs. Johansson's back.

"I knew you'd try something, you old bat."

"Jake, let me go. Papa will never let you court me if you keep this up."

"Nice try, darlin'. He'll never let me court you after all this. I'm taking you with me, like I should've done before all this." He used his arm to indicate the mayhem in the bakery.

Wrighty grunted and pointed his finger at Jake. "You think I'm going to let you go after all this, Jake? You let us down. You were supposed to shoot that bastard Charlie when you had the chance. It wasn't supposed to get this far."

"You know—" Annabelle was cut off by Jake.

"If you didn't make me wait at the edge of the forest and be 'unavailable,' then yeah, I would've shot him. Remember?"

"We needed assurance that you wouldn't go run and tell what was going on—despite it all, you're still a pussy at heart."

The women gasped at that, but the men ignored them. Jake's grip on Annabelle became tighter. Annabelle and Mrs. Johansson looked between the two men, confused and horrified at what they saw playing out. Annabelle stopped struggling with Jake because she didn't want him to press harder—a lesson she'd learned the hard way with Wrighty.

"Don't be sayin' such foul things in front of my intended, or I'll have to take you to account, Wrighty. You ain't no saint, either."

"Pfft. Don't go getting all big on me now, Jake. I might have to share some things with your *intended* and see how she feels about you then." He threw back his head and laughed as if he'd told the best joke. His laughter only provoked Jake more.

Jake shoved Annabelle behind him as he lunged at Wrighty. Wrighty bent in half, rolling Jake over his back, stood up, and dumped him on the floor. He spun around with his hands raised, ready for the punch Jake threw. As they fought, Annabelle turned around to run. Unfortunately, she ran directly into Lafayette's arms. Because everyone was so engrossed in the fighting, they hadn't seen him sneak into the room. He laughed at his luck, turned her in his arms to face outward—his hand over her mouth, the other arm pinning her arms to her waist. He quickly dragged her out of the bakery backwards, without either man noticing. Seth had come in the back door and was coming up behind Jake. When Jake reached back to throw a punch, Seth grabbed his fist and held it. Wrighty wrenched back his arm and threw a hard punch into Jake's gut. Seth released Jake's hand as he doubled over. Wrighty kicked Jake in the face, knocking him back down again.

Seth pushed Mrs. Johansson out the back before Wrighty could notice she was still there. He felt bad for Annabelle, because once Wrighty got his hands on her, she was in for a world of hurt. At least he could save her friend—she'd have one less person to grieve before this was all over. He had grown to like the poor girl.

"You have big balls thinking that you could double-cross the gang, especially me. Any last words? Because I have to get to my woman and be off before your friend the sheriff returns."

"She's not your woman, *coward*." He was on all fours, locking eyes with Wrighty. "He won't be back for a while. He's with Van Der Kamp, discussing whatever it is he needs to tell him." He spit out blood, wiping his mouth with the back of his hand. His eyes narrowed at Wrighty as he struggled to stand up. "I didn't do any double-crossing. You did. You never planned on giving me my cut, and you never planned on killing the sheriff so I could run this town. Hell, I earned the right to Annabelle, but you won't even let me have that, will you?"

"Nope. I didn't plan on you making it this far. I expected the sheriff to figure you out sooner than he did. How'd you manage that?"

Before he could answer, they heard a gunshot outside and men hollering. Reaching for their guns, they ran out the front door.

$$\sim 44 \sim$$

Charlie and Travis raced down the winding paths and through the forest as fast as they could. It was slow going, especially since they were in such a hurry. The roads were rugged and bumpy, and the some of the paths were overgrown. There were plenty of places where the horses could sprain a fetlock or catch a rock in a hoof. They needed to be careful.

Charlie knew this from traveling up these paths with Annabelle the first time. This time seemed even more harrowing than that—back then, he was running for his life. Now, he was running toward it. He had to reach her before Wrighty got there. Wrighty's temper had been out of control. There was no knowing what he'd do when he caught up to her. Look what he did to her before—all because she tried to protect herself when she first arrived. Charlie wanted to hit something just thinking about it. His horse sensed Charlie's upset—he tensed under him and whinnied. Charlie took a deep breath, trying to calm himself, and relaxed his tension on the reins and his thighs. They'd better get there in time—he didn't know what he'd do if they didn't.

They broke out into the direct sunlight as they rode away from the forest. The edge of town was in sight, and they gave their horses their head. Straining and puffing, the horses streaked across the open area, their hooves thundering on the hard ground, kicking up dust. Both riders were leaning over their horse's necks, urging them on. Nearing the edge of town, they slowed to a trot and took a look around, making sure they weren't going to be ambushed and not wanting to bring too much attention to themselves. The streets seemed fairly quiet as they moved down the middle, looking from side to side.

"Sheriff said she'd be at the baker's. I think it's toward the end of the street down there. I remember seeing it when I came to check things out the first time." He nodded in the general direction he was talking about.

They were walking their horses, so as not to raise suspicions, but something felt off. The air was too still. Travis shot Charlie a look, and Charlie lifted his chin in acknowledgement. The few people who were on the street seemed to be scurrying away. They looked around but couldn't see what the pedestrians saw, although they did sense something. Despite that, they kept moving toward the bakery when they heard shouting. A man was pulling a woman out of a shop. He had his arm around her waist, pulling her flush to his chest. He had a gun trained on someone inside as he backed out.

"Who's that?"

"Lafayette! Shit." Jumping onto their saddles, they raced down the street. Travis jumped down, training his gun on Lafayette. He was waiting for the man to stop moving so he wouldn't accidentally hit the woman, who he had now confirmed was Annabelle. He didn't get the chance, however, because someone from the alleyway took a shot at him. Charlie grabbed his gun and shot into the alley. He got Seth on the right shoulder, causing him to drop his gun on impact. Travis shot him in the heart before turning back to Lafayette.

Lafayette was looking at them with the barrel of his gun against Annabelle's temple. "Don't come closer! I'll kill her."

Annabelle's eyes were wide, but she still managed to softly say to him, "You're still mad about me head-butting you in the face, aren't you?"

"I am not!" Lafayette jerked as he shouted back at her, taking his eyes off of Travis. The gun came away from Annabelle's head—Lafayette was a notorious hand-talker. Travis took advantage of that momentary lapse by firing a shot at him, hitting him in the head. Lafayette's grip brought her down with his dead body. Annabelle screamed as they both fell to the boardwalk. Before Charlie or Travis could make it to the boardwalk, however, Wrighty and Jake appeared, side by side, with their guns drawn.

"Well, look at this." Wrighty straightened up with his legs spread wide. "If it ain't goody two-shoes, Charlie, and the prodigal son, Travis. What a fine pair you are. What the hell are you doing here?" He cocked his gun, pointing it at Charlie as Jake lifted Annabelle up from the ground and held her tightly. He positioned Annabelle in front of him so no one would be stupid enough to take a pot shot at him. He wanted Annabelle, but he couldn't enjoy her if he was dead.

"I could say the same of you, Wrighty. We asked about you, but no one seemed to know where you and your cronies were off to. Now we know." Travis nodded toward Annabelle. "You never did take rejection well, did you? Did that slip of woman hurt your manhood, Wrighty?"

Charlie had a panicked look on his face because he'd seen firsthand what Wrighty was capable of. He hissed at Travis, "Don't provoke him. He's violent."

Although Charlie didn't speak loud enough for him to hear, Wrighty took a stab at the conversation. "Better listen to goody two-shoes there, cowboy. Wouldn't want to get on the wrong side of Van Der Kamp now, would you?"

"Van Der Kamp and I have an understanding, unlike you and him. You're the one that better hightail it back to him and do some heavy kowtowing."

"Don't think so. I'm done kowtowing. You should know that by now."

"I figured. Just needed to hear you say it, that's all."

While Wrighty and Travis were bantering, Jake was slowly backing into the bakery. His hand went over Annabelle's mouth when she jerked. "Don't say a word," he whispered into her ear. She didn't say a word. Instead, she went limp in his arms as she purposely caught her heel on the doorjamb, tripping him up. He stumbled backwards as she slid down the front of him. Wrighty turned a furious face at them, shooting Jake in his forehead. For the second time that day, Annabelle was on the wrong end of the barrel, which was way too close for comfort. She gave it her best, but this time, she fainted before the spray hit her. The gunshots, gore, and copious amounts of blood overpowered her.

Charlie and Travis rushed the boardwalk before Wrighty got his bearings and tackled him. Charlie wrestled the gun out of his hand while Travis pulled his arms behind him, kneeling on his lower back. Charlie grabbed rope from his mount to tie him up, but not before Travis got a couple of punches in, subduing Wrighty's struggling. Together, they dragged him inside and tied him to a chair.

Mrs. Johansson was helping her husband into the dining area just as Travis was finishing tying Wrighty up. Her hand flew to her chest. "Oh, my." She started to look unsteady, so Travis went to her side and helped seat Mr. Johansson. "Where's Annabelle?" Her voice was warbly, and her eyes welled up.

"She's fine. Charlie's bringing her in now. She fainted when Wrighty shot the deputy. Are you Mrs. Johansson?" She nodded as he helped her to a seat. "I'll be right back."

Charlie carried Annabelle inside. She was cradled like a baby in his arms, murmuring but starting to come around. "It's okay, Wildflower. Everything's going to be all right. Shhh."

He set her down gently before addressing Mrs. Johansson. "The sheriff told me that Annabelle was safe with you. This is the first place we headed. I'm sorry we didn't make it sooner." He nodded toward Wrighty who was scowling at them.

Mrs. Johansson nodded furiously, flapping her hand, circling it above her head. "You have to hurry—there are others out there. One of them got my George—conked him on the head when they sneaked in the back to try and snatch Annabelle." She pointed through the kitchen to indicate the back door.

Charlie looked at Travis as they both stood. Travis looked down at Wrighty. "How many?" Wrighty just grunted until Travis kicked his chair. "I asked, how many?"

Wrighty sneered at him. "Like I'd tell the likes of you, kiss-ass."

Travis sighed. "All right then." He cocked his arm back, cracking his fist into Wrighty's face. Wrighty's head snapped back before dropping to his chest. Travis shook out his hand and said, "Well, let's go. I'll take the back and you take the front. They won't expect you to come back out, since you picked up Annabelle."

Charlie nodded, slipping out of the dining area, but not before he put a hand on Mrs. Johansson's shoulder. "Please watch over her again. Thank you." Before she could answer, he was gone.

$$\sim 45 \sim$$

Daniel was thankful for Van Der Kamp's easy manner. He may have made a deal with a devil but at least they were both fighting against Mack, the king of all devils. Van Der Kamp had that going for him. Daniel wasn't a fan of bending the laws, but somehow, things got out of hand, and he meant to fix it. He was just hoping the bloodshed could be kept to a low roar.

The posse rode in silence and made good time, much to everyone's relief. They still had plenty of daylight but needed to get a move-on. By the time they made it to the edge of town, the groups naturally split up, with half going down Main Street and the other half going around the backside. They were on the lookout for any strangers or anything odd in general. Very nonspecific, but by this point, they knew that less time spent talking meant a quicker showdown, and better yet, a quicker take-down.

It was the eerie quiet that clued Daniel in that the gang was still lurking in the shadows of the town. It was nearing early evening, and the sun was beginning to settle in for its nightly rendezvous with the other side of the earth. The sun was still beaming over the horizon at such a height that it made a harsh contrast between the light above and the growing shadows around. It also created a safe haven for those who didn't want to be found. Fortunately, Daniel's horse, Nash, didn't spook easily and was in familiar territory. He walked with the silent confidence of a prince returning home to his people coupled with the pride of a lion on the hunt. He knew what he was about. Daniel gave his strong neck a stroke, praising him for his stealth and confidence. Working together as one, he released the reins so he could have both hands at the ready and worked his horse with his legs and his thoughts.

Something rustled in the alleyway behind them, causing Nash to stop. Daniel drew both of his guns in response. They stilled, waiting for more sound to provide clues. They didn't have to wait long, as there was another rustle and a click of a hammer being cocked. Daniel simultaneously cocked both guns and pointed them in the direction of the noise. He had a better idea of where the sound came from, but he waited for the inevitable shift of someone trying to get a better aim. He heard it and fired. The bullet ricocheted off the building as a shot whizzed by his head.

"Damn." He shot back into the alley when he saw a figure move toward him and was rewarded with contact this time. A battle cry sounded as the man continued toward him with his gun drawn, readying to shoot. Daniel beat him to the punch and shot him in the chest. The man fell, but the commotion drew the attention of others who came to Daniel's aid.

"Sheriff. Are you all right?" It was Travis. He was on foot, gun drawn.

"What's the situation?"

"We've captured Wrighty, who shot Jake. There were two other men—a fatality and an injury. Charlie's out front searching. Mrs. Johansson said there were others but didn't mention how many. They ambushed her husband."

They went up to the body. They all looked down at it before Daniel toed it over. "Recognize this one?"

"Moris. He was the right-hand man to Wrighty, who, oddly enough, was the right-hand to Van Der Kamp. I think he," looking down at Moris, "was beginning to turn on Wrighty, but no one had much of a chance to cross him. They're lifers with him—like making a pact with the devil, only worse. Hell on earth."

They looked around them because the town was perking up. The townspeople seemed to know that the disruption was nearing its end. They looked up as the posse searching the backside of town brought one man in tow and Charlie came from the middle of town, all headed toward them. They converged, systematically walking the alleyways as well as the front and back of the shops, like a line of beaters on a hunt. They towed the prisoner along with them so as not to waste time locking him up. He hadn't provided any good information, so they gagged him on their shakedown of the town.

People were peering out of windows and doors now that the shooting had died down, and they saw a crowd of men walking the streets. They wanted to know who was there and if they were safe. People were calling out from various directions.

"Sheriff—is everything clear?"

"Who d'you have there?"

"Did the entire posse return?"

"Did you get the bandits?"

Questions were lobbed out of windows, doors, and on the boardwalk from some of the bolder men. Daniel nodded to them and held out his hand.

"Just clearing the streets, so to speak. Make sure no one's hiding in your doorways and alleyways—holler if you find anyone."

By the end of the night, they had found two other men. They locked the three men up, along with Wrighty. All of them had Wanted posters, so, despite the havoc they wreaked on the town, there were plenty of reasons to keep them locked up until other authorities could be notified and the traveling judge could officially sentence them.

✺ 46 ✺

Travis was sitting atop his horse, looking down at the sheriff, Charlie, and Annabelle. Wrighty was tied to the pommel of his saddle, flanked by two federal marshals. They were setting off for the Texas Territory, and Travis wanted to say his goodbyes. Wrighty was being extradited by Travis for his torture and subsequent murder of Sophia Goodman back in the Texas territory; the paperwork had finally come through. A judge had deemed that he needed to be tried for that crime first, and if he didn't find himself on the gallows, he'd be returned to the Arizona Territory to be judged for his crimes there. At the moment, those were less clear-cut because they involved the entire gang.

Additionally, since the Stapleton case was nearly a decade old, and it was the memory of a younger Charlie and his word against Wrighty's, they decided that they had a better chance of getting Wrighty on the Goodman case first. Besides, they'd have to admit that Charlie had been part of the reluctant robbery and kidnapping. They also would have to out Jimmy—and rob him of his revenge. Neither bode well for Charlie's reputation, with all that had happened. In any case, Travis still wanted to help Jimmy with getting Van Der Kamp's gang from within. That would blow their cover, and Jimmy remaining would raise questions—too many questions.

Travis felt bad for all that the brothers had been through. However, he felt it in his gut that Jimmy would make a fine lawman. He really wanted to see where that would lead. Allowing Jimmy this win from the inside would go a long way toward healing the young man's soul. He knew that from personal experience.

"Sheriff." Travis slid off his horse. "Been good to make your acquaintance. Many thanks for all your help." He shook Daniel's hand and turned toward Charlie. "I'll keep Jimmy safe and make sure I send word through the sheriff here. Annabelle," he tipped his hat, "You mind these good men now, you hear? They'll give you everything you want and need; just be clear about what those things are."

Annabelle blushed, looking down. Charlie nudged her, smiling. "Thanks Travis, for everything. I know I can breathe better when justice is served for that poor woman. Please stay safe and take care of Jimmy. He's like a brother I never had." She beamed brightly thinking about Jimmy.

With that, Travis smiled and put his foot in the stirrup, throwing his leg over the saddle. "We'll talk soon, Sheriff. I'll keep you posted."

The four men rode off while the sheriff, Annabelle, and Charlie watched them go. They were able to breathe a collective sigh of relief.

"Sheriff." A voice came from behind them, causing them to turn around. Mr. Johansson nodded to the three of them. "Mrs. Johansson sent me down to find you. She says she's made peach pie. I know that's your favorite. Either something's amiss or she's got some good news for you. Hard telling these days. Can you humor her and come on over?"

Daniel chuckled, shaking his head. "Hopefully she has something good to say. I, for one, would like to hear some more good news. We've had enough bad for a while."

"Yes, I'd hate to ruin the joyous occasion of Wrighty being led away." Annabelle shuddered. Charlie put his arm around her and pulled her in close. She always felt better in Charlie's arms. His big body was like a protective shield from the worries of the world, keeping her safe.

They walked in pairs back to the bakery, the wonderful smells of freshly baked goods leading them liked a Pied Piper. Mrs. Johansson was just getting the coffee off the stove as they walked in.

"Oh, good! I'm so glad you made it. Let me pour coffee. Honey, will you go bring the pie? It's cooled enough to cut."

Mr. Johansson went behind the counter to give his wife a kiss before he went into the kitchen to get the pie. She smiled back at him, patting his cheek. Charlie looked at Annabelle, sharing a smile. Daniel had given his blessing for a wedding after Charlie had asked for Annabelle's hand—he bypassed courting, given the situation they were in. They were just sad that Travis and Jimmy wouldn't be there to witness it. They knew Travis would let Jimmy know, which was a small consolation.

Mrs. Johansson poured coffee as Mr. Johansson came back with the pie. Everyone settled in and no one spoke for a few moments while they savored sugary peach goodness washed down with hot coffee. Wonderful aromas filled the air, along with groans and murmured words of appreciation.

"Mrs. Johansson, this is delicious! I hope you're able to make desserts for our wedding celebration. Would you, please?" Annabelle was shoveling more into her mouth before Mrs. Johansson could reply.

"I think Mrs. Johansson has something she wants to share with us, Annabelle," her father said.

"Yes, I do. I'm so happy and honored that you'd want me to bake for your nuptial celebration—that gives me such pleasure. Thank you—you must know I will!" She reached out, placing her hand over Annabelle's. "And, yes, Daniel, I do have something I'd like—no, need—to share."

Everyone went silent, anxiously waiting to hear what was so important. But before she could speak, Elroy came into the bakery.

"Oh, there you are, Sheriff. Sorry to interrupt, but the post came. I took his delivery for you since no one was at the jail. It's at the mercantile, but there were a couple of things for you that looked important." Elroy held up a small parcel and a couple of letters.

"Mighty fine of you, Elroy. I'm much obliged." Nodding, he took the items from him.

"No problem, Sheriff. John said he'll catch up to you after he settles in. I've got to get back to the store. I left Chandler in charge, and I can't do that for very long. Boy has the attention span of a gnat." Shaking his head, he scurried out of the bakery, picking up his pace as he crossed the street.

Daniel was turning the package around in his hands, trying to find some identification or markings on it.

"Who's it from?" Annabelle asked.

"It's unmarked." Daniel frowned, undoing the wrapping. On top of another small, wrapped parcel was a letter addressed to Daniel but with no other markings or indications of who it was from. He opened the letter, reading it silently.

Sheriff,

I won't tell you where we've gone, but know that we are not causing trouble. The evidence I promised you is in the package. Keep it safe, as I know you will need it in the near future. If I were you, I'd get Annabelle married off real quick and away from town for a while. Send her and Charlie—I'm assuming they've sorted things out—on an extended honeymoon. I also know you can afford to do so, so do it. Don't ask me how I know. I do know that trouble is coming to your doorstep, so you best take action, now.

~VDK

Daniel folded the letter up and tucked it back in the package, deciding it'd be best not to open it in front of mixed company, whatever it was.

Annabelle laid her hand on his arm. "Papa, what is it? You've gone so pale!"

Charlie knew what Van Der Kamp had told Daniel; they'd discussed it the night Charlie came to ask for Annabelle's hand. He looked into Daniel's eyes and knew the time had come. They'd have more to discuss, but not in front of Annabelle and the Johanssons. He lifted his chin in a small gesture so that the others wouldn't see the communication.

Daniel patted her hand, smiling. "It's just some legal bits. Everything will be okay, darling. I think we should get on this wedding. Let's get the preacher over this Saturday and you two can tie the knot and get on to living the lives you're supposed to live."

Mrs. Johansson seemed to read between the lines, so she picked up where he left off. "Well!" she said, straightening in her chair and bringing her hands together in front of her ample bosom. "That doesn't leave much time to get you fitted for a pretty new dress, does it? When we're done here, let's walk over to the mercantile and see what fabrics old Elroy is hoarding over there, shall we Annabelle?" She was all smiles.

"Can I, Papa?" She clutched her hands in front of her chest, her face lighting up. She was finally going to spend time with Charlie—alone. She missed sharing the cot with him, she shamefully admitted to herself. She missed his arms around her, holding her tight as she fell asleep, and she missed his kisses and the rest that they had. She felt herself growing warm just thinking of it all.

"Annabelle, dear. Whatever are you thinking of?" Mrs. Johansson teased. "I do think I see some color on your pretty little cheeks." She winked at her.

Annabelle cleared her throat. "Charlie, what colors do you like? What's your favorite color?"

"Wildflower, I like any color you choose to wear." Before she could protest, he smiled and continued. "I love blue on you. It makes the golden flecks in your eyes shine." He looked thoughtful for a moment. "Like the gold dust the miners treasure."

He almost forgot that her father was sitting there. He shook off the look of woolgathering he had, thinking about all the things he shouldn't be thinking about with regard to another man's daughter. Especially when that father was sitting right in front of him. He hazarded a glance at Daniel, who quirked a brow at him. "Ah, sorry, sir. It's just, well, Annabelle there is the most beautiful woman I've ever seen, and I feel so lucky to have her, that's all." He blushed to his roots.

"Annabelle, you go on with Mrs. Johansson and pick out whatever lovely fabric and whatnot you'll need for your wedding day. You might as well pick out a few more things, too, because after you and Charlie get married I'm sending you off on a honeymoon for a bit. I just need to talk to Charlie about some details."

Annabelle's face dropped in surprise, but a smile quickly burst out like the sun from behind the clouds. "Thank you, Papa!" She ran over to kiss him on the cheek, just as Mrs. Johansson called out to her.

"Annabelle, honey. We should go so we have some time to carefully pick out the things you'll want and need. We have a lot of planning and working to do before Saturday! Tomorrow, we'll have to inquire about some of the other ladies' help, too."

"Yes, Mrs. Johansson." She quickly skirted the table, waving at everyone. "Goodbye, Mr. Johansson. Thanks for the pie! Bye-bye, Papa, Charlie." She threw them a beaming smile before Mrs. Johansson took her by the elbow, leading her out of the bakery.

Charlie watched Annabelle leave, then whirled back at Daniel. "Van Der Kamp?"

Daniel nodded. "It's the evidence that he promised. He included a brief note, but he hints at something heading my way and me needing the evidence, soon. So either Mack is coming or someone's taking Lissa's accusations seriously. Either is bad for the two of you. He insists you get out of town for while."

"Van Der Kamp does? He's worried about me and Annabelle?"

"The impression I got is that he likes you and Jimmy and feels bad for you because of Mack. He despises him. But Mack plans on using Annabelle against me, and I can't have that." Charlie looked as if he were planning another question, but Daniel answered it for him. "Van Der Kamp's known about you and Annabelle—he's been rooting for the two of you. He actually mentioned you two getting married." He chuckled at the look of astonishment on Charlie's face.

"I'll be. I didn't think he wanted us together. He kept telling me to let her go."

"Yes, let her go so she could return home. He knew you'd be following. He has to do things so as not to raise Mack's ire or suspicion. Ironically, for the all the law-breaking he does, he doesn't hold with lying or breaking his word."

Mr. Johansson nodded at that. "And Mr. Pennington's a suspicious one by nature, as well as angry. I know, firsthand."

Again, Charlie's mouth fell open. Both Mr. Johansson and Daniel chuckled. "I got roped into baking for him when he found out I was helping my wife in the kitchen when yet another one of her girls had to quit because of Mack's unwanted attentions."

Daniel's face puckered with disgust as if he got a whiff of something rotten just thinking about the memories of his father harassing the various staff for every reason under the sky. He especially remembered all the tears from the female staff, as well as some quick departures. Mr. Johansson put his hand on Daniel's shoulder in support. Those were hard memories for all of them.

Daniel looked up. "Yes, and that's why we need to get this wedding done and you two on your way. I'd love to have you around for longer, but it won't do with Mack on the prowl. It's been enough time for him to have heard something new and to get some balls rolling."

"Or heads," Mr. Johansson added grimly.

"Look, let's not cloud this happy day with Mack. I love Annabelle and I like you for her. You're good for her, and you make her happy—that's what's important. I'm glad to welcome you to the family. When this all blows over, I'll welcome you back if you decide to return. You're only leaving because of Mack. Annabelle knows none of this, and I have to decide if and what I'll tell her."

Charlie thought about it for a moment, and memories of their arguments sifted through his mind. "You know, sir, I think you should just tell her as much of this as you can. She knows nothing of her mother and is probably making up stories about it. Knowing things will keep her safer—you no longer have to protect her on that account. Plus, she won't feel as if you're treating her like a child. Worse—that you're keeping her a prisoner of ignorance."

Daniel looked at Mr. Johansson, who raised his brows. "Daniel, I think we have a keeper here."

With that, they all laughed, nodding their heads.

"I'll tell her tonight, when I let her know what Van Der Kamp said. I've got a lot of explaining to do."

The day of their wedding was crisp and bright. The weather was perfect for an outdoor gathering as the entire town and some of the camp-side miners came by to see the sheriff's elusive daughter. Some of them thought for sure that he kept her under lock and key just because she was so pretty. A beautiful bride she was. Many said that the women back east had nothing on their Annabelle. It wasn't the lovely cadet blue dress she and Mrs. Johansson had labored on, with the wildflower embroidery details. It wasn't the way her curls danced against her slender back, shining in the sun. Annabelle's features were fine and her skin was smooth, but it was none of that. It was how happiness surrounded her the way wings frame an angel and the way her cornflower blue eyes sparkled with love. It was the way her face lit up, glowing from within, when she saw Charlie waiting for her with the preacher.

Daniel walked proudly down the aisle with his daughter, preening like a freshly groomed horse. Daniel and Annabelle had reconciled what they thought were their differences but actually were misperceptions. They also had a long talk about the situation they were in, thanks to Mack. She now knew why her father behaved the way he did and what the stakes were. She was much more supportive of his actions and he, in turn, understood how stifling he was.

Straightening out their miscommunications and misperceptions made for a good send-off. Things between father and daughter were settled and it was a joyous day. Adding to the celebration was the turnout by the entire town and the surrounding community of miners as well as the few remaining prospectors. They came to celebrate Annabelle's marriage and the sheriff they respected and admired.

Mrs. Johansson caught Daniel in between conversations. She pulled him aside, speaking in low tones.

"Daniel, I haven't had a chance to talk to you—it's important. I've heard talk." He nodded at her to go on. "The miners who come by for a bite to eat have been talking in low voices about the *mine's owner visiting*. They don't seem to know who he is, but they all have a healthy fear of him. I'm not sure what happened, but they say he's coming to settle accounts." Daniel's lips flattened. "Do you think—"

Daniel just looked at her with steely eyes for a moment before giving a firm nod. Mrs. Johansson drew in a quick breath. "That's what I feared. I was meaning to tell you the day of the pie, but things went awry when Elroy showed up. But I also figured you got some news with that package."

"Lissa's going to try to pin that prospector's murder on me, but Van Der Kamp sent evidence pinning it on Wrighty. He said that she's been shacking up with Mack and they're making plans for me. Mack's trying to get at Annabelle. That's why they have to leave so quickly. "

She put her hand on his arm, her face melting in sympathy. "I knew it had to be something. I was sure you weren't wanting to part with her so soon, even if you wanted to treat her and her lovely young man with an adventure."

He nodded, feeling his throat constrict. "I'm going to confront him this time. I won't have Lissa trying to sway me, nor me feeling all sorry for her. Annabelle knows everything and so does Charlie. He knew first and was the one who suggested I tell her everything."

Mrs. Johansson smiled the smile of a mother who sees her children making good strides. "Wonderful. Wonderful. Let's go enjoy this celebration and make the most of it. She needs to leave soon. The miners seem to be holding their breath, waiting for Mack to come."

Daniel smiled at her, giving her his arm. They happily walked back to the celebration to join the others. If anyone noticed their conversation, no one said anything. Everyone was happy to have something to celebrate, and the miners were happy to have good, free food.

Annabelle leaned her head against the back of the bench, watching the landscape go by in a blur. Her hand cradled her chin. She looked deep in thought. Charlie returned with tea and sat down next to her. He kissed her on the side of her face, causing her to turn and smile at him. Taking the teacup from his hands, she said, "Remember how I told you I was gearing up to run away when you took me?" Charlie nodded but didn't say anything. "Well, don't you think it's interesting that we're kind of running away right now?"

Charlie's eyes opened wide at that. "Well, I guess I never thought of it that way. Your pa and I thought of it as staying one step ahead of Mack, but primarily keeping you safe. From the sounds of it, he's real evil, Wildflower."

"Mmm-hmm." Annabelle turned her head, gazing out the window once again. After a moment, she said, "Did I tell you where I was planning to go when I finally ran away?"

"No, I don't think you did."

"My aunt's." She laughed at that. "But I didn't know where she lived or how to get the information. Papa was always tight-lipped about all family matters."

Charlie looked perplexed. Annabelle nudged him, "The very aunt we're going to visit now!"

"That's not what your pa said."

"No, he wouldn't. The town has big ears. But I know—I'm sure of it."

"What makes you so sure?"

"It's Papa's way of saying it's going to be okay, that we both are trying to do the right things for each other. I told him that's where I had planned to go when I was going to run away, and he about had apoplexy." She laughed. "You should've seen his face."

"Annabelle—"

"Oh, Charlie. It's all right. He knows that I know. He said they hadn't spoken for years because of Mack. It's funny that we're going to be right under his proverbial nose, isn't it?"

"I'm not sure I'd say that but, all right."

"Well, it's interesting that the day I decided to do something about getting myself out of this town it involved the idea of my aunt. Someone I didn't know. That's the day I met you, another person I didn't know. It started out scary, but it's ending well, right?"

Charlie pressed his lips into the side of her head and breathed her in. "Yup. There's a kind of ending but a new beginning, and it's all alright." He kissed her deeply, pulling her close to him. Laying his cheek on the top of her head, he thought about how he could never be close enough to her. "I love you, Wildflower."

"I love you, too, Charlie."

Together, they watched the landscape fly by them, ready for their next adventure.

ᴄᴏ Gratitude ᴏᴄ

Dear readers,

I'm grateful for you. There are many choices out there, yet you've chosen to take the time to read Charlie and Annabelle's story and allow the cast of characters who are intertwined with them to roam free in your imaginations. You breathe fresh life into my story with every page you turn, which is a gift to me and to my story.

And there are many other people I want to acknowledge as well as send gratitude their way. I try to thank them on the regular, but in relation to this project I'm giving a special shout-out to the following:

Sage Adderly-Knox, for coaching me through my limiting beliefs, fears, and old stories. You've given me a leg up when I needed one, as well as a shoulder to cry on and space to process.

Lynn Stout for being an awesome accountability buddy with a great sense of humor.

Laura Baker, for The Fearless Writer class—this is where the idea of Charlie took root. It sent me on a very different path I couldn't have imagined for myself.

Laurie Schnebly Campbell, for all the classes where I worked on Charlie and Annabelle and had supportive feedback.

Heidi Mixon for the lovely photograph and supportive friendship.

The 3 M's—my magical mistresses of the mind: M Valentine, Melissa Tuthill, and Marjaana Rinne. You are lovely women, friends, and beta readers. No joke, you saw me through some things.

Lisa Norman for her friendship and generosity, including the many times she's had to talk me out of my tree. More importantly for *The Reluctant Bandit* and my writing, she believed so much in the project that she sent me Lori Brown. And Lori, thank you for the fresh edit, dialogue, and support—both the kind and firm forms. You're a wealth of information. You both seem to understand my wacky ways and have your own wicked sense of humor that I appreciate.

Finally, my three men—Jon, Max, and Stuart. Despite my own tomfoolery, Jon has always done his best by me and has been my anchor in the storm. Love you to bits.

❧ About Me ❧

When I was little I wanted Andy Rooney's job. He got to ask questions with a splash of zany, cynic, and curious—I wanted to be a part of that. And while I love to laugh and smile, having a hall pass for grumpiness (even for a fun moment) seemed enticing if not altogether socially unacceptable (or so I was told) for a young lady. The little rebel within who battles with the good girl was all in.

While my inner scofflaw "defied" conventions, my external introvert (is that a thing?) loves wandering, wondering, and cloud watching. I'm an avid question-asker and have a strong streak of curiosity that has yet to do me in. I also enjoy learning and connecting the dots in my inner and outer worlds. I've always been a voracious reader, fountain-pen-and-paper-product enthusiast, as well as lover of wax seal jewelry and pretty, shiny objects. I love good stories and analogies, both written and spoken. Tell me your story—my spirit will listen.

I've always been told that I was an epic storyteller and have loved storytelling since I was very young. All the years of oral storytelling, observation, and random scribbles over the years finally decided to break through and find daylight. I love playing with words and now I share that in both verbal and written forms.

I frequently stand on the precipice, watching and observing, but when I'm in, I'm all in. I'm your ride-or-die girl, Thelma to your Louise (or Louie, whichever the case may be).

Coffee or tea? Yes, please.

Heidi Mixon Photography

~Thank You!~

Thank you for taking the time to read *The Reluctant Bandit*! I appreciate your support and would love to hear from you.

You can reach me at ami@amihickenking.com; visit my website, www.amihickenking.com, to read my blog and sign up for my newsletter, *The Friday Tomfoolery*; and follow me on Instagram @amihickenking and Pinterest at amihickenking.

One last thing—Please take a moment of your valuable time to review my book. Your feedback is very important to me!